DESPERATE HOUSEWOLVES

A Novel by…

Gregory L. Norris

Van Velzer Press
Americana with a Twist

To *Roxanne Dent,*

the writer I want to be when I grow up.

Chapter 1

Pilot Episode

On Mistral Lane, in the upscale little bedroom community of Hydrangea Heights, the lawns are kept green and trimmed in summer, window boxes always filled, even from December through March—sprigs of pine and holly make fine substitutes for flowers. Composting is encouraged…though out of sight, of course, as leaves left to collect in untidy piles are frowned upon by the Homeowners' Association. The houses—few less than 3,000 square feet of desirable living space—are given fresh coats of paint every four years. Nobody drives a car older than that number except for Bob Slade, who owns a '67 fastback Mustang, and it's considered "classic."

The residents employ a small army of service sector specialists—gardeners to garden and prune in the good weather, men who plow when it snows, cooks, cleaners, caterers, and personal assistants. Soccer moms wear diamond tennis bracelets when dropping off or picking up their kids at school, and joggers never take to the sidewalks dressed in anything less than their favorite designer's best.

My name is Jessie-Marie Smyth, and on the afternoon of the day I died, I had one of those revelations that stopped me abruptly in the front hallway of Number 17 Mistral Lane. Sunlight streamed through the windows in that magnificent bent that's unique to the month of September. I was sleeping well thanks to a pretty, pale pink pill that soothed a particular restlessness. I thought of Tim, my radiologist husband, and our approaching 10th anniversary. I was looking forward to seeing my three best friends for our weekly Ladies' Poker Night game, and was secure in the lie that all was right with the world.

My life felt perfect.

Through the window, I spotted the mailman in his blue uniform shorts and white safari hat across the street at my good friend Willa Forsyth's house delivering a package too big to fit in the mailbox, which was a beautiful, hand-painted plum with pastel hydrangea blossoms dripping down from her last name on both sides. A delivery of books, most likely. Willa was a romance novelist who wrote under the *nom-de-plume* of Lena LaFleur—both ironic and noble of her, considering her one experience with love and romance was with a creep named Phil Laslo, who she divorced last year.

My also-bestie and neighbor Wandalou Trueheart, fashion influencer and former Filipine beauty queen, and her police detective fiancée, Quinn Rodrigo Montoya, walked past on the sidewalk. They lived at Number 11 and were in the middle of a heated exchange.

"I'll put that in my mouth when *you* do," Wandalou said, the sharpness in her tone reaching past the open windows of my front room.

"You never had a problem with acrobatic positions before," Quinn grumbled just loud enough that I heard.

"Yeah, well, life hasn't been the same since I fled the circus," she clapped back.

I wandered into my kitchen and poured myself another cup of coffee—decaf, light on the cream, one fake sugar. From somewhere in the neighborhood arose the spirited laughter of a little girl—perhaps one of the Slade Twins, Marci and Darci, my other dear friend Isis's stepdaughters. Isis's husband, Bob, had been married before and the two girls were quite the handful, but Isis was more of a mom to them than Bob's first wife. She was more than most moms. Oh, and just to be clear, Isis was named after the Egyptian goddess of love and fertility, not those murderous radicals overseas.

My phone pinged an alert. I picked it up and read a text from Isis sent to all four of us.

Serious problem—new accent wall more like accident wall—hate it!

I started to type—*It can't be all that bad, Icy—*

Another response came in first from Wandalou. *Sounds like more Hydrangea Heights-style problems. Boo hoo! Deal with it!*

To which Willa responded with a frowning face emoji.

Yes, our problems all seemed trivial—an accent wall meant to be sunny yellow that had dried instead as baby diaper mustard, sexual boundaries being tested for expansion, and more books delivered to the front door rather than the mailbox. If you overlooked that one other big problem we didn't care to speak of that pursued all four of us, every second, like an unwanted, double shadow, life would indeed have been perfect. In September's golden glow, I almost convinced myself the werewolf curse wasn't real.

While sipping my coffee, I noticed my other neighbor from the house to the right picking the last of the season's roses from the arbor in her backyard. Regina Gowl was not a friend. In fact, she'd proven to be quite the thorn. She complained about the torque of Bob Slade's Mustang, the noise the twins made, disapproved of Willa's "salacious" novels and cast disapproving glances from the cut of her narrowed eyes whenever within sight of Wandalou. A prude who'd never been married, I often wondered if Regina had ever been *touched*. The top buttons of her matronly blouses were always fastened so tightly that it looked impossible for her to breathe.

"Rumor has it, an airline pilot bought the empty Dunkel house on the other side of *the Writer*," I remembered her telling me over the rose hedges two days earlier. "A *pilot*. Just what the neighborhood needs! Can you imagine the sort of debauchery that'll take place in Gert Dunkel's home?"

To which I'd responded, "A pilot? We'll hardly ever see him. And it isn't Gert Dunkel's home any longer."

Regina had tsked. We'd maintained a cordial détente following a few minor skirmishes in years past. Still, it was wise to never let down one's guard around her, for she was quick to take up arms and launch missiles filled with venom.

The sound of the mail slot opening for the day's delivery shook me from my thoughts. I finished my coffee, rinsed the cup, set it in the strainer, and padded to the front hallway. Among the bills—easily identified by their little plastic windows—and a catalog was a card in a severe chartreuse envelope. It was addressed to: *Resident She-Devil* in block penmanship. The address was smudged but looked to be my husband's and mine.

I walked back into my perfect kitchen in our perfect house where we had lived our perfect lives and, against my better judgment, opened what I sensed was quite the poisonous pen letter.

And I was right.

> *I know the truth about you. You are disgusting. Meet me at 7:00 on Tuesday night at the dog park gazebo with $10,000.00 or I'll tell him your ugly secret!*

All the moisture drained from my mouth. The afternoon's color evaporated, leaving a world plunged in grayness. Hands shaking, the letter dropped from my fingers. I willed it and its ugly envelope to vanish, but it didn't. A chill teased the fine hairs at the nape of my neck. I fought the shiver, failed. It tumbled down my spine and sent the room into a blur. The first tears came before things focused.

I realized my perfect day was over. Less than six hours later, so was my perfect life, and I was dead.

Not long after Jessie-Marie Smyth was murdered at the Hydrangea Heights dog park gazebo, Willa Forsythe heard a car pull into the driveway of the empty house next door. The sun had already set as the autumn days grew shorter, the twilight helped along by fast-moving storm clouds. She put down the bound galley of her newest romance novel release, *The Privilege of Passion*, and peered out the window behind the parlor's comfortable sofa. In the light from the streetlamp, she saw a pickup truck parked in the former Dunkel house's drive—black, a man's sort of ride.

The driver stepped out. And what a man he was, she saw through the deepening gloom and the tiny corner of window glass where she peeked. He wore a crisp white shirt, black suit, unknotted tie, shiny shoes, and little golden wings pinned on his lapels.

Gasping, Willa fell back and closed the plum-colored drape, swearing that she could make out the green color in his eyes. No, green was too banal a description—they glinted with the vibrancy of emeralds! It was her new neighbor, the airline pilot. Willa's heart galloped for reasons she couldn't fathom. This pilot was the kind of rugged alpha male found routinely swaggering through the pages of Lena LaFleur bodice-rippers. He was—

"*Magnificent*," she whispered.

The temptation to steal another glimpse over-whelmed her. Willa inched closer to the drapes and nudged them aside only to catch a shadow of movement at the empty house's front veranda. Another body hurried up the stairs beneath an umbrella. The umbrella was clear plastic, decorated with yellow sun faces and impossible to mistake. It belonged to Brittany Barrows, Hydrangea Heights's top real estate agent.

"And Number One *skank*," Willa grumbled.

Brittany and the pilot entered the house together. Lights next door switched on in sequence, and on the heels of her instant attraction and interest came another emotion Willa hadn't suffered since Phil's betrayal— with the very same owner of that umbrella: jealousy, just as intense.

Willa picked up the novel galley and attempted to lose herself in a tale of new love, loss, sacrifice, and redemption. But her eyes kept returning to the window. After reading the same sentence four times, she closed the book, sat up, and switched off the light.

Outside, the new storm opened up, and rain hammered the windows.

Isis Liselotte Slade, nee Cartwright, argued with one of the twins, employing the usual level voice that assured victory even more so than her title as their stepmother. "Eat your dinner, please," she said.

Face scrunched, Marci answered, "*I don't wanna*—I want pizza rolls!"

"Well, love, I want you to be eighteen, but that particular wish is still ten years away," Isis said dryly.

Darci chuckled around her fork, her plate nearly cleaned. "You're funny."

She wasn't keen on creating a rivalry between the twins, but in that instant, Isis felt justified. "And you, love, get extra dessert for eating the meal I labored to put on the table in front of you."

That got Marci interested in the succulent chop: creamy mashed potatoes with a steamed vegetable medley. "When is Daddy coming home?" asked Marci.

"Not soon enough," Isis said, which earned her spirited laughs from one twin and the other's pout.

Rain struck the dining room's windows. The first tendrils of an ominous and unexpected dread inched through the walls and embraced Isis.

"I'm telling Daddy—you're mean!" Marci complained. "I don't like it!"

Isis cleared her throat. "And I don't like this headache you're giving me. I love you, Marci, but I swear if you don't start acting more like your sister, I'm gonna snap and pop you in the oven just like in that fairy tale."

The pigtailed girl half-submerged in her chair bounded back up to a fully seated position. "Can I go in the microwave instead?"

"No, dear, that would be too quick—and I'd want you to suffer."

This cracked up both girls. The argument ended, Marci managed a decent job on her dinner. Gingerbread with whipped cream followed, mostly without argument until Darci reminded Isis about the promised extra serving. They performed the usual tasks after—dishes stacked in dishwasher, everything neat and tidy so they greeted a clean house in the morning. She left Bob's dinner on a plate under plastic wrap and put the twins to bed.

"Tomorrow night, can we have pizza rolls?" Marci whined.

"Tomorrow night, you can have leaves and pine cones if you don't like what I make for dinner." She kissed the girl's forehead.

"I love you, Mommy," Marci said.

Isis smiled. "You better. Good night." At the door, she turned back. "I love you, too, my little pains in the butt."

That flicker of joy proved brief. The rain lashing the house drummed on her nerves for reasons she couldn't explain but trusted. Since the July night she and the ladies' lives were forever bonded—and changed—Isis had learned to listen to her instincts.

Then the house phone rang, and her feelings about something being wrong proved to be right.

Wandalou let the first call go through to voicemail. She answered on the third. "This had better involve amputation or fire, Willa," she snapped.

"It does," Willa said. "Total arson. The pilot, the one who bought the Dunkel place—*he's here!*"

Wandalou examined her nails—exquisite in their bold pomegranate color. "Seriously?"

"Totally and without any romance writer embellishments, he's the handsomest thing to hit Hydrangea Heights I've ever seen. Only…"

Wandalou waited then had to say, "Yes?"

"He was with *her*."

That tone could only mean one thing, one name. "*Her*?"

"*Her*. She's over there with him right now, and I bet, like half of Hydrangea Heights's male population, it's for another notch on her bedpost."

"Termite," Wandalou spat.

"I feel like she's already ripped out my heart once, and she's doing it again when I haven't even met the guy. But I'd like to. If you saw him…"

Wandalou cast a guilty glance to the other side of the bed. "I'm sure he's divine, yeah. Listen, Willa, this isn't the best time for me to help you through another plot twist—"

"What am I supposed to do?" Willa pleaded in desperation.

"Go for a jog."

"It's raining."

"Take a cold shower. Bye." Willa asked her if something was wrong. Wandalou lied despite the nagging malaise that something was. Her gaze drifted over to the rookie police officer who'd made it down to his black boxer-briefs. Rolfe Hastings was so physically fit it should be criminal. "Willa, I'll call you back."

Wandalou stabbed off the cell phone in its jeweled case and tossed it onto the nightstand. As she did, she stole a look at the discarded clothes on the patch of floor beside the bed—Giovanna of Milan top, Carlsbad skirt, and Banolo Klonick strappy sandals, which left her clad only in her Gypsy Jones top-of-the-line lingerie. The inextinguishable fire burning in her blood—deeper, in Wandalou's soul—again ignited like an itch to that part of your own back you can never reach, the one requiring someone else's hand. "Where were we?"

Young Officer Hastings flashed a lusty smile that conjured a dimple to one cheek. "We were…" he sighed, his bedroom blues dipping lower from her face to her breasts.

Wandalou licked her mouth only to jolt at the sharpness. *My, what big teeth you have*, her inner voice taunted. *You big, bad wolf!*

She seized hold of Rolfe's face and growled. At first, Rolfe hooted and grunted back. They snapped playfully at one another's mouths. Electricity crackled over and through Wandalou's flesh. Feral energy surged through her blood and fueled her insane lust. She wanted to bite him—really *bite* him hard and deep enough to taste his blood. More so, to sip it like wine, warm and fresh while his groans of pleasure degenerated into screams of pain. Oh, how she desired—

Wandalou drew back. Officer Rolfe attempted to pursue but only succeeded in kissing the barrier of her palm.

"What—?" he sputtered.

Before she could concoct an answer, her phone rang its riff of xylophone-coconut shell notes again. Wandalou grabbed it and answered. "Willa, I said—"

"This isn't Willa, Wandalou," a man's voice interjected. "It's Tim Smyth. I can't find Jessie-Marie…"

She paced the kitchen, drank water, worried, and paced some more. Willa realized she was spinning figurative wheels in imaginary mud and devouring her own tail like Ouroboros, the legendary serpent. So what if *the skank* was next door, sexing it up with the hot pilot? Phil was a year ago, which meant...*what?* At least a hundred different notches on Brittany Barrows's gnawed-down bedpost. She didn't need a stranger, no matter how attractive, any more than she had a cheating husband. She had the heroes in her Lena LaFleur novels to fulfill her fantasies, and they were enough.

Instead of the suggested cold shower, she changed into yoga pants, a T-shirt, and slipped into her joggers. The rain had let up some and now fell in a cold, somber preview of autumn. Still, as she jogged past the Slade place and down the street, looping from Cottage Road and back to Mistral, how narcotic the night's perfume struck her senses—mowed lawn, roses, hot pavement cooled by the downpour, and those hydrangeas blooming blue or pink in every yard. In addition to sight, the curse had magnified her sense of smell. So, too, had it improved Willa's power of hearing.

So he surprised her by approaching on the sidewalk, the way he moved as though part of the waning storm. Willa dug in her sneaker soles. The pilot was now clad in jeans, expensive kicks, and a black T-shirt. The rain ran down his cheeks and added an even more shocking level of attractiveness to his dark hair, neat but showing a cowlick and a few stray spikes.

Willa gasped.

The pilot flashed a spare smile. "Hello, neighbor," he said, his deep voice matching the rest of the magnificent image presented. Those emerald gemstone eyes…how they glowed with hypnotic power.

Willa cleared her throat. "Hello."

The pilot nodded and revealed a length of clean white teeth, the gesture more wolf's snarl than actual smile. He extended his big hand with the offer of a shake. In the next second, all Willa could think about were his fingers and pleasures they were capable of unleashing.

As she reached toward him, intending to accept, Willa's phone chirped. She instead drew the offender from her pocket and apologized. "Sorry."

It was a text from Wandalou.

Are you with Jessie-Marie?

Exhaling in frustration, she typed back: *No, why?*

Tim called. No one can find her. Jessie-Marie's missing

A mile and a quarter away, Jessie-Marie Smyth's killer tossed the last shovelful of wet dirt over her body in its shallow grave.

Chapter 2

Secrets

We all have secrets.

Though she'd never admit it, my friend Isis secretly resented rearing twin girls, who were a handful, rather than their biological mother, who was a kid herself and who, one mysterious night, simply left.

My dear pal Wandalou was secretly cheating on her fiancé, but in all fairness it was under the influence of a primal, rabid call that was, truly, quite wild.

And my friend Willa, bless her heart, secretly ached to have back what Phil Laslo stole from her: a belief in the power of love.

We all shared another, far darker secret regarding what happened two months earlier on the night of Wandalou's bachelorette party. The night of the July full moon.

As for my private secrets, I took to my shallow grave the identity of my killer, who lurked in wait near the gazebo of the Hydrangea Heights dog park, and where my friends and I had taken up a rather peculiar habit.

Wandalou was the last to converge at the Smyth house, her normally impeccable presentation askew enough to suggest she'd pulled on her clothes in haste. Willa was dressed to jog. Isis wore an open trench over bright yellow pajamas.

Wandalou cast a cutting glance through narrowed brown eyes at Isis. "What's up with all of *that*, Big Bird?"

Isis scowled. "Excuse me?"

"You can thank me for the free advice and rescue later."

Isis balked. "Thank you?"

Wandalou patted Isis's shoulder. "Loose the yellow if you want to keep your husband. Fashion influencer, remember? Never off the clock. Good talk."

Tim Smyth said, "You're all here. I was hoping it was another of your girls' poker nights."

Willa and Wandalou exchanged nervous glances without commenting, though their shared look spoke volumes.

"No, no, our next poker night isn't until the seventeenth of the month," Wandalou laughed, the cackle sharp and sounding lunatic.

Isis shot Wandalou a threatening glance before taking Tim's arm. "I'm sure everything's all right," she said in the same tone she used to mother the twins. "That it's all some misunderstanding you'll both joke about after she walks through that door." Isis turned to the front entrance with its mail slot and waited.

Seconds drew out, yet the door remained shut, and the wrongness in the air worsened. They all felt it according to their expressions. One more heightened sense, this one was from the territory of the sixth.

"Have you tried her phone?" Willa asked and received another disapproving look from Wandalou.

"Of course, he has," Wandalou tsked.

Tim nodded. "Now it goes right through to voicemail."

"Do you have one of those apps that tracks networked cells?" asked Willa.

"No. With my job, I've got a work phone issued from the hospital. It's just that this is so…"

"Unlike Jessie-Marie," Isis finished.

They all glanced around at the house, each photograph and piece of framed art straight, every surface free of dust and ready for the white glove test, everything in order. The only glaring chaos came in the absence of the one who'd put such complete neatness to the place where the worried had gathered.

Alone in the Smyth's front hallway, Wandalou dialed the number. Quinn answered on the third ring. "Hey," he said. "What's up?"

Guilt squeezed unpleasantly on her insides. The hot young uniform was gone from their bed, his throat intact, the comforter and sheets spritzed with a liberal mix of her perfume and Quinn's body spray, enough to disguise proof of attempted infidelity that had been interrupted before it could be acted upon. Nothing had happened, but it almost had.

"It's Jessie-Marie," she said in a voice on low volume. "Tim's sort of freaking out."

"Why?"

"We all are. She's not home and he can't get her on her phone."

Quinn sighed. Wandalou hadn't heard any sirens in counterpoint to the storm and didn't figure the Hydrangea Heights crime report would go much deeper than a few traffic violations for this rainy night, but her fiancé didn't share the same unique insight as she and her two besties.

Wandalou's flesh prickled as she tried to explain without giving away secrets like her new powers of second-sight.

"It's just…*strange*, Quinn. You know she's not the type to go off without letting somebody know."

"Did she and the radiologist have some kind of fight?" Quinn asked.

Wandalou eyed the occupants in the other room from the corner of her eye. "No," she huffed. "You know the two of them—mom's apple pie with vanilla ice cream. They don't fight, they *debate*."

"Geeze, I wonder what that's like."

Her grip on the jeweled phone case tightened. "Unless you want to find yourself *debating* all by your lonesome from now on, Quinn—!"

"All right, fine. She drives that blue hybrid, right?" Wandalou yessed him. "I'll have my guys keep an eye out for it. Unless Doctor Smyth wants to make an endangered person report, which I'm obligated to take. Or he can wait until your friend returns home with the low-fat milk to go with that apple pie."

She fired another tsk into the phone before hanging up. Then Wandalou sashayed back to the small gathering of worried faces.

"What did Quinn say?" Isis asked.

Wandalou choked down a dry swallow and flashed an unconvincing smile at Tim. "He said that if you want, he can take a report, make it official."

Tim shrugged. "What if she only went out to the movies? Maybe that's why she's not answering the phone—because she turned it off." Silence settled over the quartet as Tim seemed to wait for one of them to back up his theory. No one did.

"What do you think I should do?" he asked.

Wandalou was the one who answered, "I think you should see Quinn and file that report."

They exited the house. The four divided into two sets of two—Wandalou with Tim to his car, the green hybrid, while Willa and Isis cut across the street to the Slade house to hold vigil.

As Wandalou clicked her seatbelt, a car turned up Mistral Lane. "Maybe that's her," she said.

The car slowed but continued past to the house next door. It pulled into the driveway and Regina Gowl, the bane of the neighborhood, got out and scurried quickly through the rain and past her front door.

They entered the Slade house, where Isis's husband Bob hungrily devoured his dinner and downed a cold beer in front of the acre of flat-screen TV in the family room, presently showing a baseball game in high-def.

"*Coaster*," Isis admonished.

Bob, his mouth full, jumped up and grabbed one of the cork-bottom wooden squares from the tray beside his open longneck. "Oh, right." After that, he narrowed his gaze on his wife and Willa. "Everything okay?"

"No," Isis said. "We can't find Jessie-Marie." She explained in an economy of words what was happening. Scowling, Bob finished his dinner while Isis and Willa snuck into the kitchen. Isis opened the bottle of white wine she'd kept for celebrations or emergencies and poured. They sat at the table where, until that night, her biggest battles had been fought with a couple of small, eight-year-old adversaries. Now a larger enemy lurked nearby.

"Do you sense it, Willa?" Isis whispered.

Willa sipped. The wine was exquisite and crisp but did little to alleviate her anxiety. "Yeah, like a kind of intuition."

"So I'm not imagining it?" Isis exhaled in relief that was really counterfeit. "All night, sitting in my stomach like broken glass and on my skin like a fever."

"It isn't just that. I don't need glasses to read anymore—my eyesight has gotten *ridiculous*. My hearing, too," Willa said.

"Poker Night," Isis said in a voice almost not there. "It's getting worse not better."

"What are we going to do?"

Isis looked into her glass and forgot how to blink. "Jessie-Marie isn't at the movies or doing any late-night shopping."

"No," Willa said.

The soft patter of footfalls drew both of their gazes toward the fridge in time to see the door open. Isis knew instantly that it wasn't her husband, who would have towered over the door's top. Mouth tightening, Isis vacated her chair and ambled over to the refrigerator. She leaned down as the crinkle of aluminum foil being lifted rose up, secretive and surly. Marci knelt on the other side of the door.

"And just what are you doing, young lady?" Isis demanded.

The girl jolted, closed her eyes, and raised her pudgy hands zombie-fashion. "Sleepwalking."

Isis folded her arms and pursed her lips. "Then how about you sleep walk back up to bed?"

Marci dropped the ruse. "But I'm starving!"

Isis snorted. "Not with those cheeks."

Marci's pleading face soured. "I am. *Starving to death!* If I don't eat something, I won't make it through the night. And it'll be *your* fault!"

Isis flashed a cold smile, touched a pointer finger to her lips, and cleared her throat. Then she bared her fangs and growled and, for a second, her eyes changed color from their usual sunny blue to black edged in silver.

"*Go to bed!*" Isis spat in a juicy, predator's voice.

Marci screamed. "Yes, Mommy!" and raced from the kitchen.

Isis coughed again and calmly closed the refrigerator door.

Marci streaked past the family room and up the staircase to her bedroom. Bob watched his game, oblivious to all but the pop-out taking place on the TV.

"Nice parenting," Willa said.

Isis smiled and returned to the table. "Yes, I thought so. Effective, wouldn't you say?" She raised her glass for a toast. Willa, her expression showing she wasn't convinced, followed through anyway.

Before either could sip more of their wine, Willa's cell rang. "It's Wandalou," she said and answered. "Hey—is there an update?"

Wandalou didn't immediately answer. "Yeah," she said after seconds that dragged past with the weight of minutes. "They found Jessie-Marie's car."

"Where was it? Is she okay?"

"They found her car but not Jessie-Marie."

Wandalou gripped the phone tightly to prevent her fingers from shaking. It had taken two tries to scroll to Willa's number as the cracks in her normally sturdy façade widened and the confidence she projected crumbled.

Quinn returned to the section of bullpen at the heart of the Hydrangea Heights police station, his movements stirring the dregs of coffee and what remained of his body spray. Wandalou's guilt surged. Quinn's handsome face projected the stern look she knew he wore when on duty. "Why would Jessie-Marie be at the dog park?" he asked, his question sounding like an interrogation.

Panic boiled in Wandalou's belly and smothered that flush of guilt. "Walking a dog?" she offered sheepishly.

"The Smyths don't have a dog," Quinn said.

"Oh, right." And then she laughed out a nervous, sharp titter that earned her Quinn's frustrated, tough guy game face at its felon-level worst.

She recovered and flashed her own version of a war mask, and a brief staring contest ensued. Quinn blinked first, as was usually the case in such instances between the two of them, but her victory tasted bitter. Quinn marched over to Doctor Tim Smyth. Wandalou secretly drank down a cleansing breath.

During twilights leading up to "Poker Night," the four friends usually quietly slipped away from wine and cheese, kitchen duties, book club reads, husbands, fiancés, and empty beds, then they'd converged at the nine-acre expanse of walking trails and the quaint gazebo for matters of a secret nature.

Today Jessie-Marie had gone there alone. Wandalou's heart, already racing around inside her ribcage like a trapped and panicking animal, galloped faster. Her guilt returned, this time over the bigger secret that overshadowed all the smaller ones.

"Do you know why Jessie-Marie would be at the dog park?" Quinn asked Doctor Tim.

"We don't have a dog, so no," Tim said.

I do, Wandalou's inner voice taunted, singing the words. *I know all about the dog park and why she went there!*

"Shut up," Wandalou spat under her breath. Both Doctor Tim and the detective/warrior chief glanced over. Wandalou again found herself under an unwanted spotlight.

"What was that you said?" Quinn asked in full interrogator mode.

Wandalou coughed and then she coughed louder. "Sorry—*ahem.*"

Quinn pointed to the coffee maker. "Help yourself."

Wandalou responded with a theatrical smile and walked over to the coffee station where a slotted tray held an assortment of sugar packets, the fake stuff, and stirrers. Tiny tubs of non-dairy cream floated in a metal bowl of water that had once been ice cubes. She pulled a disposable hot beverage cup and its safety ring from the sleeve on the counter beside the bowl and poured. The coffee landed thickly in the cup. Even the intense aroma could have cancelled out the worst hangover of her former years following a pageant loss or, more often, a win. She figured if she dumped the cup into her gas tank, she'd get at least thirty miles in the city, more for highway driving.

There was no way she'd drink it, but the ritual of making coffee gave her trembling hands something to do.

Another uniform, one of Hydrangea Heights's finest, sauntered into the bullpen. As he neared, Wandalou saw that it was Rolfe Hastings. She yelped when their eyes briefly connected then drank the coffee, finishing it in one pull.

My blue hybrid car sat alone in the parking lot. My cell phone was tucked into the catchall beneath the dashboard. Two officers with flashlights wandered the trail through the dying rainstorm and called my name.

"Mrs. Smyth? Mrs. Jessie-Marie Smyth!"

I answered, "I'm here—over here!"

But they didn't hear me, and the officers walked right past the pile of dirt the park's maintenance men used to fill in patches where unruly visitors dug holes.

Luckily, on their way back around, one of them spotted my shoe sticking out of the shallow grave where my killer deposited me, and my foot, left uncovered in their hast to escape.

My three dear friends grieved. Of course, they were all questioned, as was my husband, who was cleared of any wrongdoing—he'd spent the entire day at his hospital, which numerous sources backed up. All of my ladies had alibis, though some were more ironclad than others. Isis was with her twins, Willa her novel. Wandalou claimed to be doing her nails during the window of my murder and burial, and Quinn accepted the explanation—his fiancée wasn't the type to get her nails dirty, anyway.

Besides, none of my friends would have thrust that blade into my heart.

On the somber day of my funeral, Isis baked my favorite casserole with cauliflower and extra cheese and carried it over to Number 17 Mistral Lane before the service. My husband wore the black suit reserved for graveside matters and appeared as one of the dead himself—pale, lost, a zombie. Bob Slade wrangled the twins into the minivan, though I'd have preferred they took his other car to Peaceful Ridge Cemetery where I was to be laid to rest. I'd always secretly loved that Mustang, even if Isis didn't.

She rode with my husband. Willa carpooled with Quinn and Wandalou, who looked stunning in the black knee-length designer dress that fit her body as though it loved her.

"We're all here for you, Tim," Isis assured my husband more than once.

Words were spoken, tears cried. After, friends and neighbors returned to my house to break bread and mourn some more. Vases of sympathy flowers from the local florist crowded kitchen counters along with a bouquet of freshly cut roses from Regina Gowl, who was conspicuously absent from the day's ceremonies.

The garbage and recycling men take off federal holidays but not the loss of customers along their route, and so on the Monday morning following my funeral, Willa and a reluctant Wandalou entered the open garage at Number 17 Mistral Lane after Tim left for work—his job kept him going, so I didn't mind his keeping to his schedule.

"Why are we here again?" Wandalou groused.

"To help our friend's husband."

Wandalou rolled her eyes and picked up the paper-recycling bin while Willa rolled the two garbage barrels on wheels down to the curb. Inside the bin were the usual things—circulars, newspapers, junk mail.

"Could you move any slower?" Willa asked while working the mixed recyclables to the end of the driveway.

"You're not in heels," Wandalou countered.

"Who wears heels at six in the morning?"

"Who doesn't? Besides, Quinn normally does *this*." She thrust out the blue recycling bin at Willa. Willa sighed and reached for it, but the bin toppled to the ground and spilled its contents across the pavement. Both women leaned down to recover the mess of scattered paper.

"Seen any more of your hot pilot?" Wandalou asked.

Willa shook her head. "He must be flying the friendly skies. And I've been preoccupied."

"Yeah," Wandalou said, her expression grim.

The chug of the two city trucks sounded from the direction of the head of Mistral Lane. Willa set a hand on Wandalou's and offered an apologetic smile.

"Hurry," Wandalou said.

She grabbed at the last of the spilled paper, a chartreuse card envelope. But before returning it to the bin, she noticed what was written on it.

"She-devil?"

"Hey," Willa said. "That wasn't nice."

"No, not you—*this!*" Wandalou turned the card around for her friend to see the writing.

Willa read it clearly. By that time, the recycling truck was two houses away. "Keep that," Willa said.

She dragged the last bin down and waved at the men who got out clad in jeans, old steel-toes, T-shirts, and neon green vests. They answered with tips of their chins, that universal greeting between males that makes instant friends of strangers on basketball courts and baseball diamonds.

They tossed the recycling into sectioned metal bins on the truck and moved on. The garbage truck pulled up behind it and then followed down the lane. Willa returned the empty barrels and containers to the Smyth garage where Wandalou stood reading what was inside the chartreuse envelope, her mouth agape.

"Oh my God," Wandalou gasped.

"What is it?"

"A note from Jessie-Marie's killer!"

Isis poured three tall mugs full of coffee and carried them over to the table on a tray along with the sugar bowl and creamer and three spoons.

"You have to give this to Quinn," Willa said.

Wandalou nodded and lifted the cup to her lips.

Isis picked the envelope off the table and reread the card. "Who would send such a terrible thing to Jessie-Marie?"

Willa narrowed her eyes and reached for the envelope. "I don't think they meant to."

Wandalou huffed. "What do you mean? It's right there in front of you."

But Willa was focused on the envelope. "That address isn't a seventeen, it's an *eleven*."

"Yeah, we're always getting the Smyth's mail by mistake and they're always getting ours—you'd think our mailman would invest in eyeglasses," she said lightly and snorted, only to tense up at the implications. "Wait, that means—"

"This wasn't meant for Jessie-Marie," Isis said to Wandalou.

"It was meant for me!"

Chapter 3

Wicked Witch of the Yeast

Two months before my murder, an upscale little bakery opened in Hydrangea Heights's strictly no-neon business center. My Grains was owned by Renate Krumpt and, six mornings a week, the bewitching aroma of fresh bread and pastries wafted over the square, drawing enchanted customers in by droves. Those lucky enough to get in line early left with assortments of herb rolls, fresh bagels still warm, and donuts slathered in chocolate or stuffed with luscious blueberries and other cream fillings and dusted in powdered sugar.

Two mornings after the discovery of the mysterious card in my recycling bin, my three friends met at My Grains. Isis arrived first, the twins skipping at her side and both eager for something delicious as promised by the blood sugar-spiking sweetness in the air, Willa next, and Wandalou fashionably late, as usual.

The exterior of My Grains was as welcoming in appearance and as mouthwatering to behold as the frosted cakes under glass cloches visible through the front windows—the day's standout being a two-layer beauty covered in white butter-cream and decorated in plump slices of strawberry. The bakery itself was a soft blue in color, and the window frames had all been painted in a warm tone of coffee with cream. Customers streamed out carrying white pastry boxes tied with candy cane string.

Wandalou showed up at just after nine, according to the bank clock across the square. She cast a frustrated look at the twins, who fidgeted beside Isis. Marci performed a slow spin.

"Seriously?" Wandalou carped.

Isis shrugged. "Sue me. And don't worry, they'll behave." As soon as the words were past her lips, Isis let forth with a sharp, lunatic's cackle. "Sorry," she apologized. "I tried to pull that last line off with sincerity, but I just couldn't."

Wandalou tsked. "Come on—this place gets mobbed every morning and the owner's touchy about late arrivals."

"We weren't the ones who were late," Willa remarked, which earned her another cutting glance from Wandalou.

"Isn't this where you're getting your wedding cake?" asked Isis.

"Only if I don't piss off Frau Krumpt," answered Wandalou in a voice not much louder than a whisper. Wandalou then entered first only to freeze. The others bunched up behind her. The twins complained.

Standing directly in front of them in the immaculate, empty space was a square, tall woman with a severe silver haircut, arms folded over her apron and ample bosom, and a face that cast a January expression.

"Yes, *Fraulein?*" Renate Krumpt asked.

Wandalou managed a nervous smile. "Hello, Ms. Krumpt. I was just telling my friends that you're making the cake for my wedding."

"Only if you don't piss me off," Frau Krumpt said through a taut, spare smile. Then she harrumphed and returned to the glass counter beneath whose display the shelves were mostly empty. "You're late."

"It's only three minutes after nine in the morning," Willa boldly answered.

The frau's smile, what little there was of it, evaporated. "In Deutschland, that's late! I'm nearly sold out for the day."

Undaunted, the twins skipped over to the display case, where a handful of plain pastries sat on a tray with a few of the surviving round treats and the sad remains of half a donut. Frau Krumpt leaned down and shot the girls a menacing look through the glass. Both screamed and raced behind the protection of Isis. Frau Krumpt straightened and smoothed out her apron. "I'm afraid that's all I have left."

"We'll take it," Wandalou said.

They sat in the back drinking coffee from Frau Krumpt's self-service bar. The girls enjoyed their donuts and sipped hot chocolate at another table set before the windows.

"I was hoping to buy some pastries or a few loaves of seeded rye for my new neighbor," Willa said. "You know, a kind of housewarming gift. 'Welcome to the neighborhood,' and all that."

"The pilot's back?" Isis asked.

Willa nodded. "I think I heard him pull in last night. His truck was out front again this morning along with a moving van."

"Figured he would have hightailed it far away from Hydrangea Heights given our recent crime spree," Isis said. The shadow was back. Isis lowered her coffee cup.

"Did you show Quinn the note?" asked Willa.

Wandalou avoided their eyes. "Not yet."

"*Wandalou,* it's evidence!" Isis admonished.

"I know it is—but it's also evidence that whoever killed Jessie-Marie was really after me!" Her voice rose enough to attract the attention of the twins. Wandalou faked a smile and waved. Marci stuck out her tongue. "Same to you, kid," Wandalou said while tucking a strand of long, black hair behind her ear.

The twins returned their focus to their plates and donut crumbs. Isis shushed Wandalou.

"You still haven't told us why someone would send you that threatening letter," Willa pressed.

Wandalou picked up the half-donut from the plate in front of her. She took a bite. "My God, even that mean old witch's mutant mistakes are divine. You can really taste the love!"

"*Wandalou,*" said Isis.

Wandalou swallowed. "Fine. How should I know?"

"Because it's your secret," Willa whispered.

Wandalou narrowed her eyes. "Is it, Willa? *Mine?* Because last time I checked, it was all of ours. Jessie-Marie's, too."

"Then why didn't we get threatening letters?"

"Which means this isn't about *that* secret," Isis said. "Spill!"

Wandalou waved a hand in dismissal. "It was probably just some jealous loser from the pageant circuit. Those beauty queens are so vindictive and vain!"

"I doubt a disgruntled runner-up in a beauty pageant drove a blade into Jessie-Marie out there at the dog park."

Wandalou tipped a glance at Isis. "You never met Barbie Savina. Old Babs, she was—"

"*Wandalou*," Isis again stressed.

Wandalou surrendered. "Okay, fine. There is something else in addition to that big, fat full moon secret of ours." She leaned closer. The others followed suit. "Since…*you know*…I've had this problem. I'm not proud of it, but there are times when it shreds my last nerve and I'm sure it'll drive me insane!"

"What problem?" Willa whispered.

Wandalou confessed it all.

"You're cheating on Quinn?" Isis spat.

Wandalou waved her manicured hand and shushed her.

"With one of his fellow cops?"

Wandalou sucked down a deep breath and just as robustly expelled it. "I think the important point here, ladies, is the fact someone else knows!"

"And that someone lured Jessie-Marie out to the gazebo at the dog park, intending to blackmail her," Isis said grimly. "And when you didn't show up with the loot and Jessie-Marie did, something happened, and our good friend is dead."

"And whoever did it is still out there."

At Willa's declaration, Wandalou buried her head in her hands. "Oh, Quinn…he's gonna be furious when he finds out."

Silence briefly settled over the gathering.

"And we're no closer to understanding…or *breaking*…that other curse."

Wandalou lowered her hands and reached for the last morsel on the plate in front of her. "Damn, I could handle about a dozen more of these. That mean old *bruja* sure knows how to bang out a recipe."

"Speaking of the Frau," said Isis, "does anything about her seem familiar to either of you?"

Willa tipped a look behind the counter. The swinging door to the kitchen was shut, Frau Krumpt gone from view. "You mean apart from my time in story hour with the Brothers Grimm?"

"I was gonna say *Frankenstein*," said Wandalou.

Willa snorted. "Don't you mean *The Bride of Frankenstein*?"

"Not necessarily."

"I'm serious. Maybe it's my new heightened powers of awareness speaking, but I swear that she reminds me of someone else. I just can't place who."

"Someone who lives in a haunted old house, no doubt," said Wandalou. "Now, about that other looming problem."

"Poker Night," Isis sighed, which was their code for the full moon.

Flashing a smile that earned her none in return from Frau Krumpt, Willa scored a loaf of marbled rye and four blueberry scones that had miraculously escaped being set out for the horde of early birds who'd flocked to My Grains.

Not surprising, Willa left the bakery with the makings of what promised to be a beaut of a headache if she didn't attend to it. She washed down two aspirin with sparkling water and peeked out the living room window at her neighbor's house. The moving van was still parked in the driveway. So too was the pilot's pickup truck. Steeling herself, Willa gathered up her gift, the wrapped loaf of bread atop the pastry box, and started for the front door. As she passed the hall mirror, she caught a look at her reflection and decided on a touchup first. She tied up her mane of light brunette hair and then freed it. A wardrobe change followed. One more after that. She then swapped the sundress for jeans. Halfway to the sidewalk, the temptation to turn around and don the sundress again nearly possessed her, but she was out in the world, visible, and it was too late to question fate further.

She walked up her new neighbor's driveway. The moving van's ramp was extended, the house's front door open. A smile fixed upon her face, Willa continued to the entrance and knocked.

"Hello?" she called into the house. The empty foyer echoed and sent back her voice. Willa waited. No one answered. She repeated the question, this time louder, and received the same lack of a response. A glance around, a sigh of frustration, and then Willa entered the pilot's house.

The foyer was the same builder-beige that had been maintained for decades by Gert Dunkel. The empty rooms beyond were the eggshell paint you saw through gaps in curtains. Gert Dunkel had been one of those meek souls, as colorless as the interior of her house. Willa hoped the pilot wasn't afraid of bold paint choices when he got around to refreshing things.

She passed the living room. None of the expected furniture had been offloaded from the moving van—no leather sofa or club chairs, no gigantic flat-screen TV or boxes of sports memorabilia, all of it manly and matching the house's new owner. In fact, the entire place brooded with an atmosphere of emptiness. Nothing felt lived in, especially the kitchen. The late Gert Dunkel's relatives had picked the place clean before putting the house on the market, taking even the refrigerator. The oblong, upright gap among the cabinets hadn't been replaced. The countertops were bare, not even boasting a coffee maker.

Willa scanned the kitchen. There, in the far corner, the door to the basement stood cracked enough to show a ghost of light from below. And voices—male—drifted up the stairs. The movers, she guessed. Only what could they be moving down there?

She started toward the basement door. A few steps shy of reaching it, the door swung open, and there, with a smug grin on her thin, sharp lips, stood Brittany Barrows.

"What the hell do you think you're doing?" the skank demanded. "And why are you here?"

Willa blathered a response. "Wanted to welcome my new neighbor. A gift from My Grains."

"You're a *migraine*." Brittany closed the door behind her and assumed a defensive pose with arms folded and eyes narrowed.

Those few seconds helped shake Willa out of her shock. "I'd ask what *you* are doing here, but I can easily guess."

"What's that supposed to mean?"

Willa mimed as much skank-ness as she could stomach. *"Let me show you around, starting with the bedroom."*

Brittany's smirk tightened. "Jealous?"

"Of you? Never," Willa lied. "Other emotions, sure—disgust, for instance."

"Don't tell me that you still blame me for that ugly business," the skank sang. "That was all Phil Laslo's fault."

"It takes two," Willa said. "Like the number of faces I'm looking at."

Brittany stepped closer. "I sold this house to the new owner. I have every right to be here—unlike you. So why don't you take your sad, dry, busted-up old biscuits back to that convent of yours and write your little fairy tales."

Willa matched Brittany's advance. "I write novels—novels that readers *love*," she stressed. "And as for my biscuits being dry, I'll have you know these are the most delicious, moist, and wonderful biscuits ever made!"

She plunked the pastry box and loaf of marbled rye on the nearest patch of bare counter, turned, and stormed out of the pilot's empty house.

The doorbell gonged. Willa shifted the computer off her lap and got up to answer. En route, a hope that it was the pilot there to thank her for her housewarming gift flashed through her mind. But the smile she projected died an instant after she opened the door and saw Phil Laslo standing on the front step.

He spread his arms, all flash like a game show host and looking the part in his expensive shades, short-sleeved button-down shirt, men's Capri pants, and loafers, no socks. He'd added a diamond stud to one ear since the last time she'd endured his presence—the previous Christmas when he'd dropped by to deliver her gift: signing the divorce papers. Not small, that earring. Big enough to earn it and him notice.

"Hey," he said and peeled off the shades, revealing those slick bedroom blues.

"What do you want, Phil?" she said, not bothering to disguise the sourness in her tone.

"Why all the hostility, babe?"

"First off, I'm not your babe. Second, why do you think?"

He dialed down the slick. "Yeah, I guess. As for what I want…world peace?" Again, he spread his arms and flashed that theatrical smile. When the comedy routine failed, he came clean. "Okay, you got me. Can I come in?"

"No."

"Fine." He stepped closer and lowered his voice. "I got a call from a concerned party."

"Let me guess—*Brittany Barrows*," she said, stressing the skank's name sharply.

Phil folded half of his sunglasses and hung the other arm off the top buttoned button of his shirt. "She thinks you going over there," he tipped his chin in the direction of the house next door, "is a mistake."

"I'll bet she does."

"I do, too. Seriously, babe—" This earned him a scowl. "*Willa*, do you really think it's smart to throw yourself at an airline pilot? Dude's probably got a girl in every city around the globe. Talk about layovers!"

He cracked up at his own joke. She did not.

"How long have you been rehearsing that one?"

"Just since Brittany called. Hey, Willa…I'd hate for you to get your heart broken again." He covered the place on his chest where other men had hearts. It was all very well staged.

"No worries, Phil," she said. "You didn't break my heart. Barely made my pulse race at the best of times. *Buh-bye*."

She shut the door as he opened his mouth, ready to blather on. And oh, how satisfying it was to walk away with the last word!

After sunset, with Wandalou still not having shared the new evidence that would incriminate her, and the Hydrangea Heights PD no closer to solving Jessie-Marie's murder, Willa's doorbell again rang.

Willa opened the door. A tall figure stood outside, its identity indistinct in the poor light cast from the foyer. The man shifted a little. It was her new neighbor, the pilot. He smiled, and Willa melted.

"Hi, neighbor," he said in that deep, playful voice that pushed all of her proper buttons and more than a few improper ones.

Willa glanced down at the old pair of sweats she'd changed into following her previous unexpected visitor.

"Uh..." She slammed the door shut. The bell rang again. "Just a minute," Willa called through the house.

The minute turned out to be closer to five. When she again opened the door, clad in jeans and a flowy, floral top, the pilot was leaning against the rail in a jaunty pose, arms folded, big feet crossed at the ankles, a confident and knowing smirk on his lips. He wore a black zipped-up track jacket over a white T, jeans, and new sneakers. How those green eyes glowed in the sudden effulgence when she remembered to switch on the outside light.

"Hi," she said, feigning calm.

The pilot uncrossed his feet and straightened. She guessed he was somewhere above the six-foot mark, six-two or six-three. He smelled of summer rain and a hint of body spray or cologne applied in the perfect minimum dose. They sized one another up in silence. Willa swore he sniffed the air as though scenting her before extending his hand to complete his earlier offer of the shake interrupted on the night Jessie-Marie died.

"Joe Rhodes," he said.

She liked both names. They suited him. "Willa Forsyth," she said and accepted his hand in hers.

The pilot's—Joe Rhodes's—grip was strong but gentle, and the contact unleashed a chill through her. Willa explained that away as owing to nerves. She projected calm on the outside while inside she imagined herself coming apart. He held on. Not that she was in any rush to sever their connection. At one point, they both let go.

"I wanted to thank you for the gift—very nice of you," he said.

"Oh, *that*—it was nothing." And then she snorted an unflattering laugh that removed the confident mask she'd maintained for all of a minute and left Willa clearly horrified. She coughed to clear her throat. The hot pilot smiled.

"I've been wanting to meet you," Joe continued, either unfazed by Willa's *faux pas* or ignoring it.

"Wait, you have?"

"Since I found out I was living next door to a famous author."

She waved away the compliment and almost laugh-snorted again. This time, she caught herself before making the sound. "More like *infamous*. Do you want to come inside?"

Joe's smile turned serious. "In your house? Only with your permission."

"Yes, sure. By all means, neighbor."

Joe strutted past the threshold and took in his surroundings—the hall table with an amethyst glass vase, the indigo trim around the windows, and a framed, oversize book cover—Lena LaFleur's debut novel, *The Sweetest Kiss*, the one about the lady chocolatier who finds love during a memorable Valentine's season.

Eyes on the book cover, he asked, "Is this you?"

"Why yes, it is," Willa said. She posed beside the frame, her intention to appear cool, in control. But the frame shifted and she slipped along the wall. Willa yelped. Joe caught her as she fell. Suddenly, she was in the pilot's strong arms, gazing into his emerald gemstone eyes and chilled all over.

"Very impressive, Willa Forsyth," Joe said.

"Thanks." She again cleared her throat. Her footing restored, Joe released her. "And you—rumor has it that you fly up there." She aimed a finger at the ceiling. "Well, not in the attic. Not like a bat."

Again, Joe's face grew serious.

"Pilot. The big jets," she said.

Joe nodded. "Guilty."

"Also very impressive, Joe Rhodes."

His smile returned but now it seemed sad. An awkward silence fell over the foyer. Joe set his hands on his hips and shifted his weight from one foot to the other. "Willa?" he finally said.

"Yes?"

"I'm new in town. Don't know anyone here."

She recalled her encounter with Brittany Barrows and an ugly cocktail of jealousy and resentment mixed in her stomach.

"With my work schedule, I don't get to meet a lot of people. But I like you."

Willa brightened. "I like you, too, Joe."

"Maybe we could go into town. You could show me what Hydrangea Heights has to offer."

"Maybe have dinner," she said. "Or breakfast."

"Afraid I'm a bit of a late riser. A night owl. Or, like you said, a bat. Haven't seen the sun in…" The sentence went unfinished. "So breakfast's off the table unless it's after dark."

"Or while it's still dark," Willa said. "I know the perfect place…so long as you're not afraid of the mean old witch who runs it."

Renate Krumpt drove past the dog park and down the road through a cathedral of tall trees crowding in at both sides. She turned right and right once more. Ahead, surrounded by untended lawn, rose the ancient house with the gabled roof—that one in every town the locals are convinced is haunted.

"*It's not exactly turnkey,*" the *Schlampe*-real estate agent, that Barrows woman, said in Frau Krumpt's thoughts. "It's more…*skeleton* key."

"It is *wunderbah!*" she'd responded.

The sun had set. A sliver of waxing moon drifted over the treetops. As she stepped out of her car, a practical German import, she shot a look at the moon, which seemed to stare back like a narrowed eye.

Frau Krumpt pulled her tote along with the bag of wild things she'd gathered in the woods and approached the house. None of the windows were lit. Insects chirruped among the overgrown lawn. From somewhere in the nearby forest, a night bird cried out.

And then, as she inserted her key into the front door's lock, she heard another shout, one barely audible through the boarded-over glass of the cellar windows, from the man imprisoned down there.

Chapter 4

Race
the Moon

With only four days remaining until the first night of the September full moon, my three dear friends were no closer to understanding their dilemma let alone resolving it. Lives in the upscale community of Hydrangea Heights continued, normal on the outside and mostly oblivious to the undercurrent of wrongness that existed out of sight in the shadows.

Isis kissed Bob goodbye and sent him to work, dropped off the twins at school, and shopped at the local grocery store for the week. Her phone reminded her of an important upcoming event.

Ladies' Poker Night.

Wandalou, distraught over the prospect of telling Quinn about the crucial police evidence in her possession linked to my murder, exercised, plucked, primped, and moisturized. While her husband worked to solve the mystery of that tragic night and she lounged in their big soaking tub, performing her duties as a fashion influencer, her phone reminded her of an important upcoming event.

Ladies Poker Night.

And dear Willa, who only remembered the sweet kiss with her handsome pilot but not what followed after, jolted awake hours later than her usual early morning start time to the sound of her phone, reminding of an important upcoming event.

Ladies' Poker Night.

You see, in happier times now ended, we four would gather at alternating houses and, around tables, pour the wine, deal the cards, and enjoy a break from our routines. We played for fun not money, though Wandalou took the games and her victories more seriously than the rest. There was always dessert, and if the night was held at the Slades' place, Isis baked. If it was held at Willa's, Isis baked. Once, Wandalou offered to pick up pastries at the new bakery in town that she was convinced was owned by a witch—said witch had agreed to make her wedding cake. But by the time Wandalou pulled into the parking lot, the bakery was closed for the day and so, always reliable, Isis had baked her famous white chocolate macadamia nut cookies as a backup.

Those were enjoyable nights spent with great friends.

"It's getting worse," Isis said in a voice meant only for the two women jogging at either side.

"I'm still ripping off stray hairs leftover from the last time," Wandalou said from the corner of her mouth. "Any worse, and I'll have to invest in heavy-duty clippers. The kind dog groomers use."

The three women, dressed in tasteful athletic gear, trendy baseball caps, and new cross trainers, ran along the path that meandered past the gazebo. There was no police tape and the blood had been scrubbed off the wood, but all averted their eyes; looking directly at the scene of the crime would have broken their hearts.

"What do you mean?" asked Willa.

"Do I have to spell it out to you?" Wandalou huffed. "We're talking full-on *Yeti.*"

"No, I meant what Isis said. Worse? How?"

"The night it happened," Isis continued in a lower voice. "Before they found Jessie-Marie. One of the twins, when she raided the fridge, I lost it."

"She did. I saw it," Willa said.

"Lost it? What are we talking? On a scale of Larry Talbot?" Wandalou asked.

The others understood the reference. After the night of *the incident* in July that put we four friends in the clutches of this unwanted malady, we'd spent a lot of time researching the Lycanthropy myth—everything from historical accounts based upon unfortunates suffering from Hypertrichosis, otherwise referred to as Werewolf's Syndrome where hair grows across most of the body, to pop culture references, Instagram shorts, and Facebook clubs.

"Not even a quarter of a Larry Talbot. Maybe a tenth," Isis said. "One of the twins was lipping off."

Wandalou grunted. "Big surprise there."

"And I…I don't know. It was like a volcano went off inside me. But it was only for a few seconds, and then I…I'm not sure…I choked it back down."

"Wait. Maybe that means it's getting better not worse. That we can control it," Willa offered.

"I don't know. I'm liking my steaks rarer and rarer these days." This came from Wandalou.

Willa glanced over. "How rare?"

"Tartare."

They jogged on and passed two teenage boys who were walking along the path with a leashed golden retriever. The dog sported a blue bandana around his collar.

"What'd I tell you, buddy?" one of the youths said to the other in a secretive voice that should have been out of earshot but wasn't owing to better-than-normal powers of hearing. "You want to see fine-ass cougars, you hang out at the dog park!"

All three women stopped, turned. The two teens froze, and the color drained from their faces along with any swagger.

"Sorry," the one holding the leash apologized.

"Sorry *what?*" Wandalou demanded.

"Sorry, *ma'am.*"

"That's right," she said and did one of those head thrusts at the offender meant to intimidate.

The boys jumped back. The dog barked. My friends turned and resumed jogging. All three grinned.

The smiles drained from their faces when they reached the end of the path and the remains of the dirt pile.

"This is it," said Isis.

They stared at the earth which had been sifted and scoured for clues after the grisly discovery. A low breeze gossiped through the surrounding trees and stirred colored leaves in the broken sunlight spilling down past puffy white clouds.

"Poor Jessie-Marie," Wandalou whispered.

The breeze lifted, and—

—I called out to them, my three dear friends.

"Isis, do you hear me?" She didn't. "Wandalou?"

Nothing, then—

"What was that?" asked Willa.

Wandalou sighed. "What was what?"

"It sounded like…no, it couldn't be."

"What did you hear, Willa?" Isis pressed.

"I think it was Jessie-Marie!"

They froze, none of my friends daring to speak. I, too, grew paralyzed from the implication. Then I shook it off and called louder. *"Willa, I'm right here!"*

Willa gasped and turned to face me, but I could tell from her surprise that she saw only emptiness. "Jessie-Marie, are you here?" Willa asked to what she thought was thin air.

I tried to tell her that, yes, I was! To tell her everything. But the louder I shouted, the less she seemed to hear me, even with her ears at their new level of heightened awareness.

They sipped from their water bottles and ate power bars at the gazebo. "I swear, for a moment, it was Jessie-Marie," said Willa.

Wandalou made a face. "That's impossible."

"Is it?"

Wandalou shrugged. "Ghosts, seriously?"

"Two months ago, I didn't believe in shapeshifters, but my whole sense of wonder has recently expanded to cover that one, too."

"Point taken." Wandalou chugged her water. Isis and Willa focused on her. "What?"

"The letter," said Isis.

Wandalou turned away. "It's just that…"

"*Wandalou,*" Isis admonished.

Wandalou snapped back. "I know! Whoever did this to Jessie-Marie is still out there."

"And still dangerous," said Willa. "To you—maybe to all of us!"

"Quinn's gonna blow his top. We're talking *bat shit crazy.*"

Willa set a hand on Wandalou's arm. Wandalou shot her a look, and Willa withdrew her touch, which had been meant to console.

Isis was less understanding. "Well, buckle up, buttercup—it's past time that you told him."

"I will," Wandalou huffed. And then her defensive tone shrank. "Just not until after Poker Night. I can't handle dealing with two apocalypses at the same time."

"You'd better," Isis threatened.

"Trust me. Let's get through one end-of-the-world scenario first before I'm forced to deal with the other."

Isis and Willa cut Wandalou a break. She was right. In four nights, the world as they all three knew it could be at an end. One crisis at a time seemed only logical.

The restlessness started and grew like a fever. "I'll be back," Isis said.

Bob half-glanced over from the TV, presently tuned to the baseball playoffs. "Where you going?"

"For a jog."

At Number 11 Mistral Lane, Waundalou attempted to type a witty bit for her followers: "…looks more like George Washington's burlap underwear than designer threads," three times before giving up. She pocketed her phone and exited the house.

And Willa, who had wandered through most of the afternoon in a kind of fugue, suffered the same energy spike. Methodically, she exited the house, got in her car, and drove.

All three converged again at the dog park.

"I could run a marathon," said Willa.

Wandalou aimed a manicured pointer at the sky. "All the way to the dark side."

The moon swam behind the clouds, nearly full.

"Come on," said Isis.

They resumed jogging. The night sped by in blurs of black tinged with a hot red glare that inched in from the periphery. In record time, they'd run the circuit around and back to the gazebo. On the next lap, Wandalou dropped to all fours and sprinted ahead of the others. Willa followed suit. Then Isis caught up, tossed back her head, and howled.

Willa carried the cards, wine, and three plastic cups up to the room on the second floor. Inside, an overhead light, the only source because the space had no windows, cast its glow on a single bed and two comfortable new Queen Anne chairs upholstered in royal purple velvet. The card table had been set up with three folding chairs, unfolded. She thought of the fourth missing from the paradigm and forced a smile while setting out disposable plates, plastic forks, and paper napkins. The good china was reasonably safe downstairs, where it would hopefully stay over the course of the next three nights.

Poker Nights, her inner critic corrected. *Plural.*

The metal wall above the bed still bore jagged claw marks from the last month's visit to this place, which she despised but was grateful to have access to, like one of those big discount chain stores she loathed to enter but knew was the cheapest, sometimes only, destination to get what you needed.

Phil had insisted they build the panic room for her protection during his frequent "business trips" out of town—business trips being code for something else, just like "Poker Night." Having the panic room had kept all four of them confined during the stretch of full moon nights in August. Oh, it had gotten ugly. Not that she remembered most of it, only fragments the way a dream fades the moment the dreamer wakes up.

Bob flashed that look of frustration—a spoiled boy's scowl projected onto a man's face. Isis, dressed in a fetching burnt orange turtleneck and slacks that complimented her red hair, answered with a calm smile while she wrapped aluminum foil over the cooling metal platter of fig bars.

"You'll just have to deal with it," Isis said.

"Poker Night? Again…so soon?" he moaned. It was one final attempt to get his way. "But I've been at work all day. I just want to relax."

Oh, the digs she could have lobbed back. Instead, she reached up and squeezed his chin. Then, without words and carrying the tray, she walked out of the house.

"Do you have your phone on you in case?" he called after her.

Isis shook her head, looked both ways, and crossed the street.

"**H**ow long?" Quinn asked.

"I don't know," Wandalou said as she studied the mirror—not that the reflection staring back would endure beyond the next few hours. "I could be out all night."

Quinn sighed. "You and your coven."

She shot him a look in the mirror.

"Just kidding. But you ladies take your poker nights very seriously."

"Yes, we do." She pecked a kiss on his cheek, checked the mirror one last time, and, from the periphery, noted the shelf covered in trophies from her old beauty pageant days. The image threatened to paralyze her, bewitch her where she stood. Time was short. The sun was barely hanging on when Wandalou turned her focus toward the bedroom's nearest window.

"Gotta motor," she said.

"Do you have your cell?"

"It's off. Goodnight, Quinn."

She hastened down the stairs and out of their house. By the time Wandalou reached the street, she was in a sprint—no small feat, considering she was in a new pair of Oscar Sabatini heels, the ones with the jeweled vamps.

Reluctantly, Wandalou entered the panic room. Willa moved to fix the deadbolt in place. "Before you do, I have to pee," Wandalou protested.

Willa and Isis exchanged looks. "Do you really, or are you planning to bolt?" Isis asked.

Wandalou scowled. "Stop looking at me like that."

"Well," said Willa. "Do you have to whazz or not?"

Wandalou waved her off and took one of the folding chairs around the card table. Willa secured the door. The room thrummed in silence.

"God, I can't breathe," Wandalou griped.

"You're sitting directly beneath the air vent."

Wandalou glanced up to see that she was. "Can we at least have some music?"

"We tried that last time, remember?" said Willa. "My tablet was in pieces in the morning."

"Touchy," Wandalou fired back.

Isis, ever the diplomat, set the dessert tray on the table and served. Willa opened the wine and poured. "There, isn't that lovely?" said Isis.

Wandalou eyed the plastic cup. "Seriously? What are we? In a sorority?"

"Phi Beta Lycan," Willa snorted. "Along with my tablet, do you remember what was left of my favorite set of wine glasses after our previous Poker Night?"

Wandalou sipped. They picked at their dessert. Beyond the walls of the house, daylight vanished, and the world grew dark.

"Now what?" Willa asked.

Isis reached for the deck. "I guess we deal the cards." She shuffled, her skill exceptional. The cards merged and rearranged in a blur, the sound like music. Willa watched and only realized she was being hypnotized after her eyes stung from not blinking.

"Do you suppose it's possible that nothing will happen to us tonight?" asked Wandalou.

Isis stilled her shuffling. "Why do you say that?"

"You told us you let it slip out in front of one of the twins. Maybe it's true that we can control it. You know, hold it in as well as release the beast on our terms."

"I suppose anything is possible," Isis said. "There's so much we don't know about the condition."

"I don't actually remember being *bit*. Just those little love-nibbles on the neck."

Isis pondered the statement. "I recall things differently."

"But it could mean that our bodies are fighting it off like a cold."

Willa reached for the bottle and refilled their cups. "A toast—to Jessie-Marie."

"Here, here," said Wandalou.

They tapped their plastic cups together and knocked back sips.

"And to the three of us—three strong willed and in charge women," Isis said. They toasted again. Isis picked up the deck.

"Oh," Willa interjected. "And to we three strong-willed and in charge women beating this *cold*."

"I'll drink to that," said Isis.

They tapped their cups a third time and sipped.

"You know, I feel better already," said Wandalou. "Like it's gone from my system. *Ha—take that, she-wolf!*"

"Jacks are better to open," Isis said as she dealt the cards.

Willa tossed back her head and howled. Someone swore in a juicy, guttural voice. Then things grew blurry.

Exquisite agony seized hold of Willa. It was more than the sensation that her blood was on fire, boiling her organs in the process, or that she heard her bones *crack* as they reconfigured themselves into a different skeletal structure. No, the worst bit traveled deeper, to what Willa thought of as her soul.

She attempted to scream. Instead, another animal's roar powered up her throat, scraping tender flesh on its way. Willa leaned back so far to expel the howl that she toppled over in her chair. Floor and ceiling had become jumbled anyway. Still in the chair, she saw that both Isis and Wandalou were similarly affected.

"*This sucks!*" Wandalou spat past teeth suddenly sharper than her tongue before her howl joined Willa's in counterpoint.

At first, her attempt to rein in the wolf worked. Isis recalled meeting Bob Slade at a charity bake sale. Handsome, she knew straight away that what you saw was what you got: a single father saddled with twin girls after his wife had fled. She'd baked cupcakes frosted in homemade lemon buttercream sprinkled in spring pastel colors. Bob's girls had flocked to her table and demanded their dad buy some. He and Isis struck up a conversation. He liked her exotic name, asked if she was a goddess.

"Yes, but I'm not nearly as old as my namesake," she said coyly.

Isis didn't want kids. But at the time, she didn't really know what she wanted, and on the day they moved into the house on Mistral Lane, she'd found it. All of it. She loved the twins and their father. Their faces hovered out of focus in the building red haze before her eyes as she tried to focus on those better days. Marci was the one who always questioned and tested her authority. Nothing Isis couldn't handle, but for a terrible second, she imagined sinking her teeth into the top of the girl's head. Saliva squirted across her tongue.

"*What—?*" Isis barked, horrified.

The red stain colored everything like a filter of blood. Her vision blurred worse. But the sound of a nasal chuckle at her right helped it to focus.

"You look *so* ridiculous," Wandalou chortled.

Isis laughed, too. Wandalou Trueheart no longer appeared so impeccable in her designer best. The neighborhood's former beauty queen flashed four incisors too big for her mouth. Wandalou's nose had extended into a snout. She sported whiskers and five o'clock shadow over most of her face.

"So says she who could seriously use a shave," Isis lobbed back.

"What?" Wandalou said. She scrambled both hands up to her face, patted her thickening pelt with hairy fingers capped by pomegranate-red nails, and gasped. "Well…*shit*."

Still flat on her spine in her spilled folding chair, Willa joined the laughter. "Feels like I've just been to the chiropractor," she said in a juicy baritone. "Will somebody please help me up?"

Both of the seated women moved to assist at either side. Together, they lifted Willa, chair as well, back to sitting upright at the card table. Willa's brown hair, usually shoulder-length pretty, now spilled in a vast, unruly mess.

"*Whoa,*" Wandalou said.

"What?"

"Be kind," Isis growled.

Then Willa tipped a look at Isis and her tangled mop of red hair and let forth with a howl of laughter.

"Or not," Isis said.

"I'm sorry, it's just that it's all so…*silly*. When you think about it, we all needed a good laugh after we lost Jessie-Marie," Willa said. "A bad hair night isn't so terrible."

"No, it's not," Wandalou agreed. "Though I am really, really…*hangry*."

"Have a fig bar, dear," Isis said and offered the serving tray.

Lightning quick, Wandalou slapped the tray out of Isis's hand. The platter and its contents struck the wall. "I don't want any dessert—I want *meat!*"

Willa and Isis exchanged shocked looks before both broke up in fresh giggles.

"Yeah, Icy, you should have brought charcuterie instead," said Willa.

Wandalou joined into the guffaw. Then, all at once, their laughter shorted out, and only throaty growls filled the sealed panic room.

Little that happened after that was funny.

Chapter 5

Waxing
and Waning

Even a housewife who is pure at heart and says her prayers by night, sang the voice in Wandalou's foggy thoughts, *could turn into a wolf when the moon is full and deliver one hell of a bite!*

Her eyes shot open. At first, she confused the bright glare in the sky as coming from the full moon. Then she remembered the panic room. The blurry glow stabilized. She was on her back looking up at the overhead light. As she moved to sit, the chaos surrounding her registered. The card table had been flipped over along with all of the folding chairs. Isis was sprawled in one of the Queen Annes, her burnt-orange turtleneck that once so nicely complimented her hair ripped across the belly. The iron tang of spilled blood filled the air.

Willa—*where is Willa?*

Wandalou faced the door. Willa stood with both hands flat on the metal surface. At first, Wandalou couldn't tell if Willa was breathing. Maybe her stiff pose owed to rigor mortis. She'd died melded to the door in a frenzy to escape. "Oh no," Wandalou exclaimed in a voice losing its wolfishness.

At that, Willa roused. "Huh?" She slid down to the floor and came out of the trance.

Isis woke, too, seeming to predict that the long night was over.

"What happened?" asked Willa, still on the floor.

"I don't remember much, just a lot of growling and howling," said Isis. "I hope your handsome pilot didn't hear it."

Willa made it back to her feet and waved a hand, dismissing that one potential problem. "Oh, no, he's away until the twentieth of the month. We're good."

"Good?" Wandalou parroted and groaned as she sat up.

"I also tend to recall plenty of bitter complaining," Isis continued. "Something about *dominance*." Both she and Willa faced Wandalou.

"What?"

"You don't recall demanding to be respected as *the Alpha*?"

"No," said Wandalou. She raised her right hand to rub her eyes only to stop. Wound around her fingers were clumps of red hair.

"What's that smell?" asked Willa.

Wandalou eyed her nails without blinking. "Uh…"

"Smells what I imagine the back end of a butcher shop is like."

Isis screamed.

Willa and Wandalou looked over to see that Isis had smoothed out the shredded stomach area of her turtleneck to reveal even worse shredding in her actual stomach beneath the tatters. Willa pulled on the deadbolt. The lock resisted. At her back, Isis sucked down short, desperate sips of air while Wandalou clucked and sprialled.

"Did I do this? I didn't mean to. Oh, Isis, I'm so sorry!"

"You and your damned manicures!" Isis spat.

The lock finally released. Willa raced out of the panic room and to the master's en suite. From the cabinets, she retrieved tweezers and cotton balls. From beneath the bathroom counter, she grabbed the bottle of rubbing alcohol and, not sure why, chewable antacids. On her way through the bedroom, she pulled her phone off its charger.

From the cut of her eye, Willa noticed that dawn had broken gray beyond the windows.

Wandalou was leaning over Isis, who pushed her away just as Willa returned to the panic room. "Let me see it!" Wandalou demanded.

"Why? So you can finish the job?"

Wandalou tsked. "Stop being such a baby. Besides, I can't be sure, but I think it's sealing up."

Isis gazed down. True to Wandalou's claim, the gash had mended noticeably. Everything internal that had been exposed and hanging out was gone from view beneath healthy pink skin. The seams of the wound finished joining up as they watched. Bloodstains faded along with the noxious iron taint in the air.

Willa's right pointer hovered over the dial button. "Should I call 911?"

"*No*," both Wandalou and Isis bellowed.

"Fine."

"But can I ask you…?" Wandalou said, her arms folded. "Anyone up for breakfast? Because I am absolutely ravenous. Ready to devour my own face, that's how hungry."

"I could eat," said Isis.

Willa shrugged. "Sure."

Five minutes later, Willa emerged from the house, one sneaker on, the other lost somewhere in the shambles of the overturned panic room. Behind her walked Isis, her turtleneck torn, her hair a disaster. Bringing up the rear was Wandalou, clad in the rags of her exquisite designer labels and sporting a short mustache that the coming of dawn had failed to remove from her face.

They piled into Willa's compact, efficient car and made their early morning escape from Hydrangea Heights. One town over in Cherryvale, they pulled into a neon drive-through lane.

"Good morning," a cheery woman's voice greeted over the intercom. "What can I get you today?"

"*Everything*," Wandalou demanded before Willa could speak.

"**W**e got through it," Wandalou said around a mouthful of breakfast biscuit with extra bacon, sausage, and hot sauce.

"We got through the *first night*," Isis reminded. "We've got two more with this full moon to deal with."

"Oh crap," Wandalou spat. She reached for the tall cup of orange juice in the cardboard drink holder and slurped hers down to the ice.

Isis leaned forward from the back seat. "An interesting development, though—learning that whatever wounds we sustain during the transformation heal by sunrise."

"You're just lucky those dessert forks were plastic and not silver," Wandalou chuckled, but the joke fell on deaf ears.

"Unlike Jessie-Marie," Willa said, the statement sobering. "Whoever killed her…*murdered* her…"

"And the police still don't know who did it," said Isis. She then poked Wandalou in the ribs.

"Hey, quit it. I've had a very trying night."

"Yeah, well, you've got two more to suffer through, and then you're gonna tell Quinn about the letter!"

Wandalou grumbled and shook the ice in her emptied cup. Outside the car, the day brightened and the world woke, so far none of their neighbors the wiser for the night's travails.

"See you later, *beyatches,*" Wandalou said. She cackled once, licked her hairy upper lip, and sashayed off. "If you could only see how trashed you both look!" Then, snapping her fingers, she carried on to Number 11 Mistral Lane. Willa and Isis shrugged, nodded, and each wandered to their front doors, aware of their exhaustion.

Wearing only a pair of boxers, Quinn lie sprawled across their bed. The flat-screen on the opposite wall displayed the news of the young day on mute. Quinn fiddled with his phone and barely glanced up when she entered the bedroom. When he did, however…

"Holy…!" His eyes widened. "Rough night?"

Wandalou hid her upper lip from him behind the fingers of her right hand. "You could say that."

"You and the girls didn't come to blows over poker hands, did you?"

"No," she laughed, all nerves. "Nothing as violent as that. Certainly not as far as, say, *disemboweling* one another."

Quinn eyed her suspiciously. "Disemboweling?"

"Just to use a phrase. No, it was all in good fun, really. In fact, we had so much fun we're doing it again tonight. Maybe even tomorrow night, too."

"Tonight?" he sighed. "I thought you and I could, you know…" Quinn set down his phone and eased off the bed. He padded over to her and wrapped his arms around Wandalou, who stiffened.

"That all sounds great," Wandalou said. "But the girls and I, we're all really hurting about what happened to Jessie-Marie and need to rally."

Quinn attempted to kiss her. Wandalou pushed him away. "What's wrong?"

"You smell," she lied.

"*I* smell?" he chuckled. "You're the one with a definite whiff of wet dog and kennel in the K-9 unit coming off you, babe."

"*Quinn,*" she huffed. Wandalou stormed into the en suite and slammed the door. "*Phew,*" she exhaled beneath her breath while Quinn apologized through the closed door.

"Seriously, *chica,* I'm sorry."

"You will be when you're alone tonight," she called. "Sometimes, Quinn, you can be so hurtful!"

"Are we fighting?" he asked.

She moved in front of the acre of mirror and saw the unwanted mark leftover from the previous night's transformation, this time there like a ribbon laid across her upper lip instead of her eyebrows.

"What do you think?" she challenged while removing the hot wax pot and strips from under the sink. "I'm so frustrated right now that I could scream!"

Quinn gave his junk an absent scratch and turned in time to catch the baseball highlights on the muted TV screen. "Oh, come on, Wandalou, it isn't that bad."

Only it sure sounded so when she released one of three bloodcurdling primal screams from behind the bathroom door.

Isis entered the house and headed straight for the bedroom. She heard Bob and the girls in the kitchen, breakfast announced by the clink of spoons in cereal bowls and the usual morning conversation. Smiling, Isis continued up the stairs and into the master suite. She was behind the door to the bathroom before Bob responded to the patter of her footfalls that announced her return.

"Hon, that you?" he called.

She had stripped out of the tatters of her clothes and saw her wounds had completely healed. No trace of the night's savagery marred her midriff. "Yes, it's me."

The bathroom door handle jiggled. She'd locked it.

"Why'd you lock the door?" Bob asked.

"Privacy."

"In this house?" he said lightly. "Come on, Icy. The girls and I miss you."

"I'll be out in a bit."

"In how long of a bit? I have to drop them off at school *in a bit*," Bob said.

"You do that, dear," Isis said. "I'm kind of a mess— need a shower. Bye."

"Must have been one hell of a poker game," Bob grumbled from the other side of the door.

Willa righted the card table and chairs, cleaned up the mess of spilled pastries and wine from crushed cups, and returned the crime scene inside the panic room to its readiness for another night of enforced imprisonment while the rest of their neighbors slept.

"One night of this full moon down, two to go," she whispered, the words tasting bitter. Then, scowling, she asked, "Where's the wine bottle?"

At the drive-through, she'd eaten not one but three greasy breakfast sausage sandwiches. Those now sat like concrete—with rebar—in her gut. She returned her cache of first aid supplies to the en suite, stripped out of her one sneaker and frayed ensemble, and checked her body for lingering marks. Apart from unwanted peach fuzz on her legs that hadn't been there a day before, she'd returned back to a whole Willa.

She got out the shaving lotion and razors, ran the bath, and went to work.

After tossing the remains of her clothes into a bag and shoving that in the barrel beneath another sack of trash, Isis wandered into the kitchen and cooked. Enough lasagna was left over from the previous dinner to cover this night's, but she defrosted chicken breasts and whipped up a pot pie with fresh vegetables, a trusted method to get the twins to eat healthy.

After it was assembled and only needed to bake in the oven so that the crust was golden brown, she went to work on brownies—luscious turtle brownies that were crispy on the outside, gooey within, and topped with toasted pecans. She wondered if Frau Krumpt, the supposed witch of My Grains, found a similar sense of peace when baking. She certainly hadn't tasted the woman's hatred in those donuts.

While the brownies cooled, she baked the chicken potpie. All the while, Isis hummed a happy little tune. She set the table and then flipped through a magazine, a smile fixed on her lips. She didn't remember passing out face-first onto the tabletop and only woke to the sound of the smoke alarm warning her that dinner had become charcoal.

"Pizza," Isis said. "Get whatever you want."

Bob leaned against the fridge, tie unknotted, arms folded. "Are you sure?"

"About pizza? Quite," she trilled and picked up the dessert tray. "Brownies for dessert. Be sure the girls don't sneak seconds or they'll be up all night jumping on their beds."

"No, I meant about…"

"Poker Night? Even more sure." She kissed his cheek on her way past. "Housewives need to get free of the apron strings men tie on the oven door every now and then so they don't go crazy and start howling at the moon." She stopped suddenly and laughed a sharp lunatic cackle at her own secret joke and then walked out, leaving a slightly perplexed Bob to handle the twins on his own.

"Are we still fighting?" Quinn asked.

Wandalou pursed her lips before answering. "I'm not sure."

Quinn narrowed his gaze. "What's wrong with your face?" Wandalou sighed and stormed past him in the direction of the front door. "Your upper lip's all raw and red."

"Yes, we're still fighting, Quinn," she spat over her shoulder on her way out.

An hour before sunset, they were all back around the card table. New cups and a fresh bottle of wine were laid out beside the platter of brownies, paper plates, napkins, and plastic forks.

"Well," Isis said in a clipped falsetto.

"Well," Willa echoed.

Wandalou leaned back and scowled. "*Well?*"

"Well *what?*" asked Isis.

"We're trapped again in this hell-hole and no closer to understanding what ails us!"

Isis drank down a cleaning breath. Willa poured the wine.

"I believe the best way to fixing what's broken is to track down *you-know-who*," Isis said.

Wandalou hissed. "Don't say his name. Don't you dare say his name!"

"I agree. If we hope to be free of this nightmare, we have to find him," said Willa.

Wandalou leaned forward. "That brainless collection of biceps and washboard abs couldn't add one plus one to make two, let alone figure out a cure!"

"Agreed, though he might have some insight into the affliction that we don't. Maybe a clue that might help us to cure it."

"I doubt that," Wandalou sighed.

"Brownie?" Isis served them from the platter.

"These aren't, *you know*, those kinds of brownies, are they?" asked Willa.

"I wish," said Wandalou.

"They most certainly are not," said Isis with righteous hauteur. But on the heels of that declaration, she sat back thoughtfully. "However, that gives me an idea."

"I don't know—your last big idea put us in this mess," Wandalou said.

Isis glared. The tension hanging in the air thickened.

Willa cleared her throat. "What idea, Icy?"

Isis thawed. "Tranquilizers."

"Say what?" Wandalou asked between bites.

"What if we just slept away the nights when there's a full moon? Jessie-Marie was using sleeping pills every once in a while. Knocked her out cold for eight solid hours, she told me. Instead of putting ourselves through absolute madness, we wake up refreshed, none the wiser or worse for wear."

"Or disemboweled," said Willa, which earned her a guilty scowl from Wandalou.

"It's just an idea," Isis said.

"But a good one." Willa raised her cup. "Here's to figuring something out. Cheers, ladies."

The others followed suit. They sipped wine. Not long after, the familiar tickle itched at Willa's throat. She coughed to clear it.

"What's wrong—something go down the wrong pipe?" asked Isis.

"Maybe it's a hairball," Wandalou snickered. But the smile soon dropped from her face, because the tickle was inside her throat as well. "Hold on, girls," she said. "Here it comes."

They all tossed back their heads and expelled the building itch in howls.

On the second night of the September full moon, my three friends suffered the painful transformation, their bones and bodies reshaping, their screams contained within the walls of Willa's panic room. Once again, various staring contests and displays of domination took place that would barely be recalled by morning's moonfall. Teeth snapped. Blood flowed. The wolves hungered.

By sunrise, with the panic room in shambles, Willa released the lock and all three emerged, their clothes torn, their hair a mess, their wounds healing quickly. They traveled a town over for another drive-through breakfast and slinked back to their normal lives, exhausted by the looming prospect of yet one more full moon together.

At noon, after a brief nap, my friend Isis Slade slipped out of her house and down the sidewalk to Number 17 Mistral Lane. She cut through the garden, around the house, and to the back kitchen door. Unknown to her, my former neighbor, Regina Gowl, lurked among her roses, deadheading and snipping leaves. Regina saw Isis produce the house key I'd given her in case of necessities or emergencies and enter while my husband, Tim, was working his shift at the hospital.

What Regina didn't see was Isis disable the security system using the code I'd shared with her, sneak up the staircase to the master bedroom's en suite, and open the medicine cabinet. Tim, love him, hadn't yet gotten around to one of those rules extolled by medical professionals: when a loved one dies, properly dispose of any and all of their leftover medication.

She easily located my sleeping pills, reset the security alarm, and slipped back through the kitchen door, her intrusion unseen by all save one.

And that one set of frigid eyes glaring beneath a sunbonnet had dark secrets of her own.

"What the hell's this?" Wandalou griped at the sight of three water bottles on the card table. "Where's the *vino*?"

Isis held up the prescription bottle and gave a slight shake. "Don't mix with alcohol." She unscrewed the child-safety cap and passed one pink tablet around the table to each woman seated there.

"Better make mine a double," Wandalou said.

"I can't—Jessie-Marie only had four pills left. We don't want any unfair advantages in case this works."

Before sunset—before moonrise and ticklish throats—all three passed out at the card table. Bones cracked and reset. Yelps rather than howls filtered past lips. Willa performed the equivalent of a dog running in its sleep. Wandalou slumped out of her chair and slept curled upon the floor. Isis drooled.

The morning arrived, foggy in their minds and misty beyond the windows. Autumn's chill infused the air.

"Hungry?" asked Willa.

"Very," both Isis and Wandalou agreed.

For the third consecutive morning, they repeated their fast food ritual.

"It's over," said Wandalou.

"Only until next month," said Isis.

Wandalou whirled toward the backseat. "Do you have to be such a downer?"

Isis's expression tightened. "I'm about to be an even bigger dark cloud and remind you what this morning means, Wandalou."

Wandalou, in the act of mid-bite, lowered her breakfast sandwich and didn't eat any more of it.

Chapter 6

Good Luck to You, Wandalou

My friend Wandalou Trueheart had not pulled to a complete stop at the sign on Pleasant Street where it crossed Maple. She heard a single, short burst of the police siren. Swearing, she glanced into the rearview mirror and saw the Hydrangea Heights Police Department cruiser running with its lights flashing on her bumper. Swearing again, she switched on her blinker and stopped at the curb.

Not today of all days, she thought, her heart, already in a gallop, racing even faster.

Seconds dragged out with maddening slowness. Wandalou forgot how to breathe. She shot a look at the clock on the car's dashboard. The digital numbers blurred before stabilizing in rigid blue angles: 1:21. In nine minutes, she'd be late.

The cruiser's door opened. Out stepped a tall man in uniform and shades that she would have agreed fit him with criminal perfection on any other day. On this afternoon, at that exact moment, the fire in her belly built and incinerated her patience. She didn't have time for overzealous lawmen.

"Officer," she said and realized the window was up and she hadn't removed her license or registration from wallet or glove box.

The policeman leaned down. She caught his scent—clean, masculine sweat and either deodorant or body spray splashed with a generous dose of sunshine. It was narcotic and cooled much of the conflagration from feasting on her insides.

"In a hurry?" he asked in a deep voice—cocky, which doused accelerant on the flames and re-stoked the fire.

She narrowed her eyes and flashed her own version of his arrogant expression. "As a matter of fact, I am."

The policeman glanced around the car's interior, his eyes hidden behind his sunglasses. "I don't see any blood."

"Blood?" she repeated.

"Yeah, you know—just cause as to why you hadn't come to a complete stop at the sign back there. I don't see any open wounds that would have you racing to the hospital."

Clearly, she'd kept her wounds well hidden, especially those that hadn't healed and bled not blood but trickles of regret and disappointment. "I'll open a wound," she hissed through a fake smile and clenched teeth.

"What was that?" the policeman asked.

"I'm about to be late for a very important meeting," she said.

"Oh? Could that possibly be with your lawyer for the hypothetical car crash you caused back there at the stop sign you ran?"

Wandalou broke focus with the man long enough to shoot a look into the rearview. No traffic waited or crossed anywhere. Birds chirped in the surrounding trees.

"Or maybe you're meeting with the undertaker," he said and laughed, and *oh,* it was the laugh that really made her hate him.

1:24, the dashboard clock read.

"License and registration," he didn't ask so much as demand.

Huffing out a breath, Wandalou leaned over and popped the glove box. The registration was folded neatly atop the package of travel tissues and the blade she always carried for protection. She made sure to close the glove box completely and fished her wallet out of her tote—a knockoff, she knew, but the real thing would have cost thousands she didn't have and the cheaper version looked passable until you got up close and knew the differences.

He took them in his big, dumb hand and ran those hidden eyes over her name, her address, her license photo, which she'd demanded be retaken until she approved of the selection. Wandalou sensed his focus darting between her license and her. He clapped the doorframe beside the rolled-down window's track and straightened. "Remain right here," he commanded.

1:27.

It was considerably longer when he returned and handed back her things. "You're free to go," he said. "With a warning this time, Miss Trueheart."

Even the manner in which he spoke her name was infuriating, as though he *tasted* it more than merely spoke it. The way his eyes followed her told Wandalou he'd taken notice.

"Snap a picture, officer—it'll last longer," she said.

Unfortunately, she worried that the overzealous cop's mental snapshot would be the only modeling work she'd book in this strange, pompous little suburb where photographer Royce Benson had set up his studio.

And, sadly, she was correct.

At 1:53, she entered through the big glass door, her look-book tucked under the arm of the hand holding her knockoff Castillo tote, and approached the gatekeeper guarding the reception desk. "Hi," she said, a veneer of calm displayed. "I have a 2:00 with Royce."

The receptionist, an attractive blonde not likely much older than twenty-one but decades beyond that in sensing BS, clicked her tongue. "*Mister* Benson expected you half an hour ago. Good day."

And with that, the gatekeeper turned away and buried her face in the computer screen on the desk in front of her, as though Wandalou wasn't there.

She was down to a quarter of a tank of gas and a pittance in her bank account. Wandalou maintained her composure until she reached her car, but once back behind the wheel, her façade shattered. She smacked at the steering wheel twice before the sting caused her to rethink the outburst. She reached for the sweater folded on the backseat in case the temperature dropped and she got cold, intending to bury her face in it and scream at the limit of her lungs, only that would smear her makeup and, Royce Benson be damned, she agreed that she looked magnificent.

A shiver rolled down her spine, curiously hotter than frigid. When it passed, she inserted the key into the ignition and started the car. A quick flip to GPS on her phone, and she found herself deep in what passed for the downtown of Hydrangea Heights. She pulled into a parking lot, tore a fresh page out of the small notebook in her tote, and reached for the pen in the catchall.

Another gatekeeper guarded the stationhouse from behind what Wandalou assumed was a bulletproof, bank teller-style window.

"Can I help you?" the woman asked. She was dressed in a version of the same cop's uniform, only hers didn't love her physique nearly as much as the officer Wandalou had come to find.

"Yes, *Phyllis*," Wandalou said after squinting through the glass at the woman's nametag. "I'd like to speak to the officer who pulled me over at the stop sign on Pleasant Street about an hour ago."

Phyllis fixed her with a suspicious look. "Excuse me?"

"And I'm not leaving until I see him."

She sashayed over to the hard wooden bench, the reception area's only furniture, and sat, crossing one slender leg over the other, the pose meant to convey confidence. The gatekeeper rolled her eyes. Undaunted, Wandalou remained there. She'd already been insulted by one man's guard dog on this miserable day and refused to suffer another's nips.

After half a minute that felt considerably longer, the brute appeared beside Phyllis beyond the bulletproof window. Their short conversation passed unheard on

Wandalou's side of the glass, but she could guess the nature of it—*crazy, uppity female you pulled over demands to get in your grill.* Only when he looked up and saw her, the cop smiled.

A security door leading in and out of the police's inner sanctum buzzed open, and the brute stepped out. He'd since pocketed his shades, and she saw his eyes were brown and focused only on her. She rose and folded her arms.

"Miss Trueheart," he said.

"You remember," Wandalou said.

"You're kind of unforgettable."

His comment caught her off guard. Clearing her throat, Wandalou quietly recorded the athletic perfection of the man's body and, again, how his uniform fit in a way that suggested his clothes loved his physique.

"What can I do for you?" the brute asked.

She reached into her knockoff tote and withdrew the slip of paper. Wandalou handed it over.

"What's this?"

She patched the hole in her armor. "Read it."

He did.

"It's a ticket," she said as he scanned the note. "You owe me five-thousand dollars. That's what your little stunt cost me today. Because of you, I lost out on a lucrative modeling job that I very much needed."

"You're a model?" He glanced up. "I can see it."

Another crack formed in her defenses. This time, he filled it in.

Laughing, he crumpled up the letter. "I'm not paying this. You're lucky I didn't write you a ticket."

"I came to enough of a stop at that sign!"

"Not in my professional opinion."

"Your opinion means *squat*." She stormed toward the exit.

"Does it mean enough for me to make it up to you?"

She halted her escape. "Make it up? How?"

"Let me buy you dinner."

And that's how my future friend, Wandalou Trueheart, met Quinn Rodrigio Montoya two years, five months, and thirteen days ago.

Standing in the fog of that morning following the third night of the full moon, she remembered their dinner date.

Wandalou had booked a room at one of those chain hotels one town over in Cherryvale for a week. The place was clean with an edge of antiseptics. Once back there, she'd almost packed up her few travel cases, got in the car, and drove west, leaving him seated alone and waiting for a date that never showed. After all, what kind of relationship could they possibly share? He'd forever be the cause of her destruction—she'd needed that money desperately. And now she'd always be bitter.

But she couldn't return west. That life was over. The cardboard cartons filled with trophies in the backseat of her car proved it. In the hotel bathroom, she stared at her reflection and wondered if the frown would ever leave her face. Those days on stage and the smiles she'd worn seemed gone forever.

"*Jerk*," she huffed.

The seed of a plan generated while she showered. By the time she'd dressed, it had put forth leaves. Wandalou donned her sunglasses behind the wheel. She would have revenge on Quinn Montoya.

The restaurant he chose was called Auld Lang Sine.

"More like *Old* Lang Sine," she huffed, taking in the place across their table for two. Quinn grinned.

A gray-haired hippie wearing a leather vest, striped pants, and sandals banged away on the upright piano. Two women who seemed of equal age jumped up from their tables and danced beside the piano bench.

Quinn, who now wore a slate suit and button-down with a crisp blue tie, those clothes as perfect on his body as that galling uniform, laughed as he watched her look around. "Come on, tell me you don't like this place. It has atmosphere."

She considered him, the policeman with his happy brown eyes and boyish grin who'd taken her on a first date to the local hippie bar. When the furious music of the piano player drew her focus back, she saw that the dancers now numbered four.

"Atmosphere? By the time this is over, my pubic hair will have grown six inches and turned gray out of sympathy," she said, the words out of her mouth before she could trap them.

Quinn cracked up. "Did you just say what I think I heard?"

She reached for her water glass and feigned confidence. "I'm not big on filters."

"I like that," he said. "Care to dance?"

Wandalou flashed disgust.

"Come on—it's Simon and Garfunkel!"

"I don't care if it's *Dom* and *Perignon*," she said. "It sounds to me like armpits and tofu."

Quinn stood and extended his hand. "Please?"

Maybe it was the glint in his gaze, his hopeful expression, or even the music, which she was loath to admit was rather fabulous. But Wandalou stood and took his hand. Quinn spun her onto the makeshift dance floor around the piano. Through the haze of patchouli, perfume, and natural musk, they danced.

And Wandalou forgot all about her scheme for revenge.

"What do you think?" Quinn asked.

She batted at his hands, which were trying to cover over her eyes. The house rose before them, big and beautiful and elegant. Wandalou's stomach filled with nervous butterflies.

"Number 11 Mistral Lane," Quinn said.

Oh, she instantly loved it. Still, the yippy little dog that lived deep inside her exerted its high-pitched bark in warning. "I don't know," it said in her voice.

"What don't you know?"

Wandalou scanned the surrounding houses with their perfect lawns and trimmed hedges, fresh asphalt driveways, and upscale vibe. "Is this the best you could do?" the yippy dog yipped.

"On my salary, yeah," Quinn said defensively. "If it wasn't for my promotion from uniform to detective—and that gift from Mamma—we couldn't afford to eat. I could barely afford this. But if you don't like it—"

She whirled, saw his distress, and hated herself for putting him there. "I love it," she said and crushed her mouth over his.

Quinn's tenseness melted. He took control of the kiss, ending it. The butterflies bucked against the soft lining of her stomach when Quinn got down on one knee. He picked a black velvet ring box out of his front pocket, which explained the bulge she'd mistaken for something else.

"What's happening?" she asked.

"Wandalou Esmeralda…" His face, serious until that moment, contorted. "Seriously? *Esmeralda*? Who does that to their kid?" She smacked at his shoulder. "Wandalou Trueheart, will you marry me?"

She crossed her arms. "Before I answer, what sort of timeline are we talking here?"

"Timeline?"

"Today, tomorrow?"

He shrugged. "I don't know. Depends on what you want—a big wedding or something small and quick."

"Definitely big."

"Then when we can afford it. Which won't be tomorrow and definitely not today. With a mortgage…"

"Yes?" she asked.

"Yes what?"

"I'll marry you, Quinn."

He opened the box. The ring inside, gold with an emerald-cut diamond, was perfect. Quinn slid it onto her finger. Then, still on his knees, he smacked her ass.

Instead of destroying her, Quinn had created roots, a foundation, and Wandalou's happy new life.

She didn't have much on the day they moved in— just a cardboard box in the trunk and some luggage. As she struggled getting the box out of the car, a woman walked up the driveway.

"Here, let me help you with that," she said.

Pretty, older than Wandalou, the woman wore a smart pistachio-green top, jeans, and flats.

"Thanks," Wandalou said. "What a nice welcome to the neighborhood."

The woman introduced herself. "I'm Jessie-Marie Smyth. My husband and I live at Number 17."

"Wandalou Trueheart."

"What a lovely name," Jessie-Marie said.

They carried Wandalou's things in through the open front door and into the house's cavernous emptiness.

"The furniture's coming," Wandalou explained. "So far, it's just a mattress on the floor." She regretted the confession. But their new neighbor didn't seem boujee or judgy, which she'd expected in a place like Mistral Lane.

"If there's anything you need, my husband Tim and I are just a few doors down. The pale green house."

Wandalou considered the woman. "That's very sweet of you, Jessie-Marie."

"Oh, I wanted to say hi. Your husband—"

"*Fiancé*," Wandalou stressed.

"Your fiancé, he's a policeman?"

Wandalou smiled. "He sure is. Remind me to tell you how we met some time."

"Okay. Maybe over poker. Do you play cards?"

"Only the tarot, but that was a long time ago in my other life."

"The girls and I play. Only for fun, mind you, not profit."

"Girls?"

As if on cue, a woman's voice called into the house from the open front door. "Hello?"

"We're back here," said Wandalou.

Two women joined them, a tall, slender redhead and a brunette, both equally pretty in a natural way. The redhead carried a covered plate of what looked to be cookies, the brunette a paperback romance novel.

"I'm Isis Slade," the redhead said. "Sorry, these are not gluten-free and they have nuts."

"No apologies," Wandalou laughed. "I'm good with all that."

The brunette, Willa Forsyth, extended the paperback novel.

"Am I supposed to eat that, too?" asked Wandalou.

"Only if you devour romances. I wrote it."

"Really?"

"Really. Wandalou, you're looking at *the* Lena LaFleur," said Jessie-Marie.

The novel was autographed, the cookies the best she'd ever tasted. An hour passed in the bare kitchen with the effortlessness of a minute.

"Wandalou's fiancé is a policeman," Jessie-Marie said.

"Which means we can all feel safe at night," Wandalou said.

"Don't' worry—nothing interesting ever happens on Mistral Lane," Isis said. "Nothing frightening, anyway."

"Do you want me to go with you?" asked Willa.

Wandalou shook her head. "No, I got this. Besides, you know Quinn…I've got that man wrapped around my little finger."

"If you need me," Isis said.

"Yeah, yeah, I know." Tossing her disheveled mane of black hair back, Wandalou walked with confidence across the street and into Number 11 Mistral Lane.

By the time she reached the staircase landing, her resolve fractured. It collapsed with each step she took higher. At the bedroom door, she turned away and ordered herself to pull together. Mostly intact, she glided into the bedroom.

Quinn was sprawled on his stomach, one leg and its big foot extended out from the covers. Wandalou continued to the walk-in closet. There, she opened an expensive lacquered box and fished out the letter in its chartreuse envelope. Both had gone into a clean plastic sandwich bag over a week ago.

Wandalou crept over to Quinn's side of the bed. Looking at him splayed on his front added to her growing malaise. Wandalou's imagination painted a picture of a dead man, face down, an ending. Mercifully, Quinn's chest moved as he drew in and expelled breath.

"*Pooky*," she cooed. "Quinn?"

Quinn stirred, rolled over. He came partially awake and reached for her. Wandalou resisted.

"Funny thing," she laughed. "Well, not really funny, Quinn. The girls and I came across something that could be evidence in Jessie-Marie's murder."

She held up the plastic bag by the corner and dangled it in front of his sleepy eyeballs.

Isis had barely finished buttoning her blouse when the doorbell rang. She glanced at the screen of her phone. It was before nine. Pocketing her cell, she skipped down the stairs and answered the door.

Wandalou stood outside, her arms filled with trophies. Two suitcases sat on the top step beside her. She looked as haggard as she had when they'd parted company on Willa's front lawn. More so, even.

"Hello, roommate," Wandalou declared and walked past Isis into the Slade house.

Chapter 7
Isis
in Crisis

Wandalou breezed inside. "Get those, would you?" Isis retrieved her friend's luggage without considering the greater scope of the act. But when she closed the door, Wandalou was already at the top of the stairs.

"Wait," Isis called.

Wandalou stopped at the top step. "Yes?"

"Where are you going?"

"The guest room, of course. I'd room with Willa, but after three nights in her 'guest room,' well, let's just say I'll take my chances with Bob and the twins now since I know that would be a disaster."

Wandalou turned and resumed her runway walk out of sight. Isis struggled with the suitcases up the stairs. In the guest room, Wandalou stood at the mirrored dresser arranging her trophies.

"There are three more across the street," Wandalou said. "I left them just inside the front door. If you see him, don't worry—he'll be too busy working the case to interrogate you about me."

Isis exhaled in frustration. "I wouldn't know what to tell him anyway because, frankly, I don't know what's happening here."

"I'm taking you up on your offer."

"What offer was that?"

Wandalou faced her. "The one where you said that if I needed you, you'd be there. I need you."

"What about Quinn?"

Wandalou's expression hardened. "What about him?"

"Wandalou, what happened when you gave him the letter?"

"Oh, just the usual. He accused me of withholding evidence in an ongoing murder investigation and demanded to know why. So I had to leave out the part about the whole *werewolf thing* and told him we'd only just discovered the letter in the Smyth's recycling. Only you know my husband—he's like a pit bull. Reminded me that recycling's every two weeks and that Willa and I took out the Smyth's during the last pickup. Oh, and then there was the grilling about what I'd done to get some anonymous schmuck to blackmail me for ten grand…"

Isis gasped. "What did you tell him?"

"The truth. All of it. Every hairy, ugly detail. About the night of the bachelorette party. About the full moon and *Ladies' Poker Night*." She made air quotes with the pointers of both hands for emphasis. "About my crazed libido and my dalliance with rookie cop what's-his-name."

"I thought his name was Rolfe—"

"So not the point. So of course, he believes that part, just not the rest of it. And that's why I'm here."

Again, Isis processed what she just heard. "You told Quinn about us? The curse?"

"Don't worry—he thinks I made it all up. The dalliance with Officer Hastings, *that* part he believes. He can even live with it because he admits he hasn't been around as much lately so he'll cut me some slack. But the making up of fairy tales about the Big, Bad Wolf…that's where Quinn Rodrigo Montoya draws the line!" Wandalou snorted loudly and finished arranging her trophies. "Do you know what he said to me? The spiteful, cruel thing that man said? It was the last straw, Icy!"

Isis shrugged and listened.

"He said I was *cuckoo!*"

As she prepared dinner, Isis considered the day's twists. The brief spell of calm following the full moon she'd expected hadn't happened. After the last time—the first after Wandalou's bachelorette party—a week of quiet, ignorant bliss had played out as the moon waned and vanished from the sky. Then Jessie-Marie's murder and the building, background teakettle whine of anticipation for the next full moon tortured her while dealing with crippling loss.

She rinsed vegetables at her lovely farmer's sink, aware that the usual joy from so simple an act was missing. By now, Quinn would have the police experts scrutinizing the letter. What would they find apart from Jessie-Marie's, Wandalou's, and the mailman's fingerprints? At least the police knew the truth—that Jessie-Marie's killer had made a mistake. Wandalou was the intended victim.

Wandalou!

For the first time, it struck Isis that the killer's true target was now a guest in her house, and that any hope for the peace she needed after the vagaries of the full moon were impossible.

A sharp scream tore through the silent house. One of the girls—

Isis grabbed the knife she'd used to chop the fresh summer squash from the organic co-op by its handle and tore across the kitchen. She followed a second shriek toward the pair of French doors leading out to the patio, those doors already opened. Both girls stood frozen just past the threshold. Isis moved protectively in front of the twins.

"What is it?" she asked, not seeing the source of the twins' fright even with wide-open eyes that had forgotten how to blink.

Darci pointed at a lawn chair, aimed away from their vantage with its back raised. "There's a dead white lady in our backyard," Marci said.

Isis choked down a dry swallow and, remembering both the weapon in her grasp and the truth about the murderer's true target living under her roof, faced the source of the girls' shrieks.

Slowly, blade held before her, Isis crept along the patio's pavers toward the lawn chair where, indeed, a lady's body lay slumped in one of those unmoving poses that suggested the ghost had flown. The exhaustion that had dogged her since leaving the panic room exerted its pull. The world blurred. Isis blinked, then her vision stabilized.

She reached the lawn chair where Wandalou's pale, white corpse was laid out. The killer, Isis was sure, had claimed their second victim. Then Isis noticed a tube of sun block beside the tall tumbler filled with sweating ice cubes, chunks of fruit, and a little pink paper parasol, and when her shadow slipped over Wandalou, the seemingly dead woman jolted up. Wandalou removed her silicone earplugs and scowled at Isis.

"What? Can't a girl catch a few rays without you creeping up on her?" Wandalou reached for her drink. She downed a sip and noticed the girls, presently gawking at the reanimated corpse slathered in white sun block. "What are you two staring at?" Wandalou spat.

Marci screamed. Both girls vanished through the French doors and into the house.

Wandalou smiled. "See what a gift I am?" Then she laughed and handed the half-emptied glass to Isis. "Be a dear, Lizzie Borden, and get me another, would you? *Chop, chop!*"

Music blasted through the house—something boy-bandy with plenty of thumping drumbeats and falsetto castrato voices. Isis had been in the middle of a dream in which she was at My Grains sharing recipes with Frau Krumpt, who'd smiled throughout the exchange. Well, not smiled *exactly*—it was more of a snarl.

"Would you like to know the secret as to why everything I bake tastes so *wunderbah*?" Frau Krumpt asked.

"Oh, yes!" Dream-Isis answered.

"It's in the actual baking. Here, see for yourself, Fraulein…"

Frau Krumpt had opened the oven, and when Isis leaned down for a look, the other woman pushed her inside and closed the door.

"Let me out!" Dream-Isis demanded. When that failed, she'd begged. She was hammering on the inside of the oven door, the pounding rhythmic, when her eyes opened and the drumming of her fist segued into the latest international hit from an Asian quartet of break-dancing moppets.

Isis rolled over, the dream fading, the reality of the morning surfacing.

"What the hell is that?" Bob moaned. He was flat on his stomach, one eye opened and aimed at her.

"That," Isis sighed, "is our houseguest."

Clad in the yellow silk kimono robe her husband bought her while overseas on a business trip the year before, Isis fixed a pleasant smile on her lips and approached the guest room's vibrating, closed door. The music thumping on the other side transitioned from a dance number to a love ballad. Its ups and downs in treble made her ears itch.

Isis knocked. No one answered. She knocked louder. When that failed, she broke the protocol of polite society and turned the knob.

Music poured out, leaving Isis itchy all over now. She hastened past the oblivious figure sweating in a skin-tight workout suit and stabbed off the CD player on the nightstand.

Wandalou whirled toward her, her hair done up in a topknot. "Hey, you ever hear of knocking? What gives?"

"Right now, my last morning nerve."

Isis stormed out of the guest room, which was only slightly less in shambles than Willa's panic room had been on that morning three days behind them, and made her way down the stairs to brew the first of what she assumed would be several pots of strong coffee.

She downed the first cup of the day black and quickly, not waiting to savor it with cream and sugar, only desperate for its rejuvenating kick. Isis was still in her kimono when Wandalou glided down the staircase dressed to the nines for a day that knew no actual job beyond influencing fashion and her duties to a home she'd been banished from.

Isis steeled herself for what she had to say. The speech she'd rehearsed played through her thoughts, the words jagged. "Wandalou, we need to talk."

Wandalou sat across from her at the breakfast table, nodded sympathetically, and smiled. Perhaps their conversation would be easier than Isis feared. Maybe it wouldn't end in scorched earth.

"Yes, we do," Wandalou said in a gentle voice. And then her expression sharpened. "What the hell was that all about, walking in on me like that? And do you think you could invest in some sheets with a thread-count higher than *two*? Seriously, Icy—the ones in my room are like granite. And pizza rolls for dinner? What am I, *six*?"

Isis stared, stunned. The speech she'd rehearsed flatlined in her mind.

Wandalou reached a manicured hand toward her and patted Isis's arm. "You work on those sheets, 'kay?" And then Wandalou stood and poured herself a coffee.

Willa joined them on the Slades' back patio. "How is everyone today?"

"Fine," Isis said, the façade of her smile projected.

"Not fine," groused Wandalou.

Willa tipped a glance at Isis. The silent nod didn't escape notice.

"What's that supposed to mean?" Wandalou demanded.

"Nothing. Just worried about you," said Willa. "Any word from Quinn?"

Wandalou folded her arms and exhaled. "Screw Quinn. Or *not* screw him, which is a better plan, and which was my original plan on the night of our first date."

Again, Willa eyed Isis.

"I saw that," Wandalou snapped.

Isis waved them over to the lawn table and a pitcher of iced tea and tumblers. "Can we focus on the real reason for today's meeting?"

"*The Face*," Wandalou growled.

"Oh, yes," said Willa. "*Race the Face…*"

They sat. Isis poured. Even without her voicing it, Willa sensed the tension rising off Isis like waves of summer heat over asphalt.

"His number's been disconnected," Isis said.

"Maybe old Race has raced away from Hydrangea Heights," said Willa. "Either way, we can assume 'Race' isn't his real name—who names their son Race?"

"The big bad momma-wolf who raised him," said Wandalou. "There's nothing online—no social media accounts, nothing when I do a search except bikers and gear heads—oh, and by the way, the Wi-Fi in my room leaves a lot to be desired!" She shot another scowl at Isis.

"So that's a dead end," said Willa. "I hate to say it, but Race the Face can't help us. I think we're on our own."

"And no closer to solving our problem," said Isis.

After that pronouncement, they fell silent, the stillness only broken by the clink of ice cubes in glasses as they melted and resettled, someone's lawnmower one street over, and the sough of the wind.

"What do we do?" Wandalou asked.

"I don't know, but we've got three weeks to come up with the answer," Isis sighed.

"Anybody know an old Gypsy fortuneteller who might have a trick or two up her sleeve?" asked Willa.

"No, just a mean German witch," said Wandalou. Then she faced Isis. "Now, about tonight's dinner menu…"

It can be argued that my friend Isis Slade had the patience of a saint. And also that my other dear gal-pal, Wandalou Trueheart, could test the patience of even the holiest of souls. So yes, Wandalou had pushed Isis past even her altruistic limitations. Wandalou was, to be kind, a difficult houseguest.

She walked in on Bob while he showered and, once, while he sat in the bathroom reading the sports page on his phone and engaged in other private matters behind the door he'd forgotten to lock.

She shot intimidating looks at the twins from her chair at the family's dining table and misbehaved when Isis devoted time each weekday afternoon to assisting the girls with their homework. She helped herself to the remote—often when Bob was in the middle of watching a game or the twins their favorite cartoons.

By the end of Wandalou's first week as a guest in the Slade House, the family was sufficiently traumatized.

Bob sat on the end of the bed clad in sweats, an old t-shirt bearing his favorite baseball team's logo, and sneakers. Isis backed into the room—though it was more that she snuck in and quietly closed the door.

"What are you doing?" Bob whispered.

Isis jolted, turned. Clearing her throat, she whispered back, "Nothing. What are you doing? Don't you have softball with the guys?"

"The *guys*? You mean Quinn and Tim Smyth? That sure'll be some fun game," Bob said, his voice maintaining its low volume.

"So you're hiding out in our bedroom?" she accused.

"Well, what are *you* doing?"

Isis feigned innocence. "Checking something."

"You're afraid of her, too, aren't you?" Bob smirked.

"No," Isis said.

But then the doorknob turned, and both of their eyes shot open, and the two reluctant recluses held their breaths. The door swung open, and Marci raced in. Darci pursued.

"Close it, Darci!" Marci pleaded, her voice also in a hush.

Darci slammed the door. Both girls braced it with their backs, unaware at first of the room's other occupants.

"What are you two doing in here?" Isis demanded in a whisper.

"Just checking something," Marci said.

Darci nodded in agreement.

"Why are we whispering?" asked Bob.

A series of rapid knocks hammered the other side of the door. The girls yelped and hastened over to Isis, who took them in her arms. Bob stood and embraced his family.

"*Mommy*," the twins sang in unison.

No one had locked the door.

The door opened.

The four Slades, huddled together out of a need for strength in numbers, collectively screamed.

Wandalou strode into the bedroom. "Where do you keep the dental floss?"

Here's the thing about my friend Wandalou: Sure, she's a diva and used to getting her way. And yes, she can be difficult to live with—some might say *impossible*. But

Wandalou Esmeralda Trueheart can also be very loyal and down deep is one of the kindest people on Earth.

That same afternoon, while Bob and the boys knocked around a softball and Isis labored in the kitchen, Wandalou wandered out into the Slades' backyard and wept when she thought no one could see her. She missed Quinn. All of the bravado and bluster she'd expressed since moving out of their house was merely a smoke-screen, and that smoke was thinning fast.

She agreed the argument was entirely her creation, the rift with Quinn her fault. Regret filled her. Tears spilled down her cheeks. She loved Quinn and knew that he loved her, but Wandalou worried love wasn't enough, especially given the dark secret she and we three fellow victims of the wolf's curse shared.

But Wandalou wasn't the only mourner that afternoon in the Slades' backyard. After the cowering family had been disturbed in the master bedroom, the twins had ridden their bikes along the sidewalk to Number 31 Mistral Lane, where the Clymores lived. Gwendolyn Clymore, the twins' school friend, already entertained company in the form of pigtailed princess Cherie Bourdelais.

Wandalou noticed the two bikes first, dumped beside the chaise lounge chair she'd claimed as hers since moving in, and, at first, was outraged. Then she heard the sniffles. Wiping her eyes, she tracked them to the other side of the garden table where so many afternoons had been spent with Willa and Isis, and where the twins were attempting to console one another.

"What's this?" Wandalou asked.

Frightened, at first the twins only gaped at her. Then Darci said, "Cherie said something mean to Marci."

Wandalou folded her arms and studied the girls. She didn't really like children, but at that moment, she felt for them. The Slades were family. Loyalty kicked in. "Who's this Cherie person, and who gave her the authority to sling insults at you?"

Marci attempted to answer. Only gasps for breath emerged. Then the girl composed herself enough to say, "She called me ugly and said that I'll never be pretty."

"Well, that's just ridiculous," Wandalou said. "First of all, you're both Slade women. If you take one-tenth after Isis, you'll be too pretty to handle. And, more importantly, you've got *this* aunty to remind you not to mix prints and to steer clear of acid colors. If anything, that little viper-tongued Cherie will be flipping through fashion magazines and seeing *your* faces some day."

"Really?" Marci said after finding her voice. "I want to be as pretty as *you*, Miss Trueheart."

Wandalou sighed. "Good luck with that." She briefly indulged in more hauteur before leaning down to the girls' level. "The next time you see that shrew Cherie, you tell her that you're both gorgeous, and I told you so. And if anyone ever insults you like that again, you remember that they're jealous. Jealous of what beautiful young ladies you are."

She patted each girl's shoulder.

"You're nice," Darci said.

Wandalou straightened and assumed her defensive stance. "Don't tell anyone." She winked and smiled. Turning, she saw Isis standing at the French doors smiling, too.

Thank you, Isis mouthed covering her heart.

Wandalou nodded. Wiping her eyes, she marched around the house and down the sidewalk. Number 11 Mistral Lane rose above her. *Home*, she thought. It was time to return to Quinn.

But Quinn wasn't there, and when she tried her key in the front door, Wandalou discovered that he'd changed the locks.

Chapter 8

Oui?
Ja!

The idea came to her at the start of Wandalou's second week of exile in the Slade house. In the upstairs hall closet, while hunting for a lint roller, she'd discovered the family's collection of board games, all of them stacked neatly on the second shelf from the top beneath extra blankets and an emergency flashlight.

Among those games with dice, cards, spinners, and little figurines meant to move around squares was the beat up old Ouija board.

Wandalou reached for the box containing board and planchette only to hesitate. In the end, she drew back, turned off the closet light, and closed the door.

Downstairs, Isis stood before the mustard accent "accident" wall. Several small cans of paint and a brush were atop a folding tray table covered in newspaper. A tarp protected the patch of hardwood floor nearest the wall. Isis hummed to herself.

Wandalou descended the staircase and joined Isis in the living room. "That again?" she sniped.

Isis pulled off one of the paint can lids with the metal key. "I know I can get the color right."

The small opened can showed something more puce in color than the dab of "apricot" on its lid.

"Just don't go all fru-fru and purple like—"

Willa emerged from the Slades' kitchen carrying a tray of glasses filled with lemonade. She wore her trademark purple in the form of a short-sleeve top and gauzy slacks.

"—*Willa*," Wandalou pivoted. "Love the ensemble!"

Willa shot Wandalou a look while handing over a glass to Isis. "Fru-fru?"

"Fru...ty. Grapes are purple and they're a fruit, right?" Wandalou offered a nervous laugh before clamping down. "Forget all that." She glanced around the house to make sure they were alone and waved the others closer.

"Bob's at work, and the girls are in school," Isis said.

Wandalou hissed, "These days, we can't be too careful."

Paint brush in one hand, glass in the other, Isis moved closer. So did Willa.

"I have a plan," Wandalou said.

The paint went on the wall. While it dried, they sat around the breakfast table as Wandalou further explained the idea.

"You said it yourself, Icy—less than three weeks now until the next full moon. We're no closer to tracking down Race the Face. We're on our own. *Or are we?*"

Willa tapped her fingers against her glass. "What do you mean?"

"You said you heard Jessie-Marie out at the dog park," Wandalou answered.

Willa shrugged. "It could have been the wind."

"Or it could have been our friend trying to comm-unicate with us! What if Jessie-Marie's ghost really is wandering around, trying to tell us something?"

"*Something?*" Isis parroted.

"Yeah, like who killed her, or how we can shake the wolves off our asses."

Silence, broken only by the background hum of the fridge and a car passing down the street, fell over the kitchen as the others contemplated the possibility in Wandalou's claim.

"I think we should try it," Willa said.

All eyes turned to Isis. "The Ouija board, seriously? That's just some silly kids game we used to trot out every

Halloween. Half the time I pushed the planchette around the board—and I'm pretty sure Bob was responsible for the rest."

"Great parenting," Wandalou huffed, which earned her Isis's glower. "Do you have a better idea?"

Isis didn't. "Okay, I'm game."

"When do we do this? Tonight?"

Isis shook her head. "No. Bob will get suspicious if we play without the kids. Besides, I have dinner plans."

"Me, too," Wandalou said. She clapped Isis's closest hand, which restored the other woman's death-stare.

"How about tomorrow when Bob's at work and the twins are in school?" Willa suggested.

"Shouldn't we try to contact the dead…I don't know…at night?" asked Wandalou.

Isis's gaze drifted to the center of the table but seemed to see something other than the centerpiece of vase and the last of the summer flowers. "No. Willa heard Jessie-Marie speaking to her in the daylight. Tomorrow at eleven in the morning. Right here." Isis tapped her pointer fingers on the table.

"Here, where the four of us spent so many mornings together before Jessie-Marie was stolen from us."

Given the events of the past week—the travails associated with the full moon, new deadlines, and the sense of anxiety involving the letter, Quinn, and the resulting breakup of Wandalou's relationship—Willa hadn't devoted much of her focus on her new neighbor, the handsome airline pilot.

But on the night before the séance, Willa chanced to look down from the upstairs writing room while closing the window against the new night's briskness and saw that Joe's truck was parked in the driveway. Fresh electricity crackled through her and over her flesh. In the rush of that moment, she understood and forgave Wandalou for her indiscretion.

After the surge cooled enough for her to think, Willa noticed something else. The house next door sat dark under the dusk. The impression was one of abandonment, not new ownership. Joe Rhodes was attractive—*so* attractive! But he was also an enigma. Then Willa recalled her own secret, and her suspicion evaporated. Sadly, the most that could be said about Joe was that he traveled from place to place because of work. It wasn't like, Willa mused guiltily, he was cursed to be a creature of the night like certain other residents of Mistral Lane.

She attempted to look over notes on the new novel now that the previous was officially put to bed and off to the publisher. The latest, *Love's Oasis*—a working title she'd been unsure of but was growing more smitten with by the day—concerned a young woman who retreats to a country Bed and Breakfast to regroup after discovering her boyfriend's cheating ways and meets the inn's hunky maintenance man. Already Willa envisioned plenty of scenes with said maintenance man bare-chested and sweaty while chopping firewood, and the character had taken on Joe's face. That thought colored the one that followed. Willa tabled her attempt to further flesh out her novel and switched off the light. The new night's breeze moaned around the house in a disembodied ghost's voice.

The doorbell gonged. Willa gasped at the un-expectedness of the sound, which rang twice and loud through the stillness of the house. Suddenly cold, she hastened down the stairs to answer. Joe stood on the front step, looking as magnificent as she imagined he would cast as the hero in her new romance novel. The top buttons of his shirt were undone, revealing threads of dark chest hair. The emerald glint in his eyes comp-limented his smile. Both hinted at mischief. Willa shook off the shiver attempting to plunge down her backbone and smiled too.

"Joe!"

"Willa. Is this a good time?"

She reined in the snort before it could betray her and regained her cool. "Sure. Come in."

He walked past the threshold and she caught his scent—wild and primal with a note of pine and summer rain mixed in.

"You're back," she said.

In the foyer, he turned and spread his arms. "Miss me?"

"Maybe," she said, which seemed the right answer. The most diplomatic, at least. "Miss *me*?"

"Oh, absolutely. Couldn't get home fast enough."

She imagined him wrestling with the controls of one of the gigantic airliners, in his uniform, his strong hands guiding the plane up into the wind, high through the open skies, and then down onto the landing strip. The level of control and stress must have required an insane amount of the pilot's focus. Now, Joe's attention was trained solely on her.

"It's great to see you, Willa," he said. The pilot, used to wrangling jumbo airliners, now seemed nervous, boyishly so, which added to her attraction for him.

"Is it? What about Brittany Barrows?"

Joe's nervousness vanished. "Brittany?"

"Yeah, the skank."

"What?"

"Nothing," she quickly added. "It's just that I thought she was—"

"My real estate agent."

"Only your real estate agent?"

"Nothing more," Joe said.

"In that case…"

She bridged the distance, wrapped her arms around his neck, and leaned up, kissing him. Joe's mouth tasted cool, minty. His shock quickly passed, and he took her into his arms. Between kisses, he said, "I read your latest novel. Picked up a copy in Boston."

"And?"

"I liked it. Not big into romance novels, but I love a good story. You're an excellent writer, Willa."

The euphoria she'd kept bottled up inside until she was sure she'd burst ignited. Willa cupped Joe's cheek, drew him down for another kiss, and, for a moment at least, forgot all about her troubles.

Strange dreams filled that mysterious night, ones as veiled and terrifying as Willa suffered and mostly forgot during the nights of the full moon. In one, she plummeted out of a cloudy sky, her shrieks lost above a savage land. In another, she'd landed in a dark forest. There was a house made of stone—a very old house. No, a *castle*. Ancient. In pieces. She'd sought shelter there more from the threat of other people than the driving rain. And inside that shadowy, ruined castle, in its darkest corner, a pair of eyes that glowed blue fixed upon her without blinking.

Willa shot up in bed, at first not recognizing her surroundings in the glare of the morning's sunlight which wavered in past the bedroom windows.

The other half of the bed was empty, the sheets bunched with Joe's reverse bas-relief. A note awaited her on the pillow. She squinted, the sunlight painful and stinging at her eyes.

Dear Willa,
See you tonight.
—Joe

Short, true, but exceptionally sweet of him, she agreed, holding the letter to her heart. Willa ached in all the right spots, and exhaustion rolled over her until she noticed the numbers on the alarm clock read: 10:47.

She jumped up. The room performed a spin around her. Dressing in haste, she stumbled twice, fell once, and heard fabric rip. Even so, stopping automatically to retrieve a scarf, which she secured loosely around her neck to disguise the fresh puncture marks, doing so in a daze, and barely conscious of the act, she was out of the house and crossing the street to the Slade's by 11:04.

"**Y**ou're late," Wandalou snapped. "And what's with *this*? The 1960s called and they want their scarf back."

"Don't listen to her—she's just cranky because we're all out of caviar," Isis said lightly.

Wandalou folded her arms. "I don't eat caviar, and I'm always cranky."

Willa and Isis agreed with nods.

"So," Wandalou prodded. "What's the reason—and why are you glowing?"

Willa smirked. "A certain pilot flew in for the night."

Isis exclaimed, "*Shut up!*"

"Oh my God, it was *uh-mazing*," Willa said. "I only wish I could remember the details more. I mean, Joe … he's incredible! At least I think he was. It was so romantic and hot and everything I dreamed it would be. Only I can't seem to recall most of it. Anyway—"

"Seriously, Willa, *shut up*," Wandalou said.

Willa shot her a look.

"Séance, ladies, remember?" Wandalou said and then she clapped her hands together sharply for emphasis.

As they wandered into the kitchen, Willa stole a glance at the new accent wall and cringed. "Oh my."

"Worse than the last time," Wandalou said.

"Don't even," Isis said.

The game's box and instructions were placed on the counter. The Ouija board was opened on the breakfast table, around which so many words had been exchanged and cups of coffee enjoyed. Apart from the planchette set upon the mechanism for communicating with spirits, it could have been another of those normal mornings. A fresh pot of French roast had been brewed. The tall cups were laid out on the counter in front of the maker, inviting familiar traditions on a morning of one new and uncertain ritual.

Isis poured. They each fixed theirs the way they preferred it, and Isis led them in a toast. "To Jessie-Marie," she said.

"Here, here," said Willa.

Wandalou added, "And to the truth. May we learn who did this to our good friend and crack the secret of curing this curse."

Isis lit the candle—a pungent gardenia Bob had given her whose smell she still struggled to tolerate. They all expelled cleansing breaths and, at Isis's urging, cleared their minds.

"Since you heard Jessie-Marie's voice, Willa, I'd suggest that you reach out to her," Isis added.

Willa nodded. They each set their pointer fingers lightly on the planchette. "Jessie-Marie, do you hear me?" Willa asked. "If you're here, please answer."

At first, nothing happened. And then the planchette jostled and rolled along the board to the Yes.

Wandalou gasped. Isis urged calm with a glance.

"Jessie-Marie, is that you?" Willa asked.

The planchette rolled an inch away before jerking back to its last position.

"*Yes*," Willa said. "Oh, Jessie…*Jessie*…"

It took all of my willpower—everything I had and didn't have—to nudge the planchette. "Yes, *yes*," I cried out, but my voice faded the more I attempted to move the device.

"Oh, Jessie-Marie," Willa sobbed. "Can you tell us who did this to you?"

I pushed and pushed harder, gliding the planchette down from the upper left corner and into the letters of the alphabet. I added the last of my strength's touch to my friends' lightness, wanting so desperately to be heard. More so, to sit with them as we all had on so many other mornings when the discussions had concerned husbands, ex-husbands, and fiancés, not murders and affairs of haunted nights.

I pushed more. The planchette nudged into the alphabet and approached D.

"*D*," Wandalou gasped. "Oh my god, Darci did it!"

Isis tsked. "No, she didn't. And be quiet!"

"I don't know, just saying…twins are kind of creepy…"

Willa shushed her. I pushed harder, feeling whatever matter I had become lose its cohesion. It was too much, but I had to press on.

I had to!

Finally, the planchette cooperated, and I coaxed it down to the second row and the letter I sought. There, the planchette stayed until, caught in a wild wind that suddenly sprang up in Isis's kitchen, the Ouija board swept off the table and spun wildly away to strike the wall. All three of my dear friends screamed in surprise. The planchette clattered to the floor.

"Did you see that?" Wandalou gasped.

"More importantly, did you see Jessie-Marie's answer?" asked Willa.

Isis nodded. "The letter R."

Chapter 9
Mister Dieingly Sad

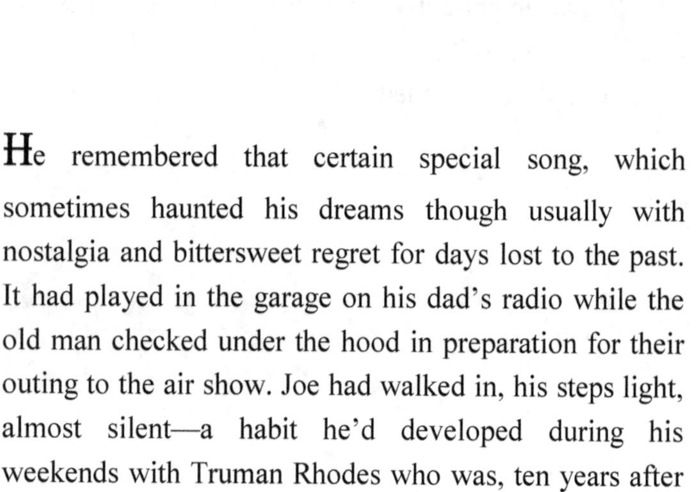

He remembered that certain special song, which sometimes haunted his dreams though usually with nostalgia and bittersweet regret for days lost to the past. It had played in the garage on his dad's radio while the old man checked under the hood in preparation for their outing to the air show. Joe had walked in, his steps light, almost silent—a habit he'd developed during his weekends with Truman Rhodes who was, ten years after Joe's birth, still a stranger.

"And now, something classic by the Critters—*Mister Dieingly Sad*," the radio host announced.

The melody had poured out of the relic on the shelf whose antenna was wrapped in aluminum foil, haunting and elegant. His dad, unaware of young Joe's presence, hummed to the tune. In that still moment, Joe understood more about his father, and the stranger checking the oil and other details wasn't as much a conundrum as he'd been ten seconds earlier. The song was sad, as promised. So, too, was the man humming it.

His dad looked up and noticed Joe standing there. He ceased his sing-along and closed the hood of the fastback Mustang, a true classic, and offered the barest of smiles to his son.

"We're good to go," his father said. "What do you say that we drive with the roof down?"

And so they had. It was one of those perfect summer mornings, the sky cloudless and the color of comfortable denim. His dad wore shades—the cool kind for pilots. The wind rippled over Joe's right arm and, en route to the airfield, he was tempted to extend his hand past the doorframe and gather up everything he could grasp to hold onto it and the memory of such good emotions. Driving in his dad's 'stang beside the former stranger, who now felt less of one, was like flying.

The airfield at Madison had been transformed into a museum. Parked on the tarmac were biplanes from another era alongside World War II fighters and jets that had flown in the Korean War. They climbed around, under, and inside for the tour. Joe's mind went into a kind of sensory overload. At the concession stand, his dad bought them both cherry colas and foot-long dogs whose grilled skin snapped pleasantly when you bit into them, and promised funnel cakes after, which they never got to in Joe's excitement to take in the air show and what happened after it began.

A set of bleachers had been erected alongside one of the landing and takeoff strips. They took their seats, his dad sporting those cool shades, and Joe, so intrigued by the concept of flight and the apparatus that put men up there knew, just knew, what he wanted to do with his life. The first of the single-engines was already in the sky, performing spins and releasing smoke in long ribbons of blue color in its wake. The second of the two planes soared up from the tarmac to join in the display of aerial stunts. The growing crowd applauded. Joe made that whistle his mother hated with fingers sticky from ketchup. Life was perfect.

The second stunt plane assumed its pattern alongside the first. The two performed spins and loops. The second discharged green smoke, and the crowd again cheered. Chills teased the nape of Joe's neck and gossiped down his spine. He had no fear of heights—he'd climbed trees in the backyard of their house to his mother's chagrin and only regretted he hadn't been able to go higher.

Up there, he mused. *That's where I belong.*

As he thought this, the same sense of foreboding that caused him to walk softly around his father sliced through his euphoria. Later in life, Joe would realize his trepidations regarding his dad owed fully to the lies his mother told about her ex-husband as a means of petty vengeance. But in the case of the air show, Joe's fears played out.

The first plane had been in the process of coming down from a loop while the second was finishing a spin. The intention, Joe understood, was that both would pass close by one another and then go their separate ways in elegant dips. That didn't happen. One plane's wing clipped the other's. In that breathtaking and terrible instant of contact, parts of both planes exploded outward, and time seemed to freeze.

Then the thunder-boom caught up. Chunks of wings rained down from the sky and the hulks of the two planes barreled toward the ground and the awestruck crowd.

Time seemed to freeze. Joe, now in his thirties, again remembered the song from that morning in his dad's garage. There were nights when he returned to that house, that day, in his dreams set to a melancholy soundtrack and woke with tears in his eyes. For the dad he didn't know and hadn't been given the chance to. For the terrible spectacle he'd witnessed on what had been a perfect summer morning. For no reason other than that, like his dad, he sensed an emptiness inside him, one that grew and eroded more of him with every season, making his own identity that of a sad stranger.

Then the explosion boomed, and he knew his attempts to control the fighter were hopeless. It wouldn't make it over the next mountain crags let alone back to home base.

"*Nuts*," Captain Joe Rhodes said before reaching for the pilot seat ejector release controls.

He held his breath. The canopy blasted off the jet's superstructure, and then he was flying—really flying. The overcast day blurred in shades of charcoal. The world beneath the doomed fighter seemed a million miles under his boots. Joe waited for the chute to deploy, and the little acid voice in his thoughts told him no, it wouldn't. *You're even more seriously screwed than you were five seconds ago, Joe-Joe!*

But the parachute did work as intended, and he spiraled to the forest floor, narrowly avoiding getting snagged on the dense canopy of branches but snapping through plenty of them on the way down. The same critic inside his skull reminded Joe that if he did stick in a tree, he was already equipped to scale his way down the trunk thanks to all those boyhood adventures in the tall pines of his backyard.

He reached the ground but was unable to indulge in more than a few seconds' worth of relief. Joe drew his service pistol from its holster and, with his boots on solid footing, swept the area for signs of the former Yugoslavian Army. In that moment, with his senses on a heightened level of clarity verging on otherworldly, he noted two observations: the first being his surroundings, a shadowy landscape he doubted got much cheerier in full sunlight if, indeed, it ever got sunny here, and, second, the utter lack of natural sounds other than the wind.

No birds sang and none squawked in complaint of his intrusion.

Operation Noble Anvil, Joe thought. He didn't feel very noble on that April morning in Eastern Europe in 1999.

He walked forward, ever alert for sounds of pursuit, of men eager to capture and parade around a downed American pilot as a trophy. But the only cracking of twigs came from beneath his own boot treads; and, still, the forest maintained its deathly silence.

Joe trudged onward. He came across a stream, runoff from melting winter snow in the surrounding mountains, he assumed. He knelt down and tested the water. It was refreshing and tasted pure. So there was that blessing, but not much in the form of others. With the sun invisible, the only gauge for direction was the moss growing on one side of certain tree trunks. This indicated the way north, roughly. He needed to be northwest, precisely. Far northwest from where his fighter had been shot down.

Joe adjusted course and trudged on.

The forest thickened. Silence crawled across his flesh. The gray day dimmed, then night crept in from the horizon. The automatic, cold professional training Joe had run on all day threatened to collapse. He pressed forward, aware of the otherworldly stillness and also of the creeping fear that things would only grow worse once the last of the day's glow evaporated.

He spotted a house—or what was left of it—right before twilight surrendered to dusk. The place could have been a victim of NATO bombing but was more likely already in a state of decay long before this date. Not a house, no—the gray stone blocks and the remains of a turret belonged to a castle!

Joe froze. The air around him, already brisk from the dropping temperature, grew glacial. It was every ruined castle from old horror movies and dark lore ever to cross his notice on TV or in books. *Don't go there*, his inner voice warned.

Even as the first raindrops fell, icy and increasing their intensity, he knew he should listen. He didn't.

Joe picked his way through the blocks of stone that littered the outskirts and moved toward the looming dark rectangle of what had once been a door leading into the turret.

The fetor of age and rot struck him instantly, a mix of standing water and wet earth that reeked of the damp underside of a log. Things grew inside the fallen castle.

But he doubted anything other than misshapen trees lived there.

"Oh hell no," Joe said aloud.

The now pounding rain at his back swallowed his voice. He turned around, seeing the downpour and just as he did, the thing lurking in the shadows reached out, grabbed hold of him, and dragged him deeper into the sour depths of the destroyed castle.

The night spiraled around him and turned red. Pain exploded over his right knee and then his left shoulder as they impacted against stone. He attempted to struggle. Somehow, the pistol was still in Joe's grip for another second despite him being whipped along the dark passage through the ruins. He fired twice in the direction of the horror that had him in its clutches. The night shattered in sharp, bright bursts of lightning. The bullets struck against slick stones of walls without windows. The sound numbed his hearing. The monster from films, TV, and old books paused and faced him, then he saw its eyes–those evil, glowing blue eyes. After that, things blurred.

It spoke to him.

"I can be merciful," it said, its voice seeming to drift up from the bottom of a well though its eyes continued to burn into him. "I can end you, or you can go away from here not alive, not dead, but in Limbo between the two."

Funny thing was the voice, in his mind more so than his ringing ears, was pure Lugosi.

Joe attempted to aim the gun and fire again—not that even a direct hit would vanquish the monster that had sucked out most of his blood. And because it had drained him of most of his blood, his limbs refused to cooperate.

"It's always the same," the horror continued. "It never changes. Always the resistance to the inevitable, as though you have a third choice. There are only the two."

It moved toward him. He heard the scrape and scrabble of its long nails across the floor's ancient stones and smelled its putrid breath ripe with his blood as it leaned down. Mustering the last of his strength, Joe raised his hand. But the gun was gone, and in its place a piece of sharp stick he'd grabbed on the slide across the ground.

One of the two glowing eyes came apart in a shower of putrid gore. Joe thrust in. A sickening crunch shuddered up his arm. The abomination shrieked in a deafening wild animal's voice before dropping down on top of him.

Another eclipse swallowed the world.

He woke thirsty, angry. A low, guttural growl powered up his bloodied throat. Joe didn't feel any pain only a burning emptiness. The dead thing laying staked and cold over him fueled his rage. He tossed the husk away and heard it hit the wet stones of the chamber's nearest wall. Joe opened his eyes. The darkness broke in gray-green tones like a view through night vision goggles.

How long have I been here?

He choked down a dry, bitter swallow. His insides had been desiccated to desert. Standing on shaky legs, he scrutinized his surroundings. The skeletons and skulls of other of the monster's prey littered corners, picked clean by both the horror and time.

Growling, he retrieved his sidearm and made his way along the passage. Instinct told him where to turn—left at the first juncture into the depths beneath the destroyed castle, right toward the door. The rectangle leading out appeared before him, lit gray by another overcast morning here at the end of the known world.

Joe approached. He strode forward into the grayness. Electricity stung his flesh. He staggered back to where the shadows pooled and looked down to see wisps of caustic-smelling smoke rise off the burn mark on the back of his hand. More rage powered up from the emptiness inside him. He opened his mouth, intending to demand answers—*what did you do to me?*

But before the words formed, his tongue grew intimate with the sudden sharpness of his incisors. Joe's teeth had become fangs, and the question emerged as a shriek broadcast through the depths of the cursed ruins that had trapped him and out into the silent forest.

At nightfall, Joe departed and made his way through the dark woods to the north. Thirsty, *so thirsty*, he came upon an encampment of the former Yugoslavian Army and satisfied both his parched throat and his anger. At least for that moment.

By day, he found dark, safe places—corners of basements or attics. At night, he traveled northwest. Eventually, Joe crossed into Germany and, from there, reassumed his identity through a series of clever lies and skills made possible by his new powers and condition.

At Ramstein Airbase, he gave his report. It was filed and then buried. He made arrangements to return home—at night.

"I can only fly at night," Joe told the man on the other side of the corporate desk.

"Night?" The HR director looked confused waiting for Joe to expand on that strange statement.

Beyond the tall windows, the city's light pollution cloaked the stars. One of the big jumbo jets operating at the airport streaked up from the tarmac and glided out of view. Joe's smile widened. The green of his eyes intensified.

"Yes, *night*."

The man glanced over the blank sheet of paper on the desk in front of him and smiled. "Well, Captain Rhodes, a very impressive resume and references. On behalf of Skybold Airlines, I'm honored to make you an offer to join our team!"

The man rose and extended his hand. Joe shook it and flashed a toothy smile.

In full uniform, he took to the cockpit. His copilot was a seasoned air force vet, the attendants both leggy and attractive in their Skybold blue two-tone colors.

"We're so glad you're flying tonight," said one of the two women as he ran through small talk and checklist.

"Yeah, we all are," said Joe's copilot.

An hour later, they were flying away from Boston toward Chicago and chasing the night.

Joe set up houses in the five destination cities he flew, all of them within easy access of the airports even factoring in normal delays.

Three months before his night of passion with Willa Forsyth, a jammed runway almost ended him behind the controls while the plane was still in flight. Joe brought her down swiftly, aware of the panic in his chest even though his heart no longer pulsed. When the plane's wheels struck the asphalt, the sun was nudging its rays up from the Atlantic. He braked, and they were on the ground.

"Take over," he ordered, and when his copilot glanced in Joe's direction, the pilot's seat was already empty.

And so, to avoid a repeat of that night, he shortened his routes. This meant selling off certain safe houses and establishing new ones.

"You'll love Hydrangea Heights," the woman leaning against the edge of the desk in a suggestive pose said. "People mind their own beeswax."

Joe smiled. Brittany Barrows gasped and tilted her head to one side. She swept a lock of bottled blonde hair behind her ear and bared her throat.

"Good," Joe said and feasted.

She tasted cheap, diluted by low-shelf alcohol and lower emotions. But she helped him secure the house on Mistral Lane, where people really did mind their own beeswax. Well, most of them did.

"The blood here is quite blue," she said on the night they signed the closing papers. "Pretty boring stuff, actually. Professionals. Some families. A cop lives over there. His wife's a former beauty pageant queen." From beneath her umbrella, Brittany indicated the house across the street.

Joe tipped a look toward his nearest neighbor, and the lit downstairs room partially visible behind a length of plum-purple curtains.

"Her?" Brittany snorted in dismissal. "*The Writer.*"

"Writer?" Joe asked.

While his new servant blathered on, her words lost in the night's cadence of rain, the writer glanced out a window and, briefly, their eyes connected. And for the first time in a long while, Joe felt something like happiness might be possible again.

She crushed her mouth over his. Joe sensed the conflagration that burned within her. Willa was different. The mark of the supernatural was upon her, too, though different from his curse. He was intrigued.

Joe followed her up the stairs. Clothes dropped along with inhibitions. He backed her toward the bed. She gasped his name like an incantation, and he salivated for a taste of her. Joe's lips sought her throat.

"*Willa,*" he growled.

She moaned, "*Yes?*"

His teeth punctured her flesh. Blood flowed onto his tongue. Joe sipped, and how sweet—*how fiery!*—Willa was. There, in her bed, he recognized the wolf's curse she carried and understood they could be more than lovers.

They were soul mates.

Before dawn, he left a note on his empty pillow and slipped free of Willa's house.

With the sky brightening, the night he never wanted to end had, and Joe hastened past his basement door, locking it behind him. He plodded to the bottom of the stairs. The coffin that was his bed waited to welcome him to sleep. He climbed in and sealed the lid shut.

And as the deep sleep claimed him, he heard that song, floating in an echo through the shadows. Only before he closed his eyes, Joe realized he wasn't so sad anymore.

Chapter 10

The Name Blame Game

"*R*," Wandalou said between metered sips of breath as she jogged the treadmill. "I bet it's the Queen of Romance's new beau, the dreamy airline pilot, Captain Rhodes."

Running the machine at Wandalou's right, Willa cast a disapproving glance to her left.

"What?" Wandalou huffed. "His last name fits!"

"Joe didn't know Jessie-Marie," Willa said in a voice that barely made it over the tank-tread whine of the three workout stations. "And he's not exactly the greeting card killer type."

"How can you be sure?" Wandalou challenged. "You've known the guy for all of five minutes."

Isis slowed her speed to a dogtrot. "I'm with Willa. It doesn't make sense in the case of her hunky pilot."

Willa smirked. "And while we're on the subject of the men in our lives and beds, what about your other police officer? *Rolfe* Hastings?"

Wandalou hissed, looked around the mostly deserted gym, and shushed the other woman. That brought more attention from the yoga mats than their conversation, which had operated on low volume. Wandalou flashed a plastic smile at the senior set now turned in their direction and added a hearty chuckle for effect. The few older society women stretching their body parts at Off Your Rockers, a workout destination for Hydrangea Heights's aging upper crust but also the only decent gym in town not overwhelmed by juice heads and lady wrestlers, returned to their routines. Once the coast seemed clear, Wandalou whirled around to Willa and leaned over the machine's handrail.

"Please don't remind me!"

"Or me," Isis remarked just loud enough to be heard. "If I listen to any more of that K-Pop noise…I think I'm starting to like it."

"The point being," Wandalou continued, "Rolfe couldn't have done it. He was with me right until I got your phone call, I'll remind you. Besides, like your pilot, my former fling isn't the blackmail-note-sending type."

"No, but he did have insider knowledge," said Willa.

Wandalou covered her lady-business with one hand and swayed as the treadmill continued its front to back roll. "How dare you!"

"I meant that he knew about the affair."

"Of course he did," Wandalou said, righting and resuming her jog. "He didn't know much else. Sort of an unskilled worker, if you get my drift. Not like Quinn. That man could…"

Wandalou stopped suddenly, and the sentence went unfinished. Then she blinked herself out of the blues before they could take control. "Rolfe didn't do it anymore than your pilot."

"I have to agree," Isis said.

Half an hour later, beneath the warm spray of the showers, Isis nudged her privacy curtain aside. Wandalou gasped and yanked it back so that only her face showed.

"Regina Gowl," Isis said.

Willa peeked out from behind her shower's curtain on the other side. "Regina?"

"The night of the murder, we saw her return to her house right after the estimated time of the crime. Do you remember how guilty she looked?"

"That old trout always looks guilty," Wandalou said. "But now that you bring it up…*that sour, spitting cobra!*"

"We don't know that she did it," Isis warned.

Willa's expression tightened. "No, but I'd bet my next book deal Regina Gowl isn't above sending blackmail letters. This fits the old dragon's profile seamlessly!"

"Only if Jessie-Marie pointed us in the right direction," Isis continued. "It's flimsy evidence. If we understood the clue, all we have is that the killer's name begins with R."

A jiggle of shower rings sounded beside Wandalou. A fourth face peered out from a gap in the stretch of privacy curtains, one set beneath blue-rinsed hair in a shower cap. "Are you discussing the last episode of *The Paddington Murders*?" Mrs. Divia Winterton asked. "I say, a perfectly riveting series!"

"Catch up on your streaming content somewhere else, Countess," Wandalou snarked and yanked the privacy curtain shut.

"*Really*," carped Mrs. Winterton from the other side.

"**R**egina Gowl," Isis said.

Willa joined her at the kitchen window. Beyond, the Slade backyard stretched, and, at its borders, were the suspect-in-question's rose hedges.

"Remember," Willa said. "We don't know for sure that Regina's responsible."

"Sure we do," Wandalou said from the breakfast table. "That vinegary old bag never had an orgasm in her life—and she's resentful of anyone who has. I have half a mind to go over there and bitch-slap her into the Fifth Dimension."

"*Look*," Willa said. Her excited tone caused Isis to lean toward the window.

Beyond the hedge, a huge pink sunbonnet appeared. It moved along the roses. The head it rested on was barely visible over the tops of the flowers and leaves.

"I have a plan," Isis said.

Wandalou stood. "What kind of plan—give!"

"One that determines if Regina Gowl is the murderer!"

After sharing the plan, Isis carried out a pitcher of lemonade and tray of sugar cookies to the backyard table. Then, with her best smile fixed in place, she approached the rose hedges where Regina worked and snipped.

"Good afternoon, neighbor," Isis sang.

Regina bolted upright, the clippers clutched in both hands, the blades extended in a menacing pose. Regina's mean face scrunched into a pout. Isis backed a step away.

"What do you want?" Regina demanded.

Isis maintained her sunny expression. "I have cold lemonade and warm sugar cookies fresh from the oven. Wondered if you wanted to join me?"

Regina sniffed the air and scanned the table, seeing that there indeed were refreshments being offered. "Oh?"

"Just being neighborly," Isis said. "We haven't talked in a while. Come on over and take a break."

Regina closed the clippers and softened the slightest. "I think I will."

Just as Isis knew Regina would. If Regina Gowl appreciated anything more than hot gossip, she was notorious for showing up at functions for the free dessert. Regina sat at the table, smelling of roses. But beneath that perfume lurked another scent, something that smelled past its prime.

Venom, thought Isis while she poured and maintained her smile. Always, she was aware of Regina's gaze, so she resisted the urge to look up when two figures darted through her neighbor's backyard and toward the unlocked rear door.

"So, how have you been?" Isis asked.

Regina reached for a cookie. "Fine."

"Just fine?"

"What do you want me to say? That the neighborhood's going to hell just like I predicted, and we all need to remember to lock our doors?"

Isis coughed.

"Something wrong?" Regina asked.

Isis cleared the tiny discomfort with a hasty swig of lemonade. "No, just my hay fever."

Regina leaned back in the lawn chair and smirked. "At least your girls are staying out of my roses since our last little chat."

That "chat," as Isis recalled, had been more of a shooting match, at least from Regina's side of the property line.

"I spoke with the twins. No more picking flowers for mommy," Isis said sweetly. "Though I'm sure you can understand why they'd be tempted—your roses are stunning."

"They are—and they're *mine*. If you ask me, those girls need proper discipline instead of constant coddling. A firm spank on the behind is in order."

Isis's smile degenerated into something she guessed was rather psychotic to behold. "Cookie?"

They snuck around the house. Once the old bat was beyond the roses and seated with her back to them, Willa and Wandalou crept up to the door and quietly slipped into Regina Gowl's lair. They entered through the kitchen. Wandalou yipped. Willa whirled and shushed her.

"*Look,*" Wandalou said and pointed at the counter where a jar of pickled pigs' feet sat beside a can of lima beans and a packet of instant rice.

"Ewww, lima beans," Willa said. Then she slapped Wandalou's extended finger. "*Focus.*"

She reminded Wandalou that they were in search of proof that linked Regina to the murder and to do it fast. They came upon the staircase.

"You head upstairs. I'll search down here," Willa whispered.

Wandalou saluted and ascended the stairs in her designer platform sneakers.

Heart galloping, Willa surveyed the surroundings. To her left was a formal dining room, the furniture severe, the space looking more for show than actual function. Willa couldn't imagine diners seated in the stiff, tall-backed chairs worried about spilling food or drink. Directly ahead, she located the foyer with a hall table and silk flower arrangement. The living room featured the expected: TV, overstuffed chairs, and recliner. Beside the latter was a folding table, and upon that a coaster, remote control, and crossword puzzle book. Hanging from the same drapery hook at the front windows that were meant for toile curtains dangled a pair of night vision goggles. Suspended from the hook on the other side were binoculars.

Willa's rage bubbled. "*Nosy*," she huffed.

Then, following her own advice, she focused. Apart from the downstairs powder room, the only other space was a small office to the right of the staircase. Inside was a sturdy metal desk—old, the kind that used to inhabit classrooms. Willa recalled that Regina Gowl had once taught Hydrangea Heights's young minds before striking a bonanza in the stock market—botulism cosmetic injections, according to Isis. Two bookshelves filled with encyclopedias and other volumes of learning dominated half the walls. A banker's lamp with a green glass shade sat on the desk alongside a paperweight of the Empire State Building and a coffee mug full of pens—most of the later, she noticed after taking to the desk's seat, pilfered from local banks and grocery stores.

Frantically, she opened drawers. Inside the central one, she discovered more pens, a calendar—one more freebie from the bank—and three pamphlets, all from some whack-job religious group calling themselves the Purists. "*Only the purest of the pure*," Willa read aloud.

Sighing, she returned the propaganda to its position and closed the drawer. If Regina Gowl had sent the blackmail note to Wandalou over her affair, the pamphlets were circumstantial but convincing evidence.

She opened the top of three drawers at the desk's right hand side. In there were tape, a stapler, a little plastic case filled with rubber bands, and glue sticks. The middle drawer contained old phone books.

"This isn't a crime scene, it's a time capsule," Willa grumbled beneath her breath.

She opened the bottom drawer. Lined yellow legal pads were stacked a dozen deep. Tsking in frustration, Willa readied to close the drawer. Just as she moved it toward the shut position, from the very edge of the pile of yellow she spied a glimpse of deep maroon. She lifted the legal pads out. Beneath them was a selection of colored envelopes and white note cards. "Oh my God," Willa gasped.

She shuffled through the envelopes—maroon, azure blue, and there, lurking beneath, one blank square in familiar, severe chartreuse. "*Gotcha,*" Willa said.

And then a bloodcurdling scream tore through the house.

Wandalou snuck up the stairs, each step higher announced by the squeak of her soles' added rubber. She made it to the top. The atmosphere in Ol' Regina Gowl's house was one of staleness, as though the walls had bottled up the essence of the viper that lived there. A scent of flat perfume hung unpleasantly against the powdery smell exuded by plug-in air fresheners.

In the bathroom, she discovered the usual and expected—toothbrush, denture cup, and one-ply that Wandalou figured must scrape tender flesh like sandpaper. She made a quick pass through the medicine cabinet, only to recoil at the various tinctures and lotions meant to cure or soothe fungus and hemorrhoids.

The master bedroom was orderly in appearance but looked tired in the emotion it unleashed. A dusty rose comforter was faded and thin. The furniture was clearly from another era but not cheery in the way of cherished antiques. She did spot a lint roller on top of the dresser beside a mirrored tray with a few baubles and broaches laid across the glass, and the urge to pinch it tempted her. But then she remembered Willa's prompt to focus and instead busied herself by opening drawers. That, however, ended when she exhumed Regina's girdle from one. The thing was a beige-colored torture contraption.

Wandalou shut the drawer and wiped her fingers on the hem of her stylish glacier-blue House of Landau hoodie. She turned toward the nightstand, upon which a set of binoculars sat.

"Oh, you voyeuristic, tight assed…" she spat at the empty room.

A hasty inventory of the nightstand drawer's contents revealed lip balm, aspirin, hand lotion, and a small devotional book titled *Practicing Purity*.

"Purity? The one thing missing from this drawer is the one thing you need most, Regina," she said. "*That,* and extra batteries."

She straightened and approached what she assumed was the door to a walk-in closet. Wandalou felt along the wall, located the light switch, and screamed.

"How goes the botulism biz?" Isis asked. She refreshed their drinks. "No wrinkles, I hope."

Regina's expression soured. "Is that supposed to be funny?"

Isis lowered the pitcher. "You tell me."

"No, it wasn't funny at all. In fact, your comment was rather cutting. I'm sure you know I sold my stock shares right before the big Botulism Boom when they realized it could help with migraines. I lost out on a fortune!"

"Oh, I do apologize. I really didn't know. I'm sorry for your loss."

Regina sniffed. "I'm sure you are. Do you think that living here is cheap? Every year, the property taxes get worse—and I'm on a teacher's pension. And it's not just my own needs but the charities I support!"

"Oh?" Isis prompted, glad for a new avenue to continue talking and keep Regina right where she was longer. "Pet shelters and the needy?"

"No, nothing as lame as that. I'm talking about *real* charities for things that matter—like keeping people's naughty parts in their pants and out of sight, where they belong!"

Isis narrowed her gaze. "I didn't know you felt so strongly about such matters."

"*Religiously*," Regina said.

"And do those same religious beliefs about carnal pleasure also include worshipping the almighty dollar?"

"The Purists of Purity say nothing about making an honest buck."

"What about a dishonest one?"

Regina tossed the half-eaten sugar cookie onto the table in front of her. "Hey, what is this? Some kind of third-degree?"

Isis worried if she'd overplayed her hand. But right after that, the point became moot, for the air trembled with a muffled scream … and that clarion call originated inside Regina Gowl's house.

Regina's narrowed eyes snapped fully open. "What the H-E-Double-Toothpicks?" she fired off before rising and racing away with unexpected agility and speed.

Isis pursued. "Wait—have another cookie first!"

Regina made for the back door, only to stop and retrace her steps. She snatched the clippers up from where she'd left them stabbed blade-down in the ground and, holding them like a weapon, stalked into the house.

Willa raced up the stairs. "*Wandalou?*" she called in a whisper.

"In here," Wandalou answered.

Willa tracked her voice into the master bedroom. "*Wanda—?*"

"The closet," Wandalou said.

Willa hurried over to the door. "What's with the voice lessons?" Wandalou stepped aside. Willa saw what the closet contained and screamed too. The outburst incited another shriek from Wandalou.

Instead of clothes, the closet held shelves of dolls with porcelain faces, little red smirks, and vacant stares. There were sailor dolls, dolls in candy striper and police uniforms, and bride and groom dolls. Dolls—*hundreds* of them—were posed upright and covered every inch of available space.

Wandalou clutched at Willa. Willa yelped. "Come on, let's ditch this insane sideshow," Wandalou said.

"Agreed."

They turned and started toward the bedroom door and escape from the asylum they'd uncovered, only Regina Gowl blocked the way, and she was armed with what they at first mistook for a sword. A big, sharp and lethal dealer of death.

"What are you doing in my house?" Regina demanded.

"A cup of sugar," Willa said around a nervous laugh.

"Yeah, we wanted to borrow a cup of sugar. That's it." Wandalou released Willa. "The door was unlocked. But we don't need sugar now, nope. You're busy, so we'll be going. *Ta.*"

They took two more steps toward the bedroom door only to freeze and scream when Regina swung the clippers in a threatening arc that sliced through the staleness in the atmosphere with a switchblade's cutting song.

Wandalou and Willa jumped back.

"The Whore," Regina hissed, aiming the blade at Wandalou.

"*Hey—!*"

"And the Other Whore." Regina pointed at Willa.

"*Hey—!*"

Regina smiled. "I've seen that steamy trash you write. Don't even try to pretend that you're pure."

Willa folded her arms. "Those are wholesome and happy reads designed to empower women and help them experience pleasure." She leaned in closer. "And at least I don't have a shrine full of creepy dolls!"

Wandalou snapped her fingers for effect. "Yeah, take that!"

Regina walked her hauteur back a degree. "They were gifts from my students. Word got out that I referred to them as 'my little dolls,' so at every Christmas and graduation, more of them piled up on my desk. It's not like I'm hoarding them. I don't have a problem." Then she returned to the matter of the moment. "Unlike the two of you, who've invaded the sanctity of my home! Which gives me every right to defend myself and my property!"

Regina raised the clippers. Before she struck, she suddenly froze.

"Not another move," Isis said at her back. "What you're feeling now is the .22-caliber I keep on the top shelf of my hall closet for…you know, those *just in case* moments. Presently, it's aimed at your right kidney, where it can do an H-E-Double Toothpicks lot of damage if you don't immediately and very carefully lower your weapon and hand it back to me."

Eyes wide, Regina did as instructed. Isis rounded Regina holding the clippers in one hand and air in the other. She raised the two fingers she'd cocked into a fake gun, pointer and middle, and blew on them like some Old West gunslinger.

"You tricked me!" Regina spat.

Isis shrugged.

"How dare you?" Regina eyed the other two intruders. "Breaking and entering's a crime, you know!"

Willa stepped forward. "And so's murder, Regina."

"Murder?"

"I know you killed Jessie-Marie," Willa snapped, getting right in Regina's face. "I found the proof downstairs—the same envelope and card that were sent to Jessie-Marie that you intended for Wandalou!"

Regina backed away. "No, it isn't what you think. I didn't kill her. I swear, *I didn't kill Jessie-Marie Smyth!*"

Chapter 11
What Happened That Night

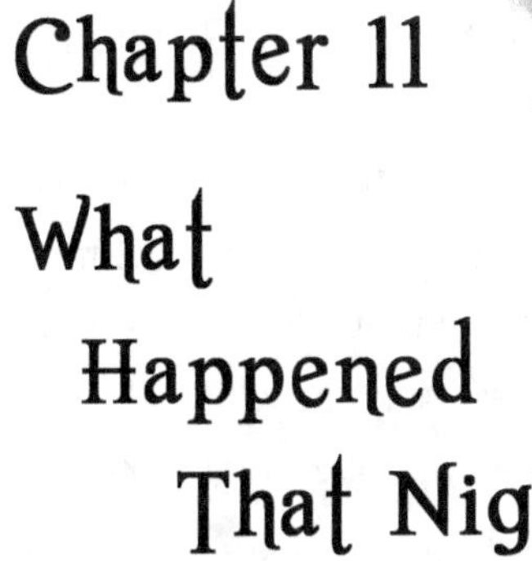

Quinn stepped into the kitchen. Wandalou's heart pounded in her chest, but she attempted to maintain a calm façade and mostly succeeded. Their gazes crossed, converged, and held for several tense seconds, then Wandalou blinked first. Quinn cleared his throat and continued to the kitchen table where Regina sat under unofficial guard by Willa and Isis.

"What's going on here?" Quinn asked in that gruff, all-business tone.

"Regina has something to tell you," said Isis.

Regina shot her interrogator a dirty look before answering. "Yes, Detective—I'd like you to arrest all three of these miserable hags for criminal trespassing!"

"*Hey—!*" Wandalou complained.

"*Hey—!*" Willa added.

Isis not so subtly kicked the chair where Regina sat. "Let's try to stay on point, shall we?"

"Fine. All right!" Regina tossed the lone chartreuse envelope onto the table. "I did it. I sent the blackmail note. But it wasn't meant for the Smyth woman—damn fool mailman can't read numbers, apparently."

Quinn processed what he was hearing. "You're saying that it was you who tried to put the squeeze on my fiancée?"

"For her disgusting dalliance with that rookie police officer, yes," Regina blurted out.

Quinn said, "Regina, I think now would be a good time to remind you that before you go any further, your lawyer should be present."

"I don't need a damn lawyer," Regina barked. "Because I didn't kill Jessie-Marie Smyth! The worst I did was try to shake a few nickels out of that loose woman you're engaged to—"

"*Hey—!*" Wandalou protested.

"*Hey—!*" said Quinn.

"—and meanwhile, they're taking liberties breaking and entering!"

"The door was open," Willa said.

Regina eyed Isis. "Was the Smyths' back door unlocked when you broke into their house, *hmmm?*"

Isis did her best to mask her surprise at Regina's accusation and mostly succeeded. "I have a key. I check in from time to time on Tim to make sure there's food in the fridge. It's true, I go over there unannounced on some mornings, but only to be a good neighbor." She delivered the last line with a glance at Regina.

"Can we get back to the blackmail note—and Jessie-Marie's murder?" Quinn ordered.

Regina's expression tightened. "If I'm guilty of anything, it, too, was in trying to be a good neighbor."

She sat in the interrogation room, a fresh bottle of water unopened in front of her, Phyllis taking notes and filling out reports while Regina answered questions. Quinn opted to stand—an intimidation tactic. Outside the door, a body dressed in Hydrangea Heights blue leaned in for a look. From the cut of his eye, Quinn saw that it was Officer Rolfe Hastings.

Quinn tipped a threatening look at the small square of reinforced glass. The uniformed man hovering outside vanished. Ten days of the worst duties had, apparently, impressed themselves upon the rookie policeman. And if they hadn't, Quinn could always claim budget cuts for an interruption of janitorial services and assign Hastings to clean toilets when he wasn't redoing paperwork already sufficient the first time or manning the most boring of traffic traps.

Quinn turned back to his suspect. "I don't need to tell you this, but you're in serious trouble, Regina."

Regina maintained an air of authority from the chair where all who were interrogated in the room sat. "I don't have to say another word."

"No, you don't," Quinn agreed. "But this is now official police business. Just know that *how official* it becomes is entirely up to you. You've already confessed to blackmail and surrendered the evidence that proves it. You've stated you didn't kill Jessie-Marie Smyth."

"Because I didn't."

"Fine. So tell me why I should believe you."

Regina's thin lips curled into a humorless smirk. "I could get a lawyer. I'm good friends with the Purist of the Pure."

"The cult?"

"They're not a cult! They only believe in spreading their message—and damning to fire anyone who disagrees."

Quinn and Phyllis exchanged looks.

"They'd love to take this one on. The fiancée of the detective harassing me sleeps with the new cop in town, and said detective goes all Old Testament on the witness who pointed out their fornication."

Quinn scratched his head. It was time to change tactics and drop down to Regina's level to remove the intimidation that got her to put up her back, and so he sat.

"Okay then, call," he said. "I only want to know the truth about what happened that night."

Her bluff bested, Regina's smugness deflated. "Okay, yes, I did go to the gazebo at the dog park that night. I know that's where Wandalou went to jog sometimes with her gaggle."

"You mean Willa Forsyth, Isis Slade, and Jessie-Marie Smyth?"

Regina nodded.

"What time did you arrive?" Quinn pressed.

"It must have been around 6:30 that night. It had just started to rain."

"Where did you park?"

"Father down the trail. I didn't want her to see my car. I didn't want her to see *me*."

"Why not?"

"I was having second thoughts about the whole thing," Regina continued. "Believe it or not, I'm not a pro at extorting money from other housewives!"

Quinn exhaled through his nostrils. The sound restored some of Regina's flame.

"What's that supposed to mean?" she demanded.

"Continue. So you parked out of sight. Then what?"

"I got out of my car. And then—"

She was back there on that night, stepping out into the rain. As Regina relived the events through conversation, so, too, did she through memory. She flashed to the cold drops striking her neck and top of her head, one splashing the very crown where her hair thinned as though the bald spot were a bullseye.

Her pulse quickened. For the first time since concocting her scheme, Regina questioned its merit. But the plan was now very much real, and it was too late to turn back. Even so, the prospect of an additional ten-grand only got her as far as the cluster of low-hanging maple branches that disguised her car's presence from the gazebo's vantage. Her legs refused to cooperate when she ordered them onward to her intended goal.

The wind gusted, scattering rain into her face. Regina remained behind the cover of the leaves and wished she'd thought to bring along an umbrella. More so, that she'd never gotten to this point. Even after collecting from the police detective's whore of a fiancée, she'd have to live in the same neighborhood as them for whatever remained of her life. And, as more than one of her past victims had emoted, Heaven didn't want Regina Gowl, and Hell was afraid she'd take over.

She waited; time dragged on with a maddening slowness. Right when she was about to jump behind the wheel and motor away, headlights strafed the early twilight's deepening gloom and a car pulled up to the gazebo.

Only it wasn't the princess's little sports car, as she'd expected. No, it was the very practical blue electric hybrid driven by her neighbor to the left. Confirming this, Jessie-Marie Smyth stepped out. As Regina watched, unseen by the new arrival, Jessie-Marie glanced about, closed the car door, and hurried through the rain and beneath the shelter offered by the gazebo's peaked roof.

Her? Why is Jessie-Marie here and not the beauty pageant queen? Regina's mind raced in counterpoint to the rapid cadence of her heart.

Then it struck her—the four of them! Jessie-Marie, the porn writer, the stepmother of those flower-stealing twins, and the beauty queen were all in cahoots. Wandalou Trueheart had conned the doctor's wife into fighting her battles. *Doctor?* Tim Smyth spent his days sitting in a dark room reviewing X-rays. He was more of a movie projectionist than a real doctor. Regina frowned. More so when she noted Jessie-Marie had traveled light by a meaty, neat ten thousand clams, according to her empty arms.

Regina made a fist and shook it.

It was clear by her neighbor's worried face that she was aware of some part of the details that had brought her to the gazebo—if not all of them. Then it struck Regina what was even likelier to be the cause—their idiot mailman had confused house numbers again. The wrong she-devil had received her blackmail note! Which made perfect sense as to why Jessie-Marie Smyth was standing on the gazebo instead of the she-devil Regina meant to squeeze. And which also begged the question of what Jessie-Marie Smyth had to hide that was big and dark enough to make her keep this meeting.

Nothing that Regina could guess. The Smyths were so milquetoast that she considered them even too pure for the Purists. *It's gotta be something pretty darn Machiavellian,* Regina thought. *Probably about the husband and his job. Oh, I wish I knew!*

Regina observed Jessie-Marie pace the gazebo, her worry clearly deepening. Heat rose up Regina's throat, part of it owing to the curiosity over the nature of whatever it was Jessie-Marie hoped to hide, the rest mostly anger over the windfall denied her by the mailman's stupidity. A meager portion could be blamed on the voyeuristic nature of her position among the cover of tree branches, the same pleasure she experienced whenever she donned her night vision goggles or peered out through binoculars at the goings on along Mistral Lane.

The cracking of a twig sliced through the air. Regina froze. It was somewhere nearby. Jessie-Marie heard it too, and tracked the sound toward the place where Regina hid.

"Is somebody there?' Jessie-Marie called.

Regina held her breath. And then she felt a slither over her flesh that confirmed someone *was*—someone else hidden among the dog park's shadowy places. She turned and looked around. No one was there. Nobody that she could see at least. When she glanced back, Jessie-Marie was on her way down the gazebo steps.

Panicking, Regina fast-marched back to her car, got in, and tore away.

"**A**nd that's it?" Quinn asked.

Regina blinked. "What do you mean—isn't that enough?"

"You didn't see anyone else?"

"No."

Quinn rose from his seat, set both palms flat on the table, and leaned down. "And then what did you do?"

"I drove around. I was upset!"

"*You* were upset?"

"Yes," Regina defended. "I hit the Burger Shack drive-through in Cherryvale, the one on Route 28 right outside Hydrangea Heights, and ordered a shake. Vanilla. *Small*, if you need to know."

"And how did you pay for it?"

"With my debit card."

Quinn tipped a look at Phyllis, who nodded. "We're gonna check that with your bank."

"Why?" Regina snapped. "Are you my new dietician? My new loan officer?"

Quinn's detective face returned. "No, Ms. Gowl, to establish your whereabouts at the time you claim. That drive-through puts you at least fifteen minutes one way off, half an hour roundtrip."

"Oh," she said. "Go ahead, make your call. And while you're at it, ask yourselves another question that should prove I'm innocent in all this."

"You're not innocent in *all* of it," Quinn reminded.

"I am about the part that matters—Jessie-Marie Smyth's murder! My bone density's only about half of what yours is and a lot less thick than our mailman's skull. With osteoporosis, how the hell do you think I offed the victim, carried away her body, and buried it in that dirt pile? Huh, Detective? Answer me that!"

The security door buzzed open. Quinn stepped out, his face grim. He approached the trio huddling together on the bench; they rose at his approach.

"So, did you beat the truth out of that old bat?" Wandalou asked.

Quinn eyed her but didn't respond.

"Well?" she pressed.

"You know that I can't discuss any details of an ongoing investigation," he said in his best professional tone.

Wandalou folded her arms. "What do you mean 'ongoing?' You're not buying her excuse that she just slinked out of there while Jessie-Marie was still alive, are you? Her own confession places her near the scene of the murder."

Quinn turned his attention to Isis and Willa. "I'm gonna need all three of you to make official statements. Why don't we start with you, Isis?"

Isis moved to follow Quinn but Wandalou intercepted and cut in line. "Why don't you start with *me*?"

"Okay," Quinn said.

"But before I give my statement, I want yours."

Quinn again faced her. "Excuse me?"

"Yeah, uh-huh, why don't you explain why you haven't returned any of my texts."

"You mean the ones that read *blarp, blorp, ding-dong*?"

"Damn auto-correct," Wandalou grumbled. "I wrote 'I miss you.'"

"And the ding-dong part?"

"'I miss you, ding-dong.'"

"You've sure got an odd way of showing it," he said in a voice meant only for her.

Wandalou snorted. "Me? What about those changed door locks, Quinn?"

"That's all *you*, babe."

"*Babe?* Clearly, I'm not your babe anymore. Message received, Mister Montoya," she said and turned away.

"You don't understand," Quinn said. "The locks. I didn't change them because of what you did. I had them changed for better ones after Jessie-Marie's death because I wanted you to be safe when I wasn't there. I placed that work order with the lock guy way before…well you know."

Wandalou stopped. Her righteous rage instantly dispersed. "Quinn?" Turning slowly, she approached him.

"Come home, Wandalou Trueheart," he whispered.

"I want to."

Quinn nodded. "Then do, as soon as you tell me the truth—and no more of this werewolf nonsense."

His words struck Wandalou like a slap. "*Nonsense?*" she exclaimed. "I hope you enjoy sleeping alone tonight." And then, to Isis's chagrin, she added, "I'll be in my room at the Slades'!"

"Do you believe Regina?" Willa asked.

Isis lowered her wine glass. At the other side of the patio, Bob grilled steaks clad in his Kiss the Cook apron, a snapshot of the normal world in contrast to the dark, secret reality the three seated around the backyard table shared. "If Regina didn't kill Jessie-Marie, the murderer is still out there."

Wandalou whispered, "Do you think it has something to do with…*you know*," and then very quietly, she howled like a wolf.

Both Isis and Willa shushed her. Bob glanced up from the sizzling feast he was preparing, smiled, and waved with the big meat fork.

"What I think," Isis said, regaining her theatrical smile for the benefit of others not in the know, "is that we're no closer to getting to the bottom of either Jessie-Marie's murder or…*you know*." And then she howled, too, which earned her the ire of her two companions and another glance from Bob.

"Are you ladies checking me out?" he joked, all cool.

"Yes, Bob, it's that sweet ass of yours," laughed Wandalou.

Bob grinned and flexed his butt in the old pair of cargo shorts that showcased the firmness of his glutes to perfection then returned to grilling.

"Something smells good," another man's voice joined in.

Willa tracked it to the corner of the house, where Joe materialized under the gloom of the new dusk. Energy surged through her insides. She jumped up and said his name.

"Mind if I join you?" Joe asked.

Willa walked him over. "Good, you're here. I want to introduce you to my friends."

Joe ambled over, stopping first at the grill. He and Bob shook hands.

"Bob Slade," their host introduced himself.

"Joe Rhodes."

"Stay for dinner, Joe?" Bob offered. "My wife's whipped up her famous potato salad. You look like a meat and potato kind of dude."

"Meat, for sure," Joe said.

Willa's eyes bulged and she flashed a woman's excited smile to Wandalou and Isis.

"Dial it down about ten notches, *Crazy*," Wandalou urged corner-of-the-mouth.

"Oh, right," Willa said.

Joe sidled up to the table and Willa made introductions. "Ladies, this is my…"

Silence followed until Joe broke it. "—neighbor, Joe Rhodes," he said while shaking hands. "Also, I'm her boyfriend."

"Yes, boyfriend," Willa said around a nervous giggle. "He's my boyfriend. *Oh my God, I have a boyfriend!*"

"And quite the hot one," Wandalou said coolly.

Joe smiled. "Thanks."

"No, thank you," Wandalou continued. "Our girl Willa deserves someone who makes her feel like doing cartwheels while lighting fireworks out of her—"

"Wandalou," Isis interjected. "Here's a thought—why don't you invite Quinn to join us?"

Wandalou's confidence sagged. "Quinn?"

Isis's and Bob's eyes met across the distance.

"Yeah, give him a call," Bob said. "We've got more than enough for another friend at the table."

Joe sat. Wandalou picked up her phone. Her fingers hovered over the screen, but in the end she set the phone back down.

"So, Joe, tell us all about you," Wandalou said.

He held Willa's hand under the table as they talked. A cold beer delivered by Bob sat in front of him, mostly untouched. Every now and then for show, Joe raised the bottle to his lips. None of the old pleasures of food and drink interested him anymore.

"Where are the twins?" Willa asked.

"Sleepover at a friend's."

"How nice for them. And for you and the grill master," Willa said.

Joe listened, smiled, and commented when appropriate. When the food appeared on the table that the five of them squeezed together around, he made the excuse that he'd already eaten and wished he hadn't.

He enjoyed the company, especially Willa's, despite realizing that the night beast lurking within her dormant, just beneath the surface, also slept inside her two closest gal-pals. *Interesting.*

Chapter 12
What Happened That *Other* Night

Before long, it struck Wandalou that she was the odd number at a table with two sets of evens. Though no one in either couple brought this fact to her attention, Quinn's presence at the meal would have balanced out the night ideally, and the longer she fought to deny how much she missed him, the worse the emptiness inside her grew.

She set down her napkin and said, "Excuse me."

"Where are you going?" asked Willa.

Wandalou tsked. "*Novelists*, always so interested in answers. Leave a chapter out and call your next book a mystery!" With that, Wandalou continued in past the French doors, through the Slade house, and out the front door. She crossed the sidewalk and approached Number 11 Mistral Lane. Quinn's SUV was parked in the driveway. Wandalou hesitated before ringing the bell.

She waited, her heart in a gallop, her armored exterior threatening to crack. The house—how she wanted to experience its embrace welcoming her home. Home to Quinn. But the door with its new lock remained sealed, and she imagined herself as a visitor, not one of its family.

Then the door opened, and Quinn stood in the gap. His tie unknotted, he'd shed his shoes and wore black socks. One big toe poked through a hole in the frayed cotton. Surprise in his eyes, Quinn said, "Wandalou?"

Her instinct was to breeze past him and into the house, which was still half hers. Instead, she sought permission. "Is it okay if I come in?"

He answered with a tight-lipped nod and vacated the threshold, bidding her to enter. Wandalou stepped in, all nerves and aware that her condition showed in her body language.

"Hell of a cookout over at the Slades," she said. "We missed you."

"Was I invited? I don't seem to have gotten the notice. Not even a text," he said.

"My bad," Wandalou said. "It isn't too late if you want to join us. Willa's new boyfriend's there. You know, the airline pilot. He and Bob seem to have hit it off. I think you'd like him, too. Then the three of you could hang out together."

"Yeah? And do what?"

"Scratch something," she laughed.

Quinn didn't lighten. "I'm not up to company. I've had a long day, and I already ate."

"I can smell the peanut butter on your angry comebacks."

Quinn sighed. "Maybe I wouldn't be angry if I understood what the hell was going on around this neighborhood better—and what was happening with my fiancée."

"I told you the truth," Wandalou said.

"And I believe you about Rolfe Hastings."

"Hey, I told you it was a mistake and that nothing really happened between us!"

"I believe you."

"So why can't you believe me?" She folded her arms only to comprehend his words. "Wait, what, you do?"

"I absolutely do and accept your apology along with your promise that you won't cheat on us again. You get *one* free pass, Wandalou."

A smile of relief tempted her lips. "So we're good?"

"No, we're not good," he said and, turning, marched away into the kitchen.

Wandalou pursued. As she'd already gathered, the open jar of crunchy peanut butter sat on her exquisite Dahlgren kitchen table with inlaid tile beside a loaf of white bread and a half emptied glass of milk.

"What's the problem then?" she demanded.

He spun and aimed a finger at her. "Bad enough that I can't trust you in my bed, but I know you're somehow tangled up in the murder of Jessie-Marie Smyth!"

She didn't respond, which only worsened Quinn's frown.

"What aren't you telling me?"

Wandalou inhaled a deep breath and then just as deeply expelled it. She sat down in one of the Dahlgren's comfortable chairs and extended a hand for Quinn to join her. He did, taking the chair backwards in that pose of Old West cowboys and film noir police detectives. This wouldn't be a clearing of the air or even a conversation; it was yet one more interrogation.

Her defenses ramped up. Wandalou focused on the jar of peanut butter instead of Quinn's narrowed eyes. "*Crunchy?* Seriously? You might as well eat birdseed."

"Wandalou…"

"Or kibble. The way that stuff gets between your teeth—"

He slapped his palm down hard on the table. Everything on top of it jumped—peanut butter, bread, and milk. So did Wandalou.

"Okay. So, a little more than two months ago…"

She lowered her sunglasses, a chic new pair from Trendi, and scrutinized the sign. *My Grains.* According to the local buzz, this new bakery was the best place for artisan breads, finger pastries, and the one major bullet point she hoped to check off her list.

Wandalou didn't give the place much hope. The exterior was an unflattering shade of blue, and the name on the sign a poor choice. *Headachey*, her inner critic snarked. Still, she'd read plenty of local reviews to convince her to give this place a try. Then she inhaled the sweetness of the air, and Wandalou's doubts collapsed.

She'd hastened through the door and into the long line of customers clearing the shelves of warm loaves and delectable breakfast pastries.

It was inevitable that her patience would fray. It did. Wandalou checked her Vartiere gold lady's watch. Ten minutes passed and she was only halfway to the glass counter. No one removed themselves from the line, opting for other breakfast destinations. The air was sugary, so absolutely *delicious*, that she grew lightheaded and insanely hungry. Around her, customers drank coffee and ate donuts at the tables and conversed in low voices. The person standing in line behind her cleared his throat. Wandalou shot him a threatening look, only to realize she had, at long last, reached the glass counter.

Wandalou strode up and froze. The face looming above the other side of the glass case threatened to turn her to stone.

"*Vhat do you vant?*" Frau Krumpt demanded.

Wandalou forgot how to talk. "Uh…uhm…"

"*Next,*" Frau Krumpt announced.

Wandalou coughed up her voice. "I'd like to talk about wedding cakes."

"*Vedding* cakes?"

"Yes, *vedding* cakes," Wandalou said.

"Have a seat," the woman didn't ask so much as demand.

Wandalou nodded and sat at one of the few empty tables. There, she waited, and while she did, she pulled out her phone and attempted to work.

After what seemed an unforgivable long while, the German woman took the other chair. Frau Krumpt's steely blue eyes bore into her. "Who are you?" the woman asked.

Wandalou feigned confidence. "I'm an influencer."

"What are you doing?"

"Influencing."

"That's a thing?"

"Yes, it's a thing." Sighing, Wandalou slipped her phone into her designer tote and worked up the courage to meet the older woman's gaze. "Look, I hear you're the best bakery within driving distance of Hydrangea Heights."

"I'm not bad," Frau Krumpt said.

"Are you up for the job?"

"Very."

She described what she wanted—white cake, not yellow, three tiers with vanilla buttercream and lots of decorative swirls, fresh strawberries, and a tasteful bride and groom topper.

"*Ach*," Frau Krumpt sighed.

"What do you mean '*ach*'?"

"Nothing, just my back. And *vhen* is the happy occasion to take place?"

"We haven't set a specific date but soon."

"How soon?" Frau Krumpt pressed.

"Can I get back to you on that?"

Frau Krumpt stood. "You do that, but always remember that I am a very busy woman. My business and other matters don't leave me a lot of time for lollygagging."

Wandalou grinned. "It's rough in those deep woods at your gingerbread house with all those kids, right?" The words were out of her mouth before she could trap them, a bad habit she'd yet to break.

"*Vhat?*" Frau Krumpt bellowed.

All other conversations in My Grains shorted out.

In a sheepish voice, Wandalou said, "Nothing."

"I despise gingerbread, and am not looking forward to *Weinachtsfest*, if you must know. And as for *Kinder*, there is only one who goads me." Frau Krumpt's eyes narrowed. Wandalou shrank from her gaze. "I *vill* require a week's notice for the cake. And one more thing."

"Yes?"

Frau Krumpt leaned forward, and Wandalou froze. "Don't piss me off, Fraulein."

Wandalou nodded. "Okay."

"I can't hear you, *leetle mouse*."

"Yes, ma'am," Wandalou repeated not much louder.

"Much better." Then Frau Krumpt returned to her bakery counter, where the line had reformed.

Shaking, Wandalou slunk out of My Grains. Halfway to her car, she regained her swagger. She withdrew her phone and dialed. "*Vedding* cake, check," she said while the number rang. "And remind me to warn my fans about the temptation to wear *Dirndls* come October."

"Hello," Isis chirped.

"Yeah, girl. Bachelorette party. You're on it. And make sure it's unforgettable. I see one cucumber sandwich, and I'll shove it up your—"

Isis quickly set down the English cucumber she happened to be selecting for the family dinner salad. "Understood, *unforgettable*, right," she said into the phone.

"Something so *epic* that we'll be talking about it for the rest of our lives. Ta." Wandalou hung up.

Isis slipped the phone into her tote and pushed the grocery cart out of the market's produce section.

*E*pic. Isis exited the ladies' locker room at the flashier of Hydrangea Heights's two gyms, Extra-Own. Rumor was that the owners had named the place after a jumble of the words "estrogen" and "testosterone," and Isis believed it. Men with glistening biceps and six-pack abs grunted and sweated at the weight benches. Women who looked ready for wrestling rings and combat worked out on bikes or ran marathons on the line of treadmills. It was all very intimidating. Off Your Rockers, the other gym catering to the town's upscale senior set, seemed more her speed.

She almost returned to the locker room and, from there, her car. But beyond the tall windows that gave anyone in the parking lot a decent show of the happenings inside, the humid July day had opened up. Rain spilled down in sheets, making the outside world a blur.

"Oh, *poo*," she cursed under her breath.

But it was, as she often stated or thought, what it was. Another summer day in Hydrangea Heights. The twins were with their dad at the water park three towns over likely getting plenty of water according to the unexpected summer soaker. She had another six and a half hours of Isis Time, according to the wall clock. She hadn't planned on getting soaked at home, but a march through the rain was inevitable.

And then he walked in.

Isis froze, unable to blink or, at first, breathe. The man strutted over to her, so physically attractive, in a pale blue tank and loose-fit cotton shorts, expensive sneakers, no socks, that it physically hurt to look at him. Isis did, unable to break focus. His blond hair was neat on the sides, one length longer on top, wild but controlled in the same instant. His eyes were a faded blue, almost gray in color—no, *silver*. And as for the body that inhabited those workout clothes…

"Are you here to sweat?" he asked, his voice a deep, manly growl.

"Uh…" Isis blathered.

He flashed a crooked smile, real cool, that showed off a length of clean white teeth. Clearly, he was a man used to such reactions from others blinded by his dazzling looks. Those overwhelmed by them.

Isis came out of her trance. "I was hoping to catch the next aerobics class. Are you leading it?"

Cocky, the man folded his arms and shifted his weight from one big foot to the other. "What if I am, Red?"

And that's how it happened, their aerobics class for two. The demigod conducted a hell of a workout set to the music oozing out of the overhead speaker.

"Sweat, sweat, *sweat*," he urged Isis.

Sweat, she did. Isis Slade was happy in her marriage to Bob and loved their little family, even if the twins sometimes tested her right down to her last nerve, Marci especially. But she wasn't dead. Far from it, and so she noticed the man's sweet moves, the poetry of his muscles, the sex in his dance steps. When the twenty-minute session reached cool-down, a lusty grin spread on his lips. "I caught you checking me out, Red," he said.

Embarrassment rose up her throat and warmed her cheeks. "I swear…"

"And don't think I didn't notice the wedding ring," he taunted.

Isis folded her arms. "Now see here. You might be an asset to this gym—"

"Oh, I don't work for the gym. Just figured I'd help out the hot redhead and shake my shit."

Isis's defenses sagged. "You're not the aerobics instructor?"

"No, I'm new in town and at a loose end. Figured if they saw me in action, they'd trip over themselves to hire me on the spot."

Isis indulged in another glance down before lifting her gaze back to those pale blue-silver eyes. "I don't know about the gym, but I'd like to hire you."

"You would?" he said, not shying from the mischief in his tone.

"How would you like to *shake your shit* for a private bachelorette party of four?"

"I'm your guy," he said and extended his hand. "My name's Race."

At five, the limousine Isis hired collected Wandalou, Jessie-Marie, and Willa, and spirited them in luxury to Bungalow 7 at Duncan's Point on Hydrangea Lake. The waiting list in summer months to book the exclusive venue was two years into the future, but there'd been a last minute cancellation, and Isis knew the manager whose daughter attended the twins' school.

The day was one of those bright early July beauties, low humidity, only a few fluffy white clouds in the sky, and the night promised to be the same. The bungalow's tall windows and outside deck faced the water, and the view was stunning. Comfortable furniture, a fridge stocked with plenty of upscale appetizers, desserts, and bubbly, Isis wandered through the spacious and sunny rooms.

All was perfect.

The limousine pulled up to the bungalow's flagstone walkway at 5:17. Wandalou's head and shoulders gyrated up through the open sunroof, a hot pink boa draped around her neck. "Mamma's here!" she announced loud enough that those in Bungalows 1-6 heard.

She danced out of the limo ahead of the others. At the door Isis handed her a glass from the tray, the first of several colorful, fruity drinks with tiny paper parasols.

They played the usual games that involved drinking, like the Newlywed Game in which Isis had emailed a list of questions to Quinn, and for every one Wandalou got wrong, she had to take a chug and after every one she got right, the partygoers did.

They played the usual games that didn't involve drinking, including the Ring Scavenger Hunt in which Isis had hidden several plastic toy diamond rings around the bungalow behind throw pillows and lamps, and anybody who discovered one won a prize.

"Oh my God," Jessie-Marie gasped after she opened her winning envelope, the toy ring displayed on her hand. "It's a membership to Extra-Own!"

Wandalou snatched the envelope out of her friend's hand. "No, it's a cucumber sandwich!" she spat, her focus aimed at Isis.

Jessie-Marie took back the envelope. Isis made a tray pass with individual tiramisus.

"So luscious," Willa moaned.

Wandalou pouted.

Isis patted her shoulder. "Fear not, bride-to-be. You asked for unforgettable, and I think I delivered on it."

"Oh?"

About twenty minutes before the sun set, a knock hammered against the bungalow's front door.

"This is the police—*open up!*" a man's deep voice demanded.

Jessie-Marie and Willa exchanged nervous glances. Isis calmly answered the door. In strutted a demigod with expensive shades over his eyes dressed in a black police uniform that fit his ripped physique in a way that should have been criminal.

"We've received serious complaints about a party that's gotten out of hand," Race said, real cocky. He sidled up to Wandalou. "You in the pink boa, are you the leader of this girl gang? 'Cause you sure look like trouble."

Wandalou snorted a laugh. "Nice uniform."

Race smiled and flashed teeth. "You like it?"

"Too bad it's a fake, like this raid," she answered, matching the cop's cool.

"Says you."

"Says the fiancée of one of Hydrangea Heights's finest."

"In that case," the cop said. He took a step back, reached down, and, in one deft yank, tore his uniform pants off their fasteners. "Let's lose the uniform!" Underneath, he wore an American flag thong.

Jessie-Marie squealed. Isis dialed up the tunes on her tablet—something foreign that reminded her of bubble gum called K-Pop that was, according to Quinn, Wandalou's favorite music.

Race the Face gyrated and danced to the beat. More of his clothes came off, including his shades to reveal those pale, near-silver eyes. The four friends joined in and moved to the music and around the hot stripper. Champagne got uncorked and poured down throats. Laughter and shrieks played in counterpoint to the beat.

And outside, over the lake, a full moon rose into the new night's sky.

Race the Face was performing a cheesy version of a lap dance over Jessie-Marie when he jolted, tossed back his head, and let forth with a howl that shook the bungalow.

"That's right," Wandalou hooted. She howled, too.

Then Jessie-Marie screamed, and when the others looked, Race the Face wasn't dancing but contorted, clad only in his American flag thong.

"What the hell—?" asked Wandalou.

A low, throaty growl played beneath the music. Isis walked over first, intending to help but not yet understanding the jeopardy she was in—that they all were in. She set a hand on Race's bare back, which had been hairless when she'd started toward him but now sported a few layers of blond peach fuzz.

Race whirled. His eyes glowed silver. His salivating mouth hung open, and it was filled with sharp teeth.

"My, what big—" Isis started to say.

Race was upon her, biting at Isis's neck.

Isis screamed.

Wandalou screamed.

Willa screamed.

A few minutes later, all three of the party guests and its star were down, their throats ripped open.

"**...a**nd then, the next morning, we all woke up," finished Wandalou.

Quinn listened, at first not speaking, his eyes wide and trained unblinkingly upon her.

"Now's when you ask me questions," she added.

Quinn blinked. "You woke up the next morning after the stripper ripped all of your throats out?"

"That's how it works. The curse or whatever you want to call it. Last time, I tore out Isis's stomach and come sunrise, *boom*." She snapped her fingers for effect.

"And this guy Race—"

"Race the Face."

"He just left?"

"And we haven't been able to find him. If we did, we might figure out how to reverse it. You know, stop it, *cure* it so we're not baying at the moon and looking all Lon Chaney Junior three nights a month!"

Quinn stood.

"Hey," Wandalou called after him. "Is that all you want to ask me?"

Giving one low key sentence as an answer, Quinn marched up the stairs. She heard the bedroom door quietly shut.

She stormed out of the house and back across the street. They were no closer to solving the werewolf's curse or unmasking Jessie-Marie's killer. Not quite as important but certainly galling, Quinn's only suggestion was that she see a shrink as soon as possible. He knew of a good one who worked with the Hydrangea Heights Police Department.

Chapter 13
Willa and the Killa

The suspicion of murder was dropped, but Regina Gowl was far from innocent. The charge of blackmail struck as did one of involuntary manslaughter. Regina's court-appointed lawyer made bail on her client's otherwise spotless record and also the fact that Gowl wasn't a flight risk—after all, the former botulism mogul was practically penniless since and hadn't collected on her scheme to bilk the detective's estranged fiancée out of the money. But, as she was mostly penniless and unwilling to put up her house as collateral, Regina Gowl was remanded to prison to await trial.

Life on Mistral Lane continued to operate under a pretence of normality. Five days a week, Isis drove the twins to school while two days and nights more, the Slades' houseguest further frayed nerves and wore out her welcome. Tim Smyth pulled twelve-hour shifts at the hospital and was rarely seen except when he came home or left for work. Willa wrote her new romance novel and dated the handsome pilot next door, mostly unaware of certain of his peculiar habits, which registered as fog whenever she pondered them, like fragments leftover from a dream.

And for three of the neighborhood's residents, the date on the calendar slipped past the first of October and inched closer to the night of the next full moon.

"It's starting to drive me crazy," said Willa.

"So's that scarf you're wearing," said Wandalou, who was seated at the Slades' kitchen table, a fashion magazine opened before her.

Willa turned away from the windowpane and shot over a cool expression.

Wandalou feigned innocence. "What? I'm only trying to help."

"Help? How?'

"*Hello*—fashion influencer influencing."

Willa sighed. "It's gonna be here in eleven days."

"Why are you suddenly wearing scarves?" Isis asked. She stood at the stove checking on the molasses cookies which were almost ready to come out of the oven.

"You, too? Can we focus on the real problems about to crash down on us and not worry about my wardrobe choices?" Willa shook her head while changing the subject. "Lord, do those cookies smell divine!"

They attempted to strategize. No new leads pointed to Race the Face. The best they could come up with right then was Willa's panic room and the ruse of Ladies' Poker Night.

"If I have to spend three more nights in there, I'll kill myself," Wandalou griped. "I swear it! I'll bite my own head off if I have to!"

"Don't worry, I'll probably choke you before it gets to that point," said Willa.

"Chew my own head down to my neck!"

"With this very scarf, actually!"

The timer pinged. Donning big paisley oven mitts, Isis sang, "Who wants cookies?"

With nine nights to go, Willa struggled to maintain focus. She tinkered with the fourth chapter of her new novel, stalled, and instead tried to distract herself with banal house-related matters. She got out her winter wardrobe, vacuumed, and dusted.

While wiping down the hall mirror, the strangest thought crossed her mind: that her reflection wouldn't be in the glass. For a terrible instant, it wasn't. Then Willa blinked, and her worried face stared back.

And so, too, did the image of the scarf around her neck.

She peered at it. Numerous times, she reached up intending to undo the loose knot that held it in place around her throat. In each instance, her focus drifted, and the scarf remained there.

At one point, Willa blinked and the daylight that was streaming through the windows evaporated. Twilight fell around the house.

"It sure gets dark earlier and earlier," she mused aloud. She wondered if she'd been hypnotized. The thought was there one instant, gone the next. Whatever the source of her bewitchment, Willa hadn't thought about the full moon in untold minutes, and for that she was grateful.

The doorbell gonged. Willa woke fully and answered it. Outside, standing framed by the new night, stood handsome Joe. Saying nothing, he stepped past the threshold and into the house, his expression stony, difficult to read. They faced one another. Then Joe smiled, and she noted how white his teeth were, how sharp.

Willa smiled back. Joe removed Willa's scarf. They kissed. After that, he removed the rest of her clothes and she his. He playfully chased her around the house. Willa laughed at his antics. They streaked naked up the stairs to her bedroom. There, they made love in a variety of acrobatic and contortionist positions, all the while laughing and groaning and talking dirty. She'd never had so much fun! Certainly not with Phil Laslo, that creep.

While flopped on their backs across Willa's bed, another dark cloud challenged her joy. Thinking about Phil wasn't nearly as somber a topic as the full moon, but it originated in the same territory.

"What's wrong?" Joe asked.

Willa twirled a finger through his lush chest hair and gazed up at the ceiling. "Oh, the usual. I'm stuck on chapter four of the new book, I can't shake the feeling of being betrayed by my ex, and there's the moon."

"The moon?" he asked.

"The full moon. Joe, I have a secret. A *terrible* secret. One that seriously affects us both." She glanced down from the ceiling and into his eyes, which glowed preternaturally emerald.

"That's one of the many qualities I love about you, Willa."

"You...*love?*"

He leaned over. "I love you."

And then Joe crushed his mouth over hers and she forgot all about the moon, also the scarf and why she wore it. He suggested they make love in every room of Willa's house. They did.

"Next time, let's sleep over at your place," she said, out of breath in the downstairs powder room, the last stop on their marathon tour.

"No, I still don't have any furniture," Joe said.

"Except a bed, right? You at least have that over there."

He brushed his thumb over her cheek. "It's meant for one and isn't very comfortable."

Willa noticed that Joe didn't cast a reflection in the mirror above the pedestal sink and suddenly understood that he had a terrible secret of his own. It probably should have mattered, she knew this somewhere deep in her heart, but she'd never been happier than at that moment and guessed she could live with it.

The grayness of an overcast dawn seeped past the bedroom windows. Willa rolled over and instinctively reached to her left. The other side of the bed was empty. She stirred from the fog inside her head and settled onto her back. Her eyes inched open to see an insane vision escaped from a nightmare standing over her.

"What the hell—?" she rolled away just as the wraith raised the blade.

"Die, *bitch!*" the blonde woman standing at the side of her bed roared.

Willa reached up, seized hold of her attacker's wrist, and deflected the point of the blade into the mattress. In the rush of clarity that followed, she recognized two vital details: the knife was made from wood and the assassin's identity.

"Brittany?" Willa gasped.

Brittany Barrows smacked her with her free hand. Willa gasped again. Then Brittany raised the wooden implement—a stake, Willa realized—and readied to drive it into her. Willa rolled across the bed and made it to her feet. Another observation registered: she was still naked following her nightlong romp with Joe.

"Are you crazy?" she shrieked.

Brittany's shock paused her momentarily from pursuing. "*Me?*"

"Yes, you!"

"I'm not the one sleeping with a *creature of the night!*"

Willa crossed her arms. "No? Then explain Phil Laslo."

"He's a different kind of bloodsucker. He's not a…"

And then Brittany screamed and came at her. Willa was ready, because the prize she'd won in the scavenger hunt on the night of the bachelorette party had been self-defense lessons at Sensei Schulman's dojo. She fired a strike at Brittany's wrist, let loose with a war cry and quickly followed up with a punch to her would-be killer's breadbasket. Brittany dropped the stake and staggered back. Willa recovered the crude weapon and pressed it against the skank's throat. Eyes white and wide, Brittany surrendered.

"Okay, okay, you win," the other woman gurgled out against the pressure of the stake. "*Gawd.*"

Willa seized hold of a hank of Brittany's blonde locks and yanked. "You'd better explain yourself, *Buffy!*"

A measure of Brittany's fire re-ignited. "Me? Why don't *you* explain yourself?"

"*Me?* I didn't break into your bedroom and come at you with a big toothpick!"

"No, but you have been bumping uglies with a *vampire!*"

Willa gasped. "Are you insane?"

"Are you blind?"

"How dare you," Willa said.

Hands still raised, Brittany stood. "You've been under his spell, like I was. If he isn't stopped, you'll be one of the undead too. You don't want that, do you? To become a vicious supernatural predator?"

"You're a little late for that," Willa snorted.

"Huh?"

Her grip on the stake tightened. "Give me one good reason why I shouldn't drive this through the place on you where other people have hearts?"

Brittany flexed her chest. "I'll give you two."

"Plastic surgery won't get you out of this!"

"Fine. If not for Doctor Shapiro's excellent work … one, you know I'm right. All you have to do is look at those bite marks on your neck," Brittany said.

"And the second reason?"

"Two, because…*hey*, what's that thing standing behind you?"

Willa spun around. "*Wha—?*"

No one was there. Brittany seized the opportunity provided by her distraction to bolt from the room.

"*Skank!*" Willa spat and pursued.

She exited the bedroom and raced down the stairs. Brittany sped through the front door, not bothering to close it behind her. Willa made it as far as the bottom step before remembering her state of undress. Squealing, she backed into the house and nudged the door shut with her bare left foot whose nails were painted in her favorite shade of plum-purple.

Quinn and Officer Rolfe Hastings took her statement. "Why do you think Ms. Barrows targeted you?" Quinn asked.

She'd hastily pulled on jeans and a dark turtleneck that masked the bite marks on her neck. "We have, as you know, a history," Willa said.

"Your ex, Phil Laslo," Quinn said. "But doesn't that mean you should be the one driving a stake through *her* chest?"

"The thought has crossed my mind," said Willa. "Look, I'm no licensed therapist, but she's obviously *foobared-in-the-head*. I wouldn't be surprised if Brittany Barrows was the one who shivved poor Jessie-Marie and I was meant to be her next victim."

Quinn considered that idea. "Attempted murder is serious enough."

Officer Rolfe had bagged and tagged the evidence. The wooden stake went blurry before Willa's eyes. A wooden stake? The skank would have made out better with silver bullets. After all, did Brittany think she was a—"*Vampire?*" Willa whispered as all the rest that she hadn't told Quinn slipped out of the fog in her mind.

"What's that?" Quinn asked.

"Nothing, only that she was spouting some insane nonsense about me."

"This whole neighborhood's gone *loco* in the past month," Quinn said. "I'm assigning Officer Hastings to watch your house until we have the suspect in custody."

"No, that won't be necessary," Willa said.

"It's not up for debate." Quinn nodded to the rookie, took the evidence bag, and walked Officer Rolfe to the door. Even before they were gone, a seed of worry germinated in her stomach and quickly grew to put forth poisonous fruit. What if Brittany Barrows *had* killed Jessie-Marie? That R easily could have been a B. And what if the skank had kicked off the most recent leg of her crime spree one house over?

"*Joe*," she said aloud to the empty room.

She started toward the back door only to stop at the downstairs powder room and approach the mirror. She nudged down the turtleneck, and there was the proof.

The man she loved and who loved her *was* a vampire!

The spell threatened to seduce her back into its dreamy embrace. "No," Willa huffed.

The truth was bitter, yes, but it didn't cancel out the desire in her heart. She resumed her march out through to the backyard. There, she peered around the corner of the house to see the Hydrangea Heights PD black and white parked in front at the curb. Willa snuck past the hedges to Joe's kitchen door. She found it unlocked. She entered. The kitchen was just as empty and untouched as the last time she'd visited. But, to her relief, she found the basement door secured from the inside, which meant Joe was down there sleeping safely and secure if not necessarily *alive* according to the medical definition.

"Brittany Barrows?" Wandalou asked. "Sunny umbrella Brittany Barrows?"

"Yes, sunny umbrella Brittany, the one and the same," Willa said. "And the way she came at me…thank goodness for Sensei Schulman!"

Isis held up the coffee carafe in one hand, a bottle of red in the other.

"That," both Willa and Wandalou said pointing at the cabernet.

Isis poured. The three retired to Willa's parlor with its plum-colored drapes and overstuffed furniture. Willa peeked through the curtains.

"Is *he* still out there?" Wandalou asked.

"If by 'he' you mean Officer Hastings, yes."

Wandalou tsked. "Stupid Brittany Barrows!"

"More to the point, do you think she's the one who killed Jessie-Marie?" asked Isis.

"I did. At least at first," answered Willa.

Wandalou eyed her over the top of her wine glass. "And now?"

Willa shrugged. "I'm not so sure."

Suddenly, Isis was directly in front of her and projecting the same firm look Willa had seen her use when disciplining the twins. "And why not?"

Willa attempted to shrink from Isis's gaze, but then Isis added her tough-mom scolding tone and Willa froze.

"Come on—fess up!"

"All right, sheesh!" Willa said. "Because of...*Joe*." She whispered the last word.

"It sounds like you said 'Joe,'" Isis said.

Wandalou lowered her glass. "I heard 'toe.'"

"What does toe—I mean *Joe*—have to do with Brittany Barrows trying to drive a stake through your chest?"

"Because toe—I mean *Joe*—is really a..."

"He's a what?" Isis demanded.

Willa hesitated. Fear of their reaction to her answer held her speechless.

"I know, he's a *Socialist*," said Wandalou.

"No."

"He's a mime?"

Willa shook her head. "Does my boyfriend look like the type who mimes walking against a nonexistent breeze?"

"Don't tell me he's vegan!"

Willa exhaled and said, "No, Joe's a vampire. There, I said it! God, sometimes the two of you can be so *judgy*!"

A stunned silence settled over the room. Arms folded, Willa waited for either of the others to comment. Wandalou answered first—with a cackle.

"Vampire?" she said. "Damn, girl, you should use that one in your next novel. *Hot airline pilot by day, bloodsucker by night...*"

"No, you got it backwards. He flies at night and only drinks blood occasionally—when he isn't working, and never on the job. Or *rarely* on the job, I think."

Wandalou cackled again and finished the contents of her glass in one gulp. While reaching for the bottle to pour out more, she glanced up to see Isis had not softened from her stance. "Seriously?"

"I believe you," Isis said.

"What?" said Wandalou.

Willa sighed, not in relief but because the last sip of air bottled in her lungs began to boil. "You do?"

"Unfortunately, we know that werewolves are real, and if our experience with the Ouija board is to be trusted, ghosts are, too. So why not vampires?"

"He's not a bad vampire," Willa said. "Not like you see on TV or the movies. I mean, Joe didn't ask for this any more than we did."

"He told you this?" Isis posed, with that question sounding more like drilling for answers than conversation.

Willa shrugged. "I think he did. Happened over in Europe. The point is, he's not any more dangerous to the neighborhood than we are."

"That one over there ripped out my stomach and, I'm pretty sure, part of my small intestine!" Isis said, aiming her right pointer finger at Wandalou. "Don't tell me we're not dangerous. If it wasn't for the panic room, there's no telling the level of carnage we could unleash on those we love!"

"That would explain the scarves and also that turtleneck sweater," Wandalou said. "By the way, the Beatniks called and they want it back."

Isis glared at Wandalou.

"*Hello*. Style influencer…I'm trying to influence. And don't think I didn't hear that 'small intestine' dig."

"Come on, Icy," Willa pleaded. "You've met Joe. You know what a good man he is."

"I know nothing of the sort," Isis said. "And if what you say is true, he isn't a *man* any more, is he?" Turning, Isis stormed out of the room and toward the door.

"Wait," Willa said, catching up. "Does that make me no longer a woman—or the friend you knew before the night of the bachelorette party and what Race the Face did to us?" Isis didn't turn around or comment. "Does that mean you're no longer Isis Slade, wife, mother, friend, and all-around suburban goddess?"

Isis slipped out the door and away from the conversation. Though Willa couldn't see her friend's face, she suspected that Isis was crying.

"What twisted her panties into such a bunch?" Wandalou asked.

"Maybe it's the fact that we're little more than a week away from the October full moon."

Chapter 14
The Zeitgeist

Willa picked up her phone and dialed. After three rings, it went to voicemail. *"Hi, this is Isis Slade. I can't take your call right now, but if you'll please leave a detailed message, I'll get back to you as soon as I can. Bye."*

After the beep, Willa said, "Hey, it's me—*again*. I know you're upset with me, but we really need to talk. I can't risk saying anything here more detailed than that."

She tipped a look at the nearest window. Outside, the neighborhood darkened, the dusk helped along by the brisk October grayness. The leaves in the maples showed plenty of color. A chill teased the nape of her neck. She fought it, failed. After the shiver tumbled down her spine, she glanced out the front-facing window to see the police cruiser still parked there, though a different officer had taken over guard duties.

Willa supposed Isis had good reason to be hacked off. What she and Wandalou had witnessed that afternoon was their friend's Mother Tiger instinct kicking in. A vampire in the neighborhood? That didn't exactly jibe with girls' soccer games and family barbecues—any more than a trio of werewolves.

She turned; Joe stood in the foyer. Willa screamed and quickly covered her mouth. Joe raised a finger to his lips, urging silence.

"There's a police car in front of your house," he said. "I was worried."

"I was worried, too—for you."

She moved toward him. Joe caught her in his arms. She held tightly, aware of the cold in his touch and the heat for him that ignited inside her. They kissed, and when they parted, Willa gazed deeply into his eyes.

"So…the cops?" Joe asked.

She told him everything, including that she'd confessed all to her two dearest besties. "You can trust them," Willa finished.

Joe scowled. "I don't know that."

"Do you trust *me*?" He nodded. "Good, because there's more. What I'm about to tell you might sound crazy…"

He brushed a stray lock of her brown hair back behind her ear. "You mean about you and your two gal-pals being werewolves?"

She broke their embrace, tossed up her hands, and performed a 360-degree turn. "Talk about *anticlimactic*!"

"Oh, don't you worry, Willa," Joe said. "I've got plenty of *those* coming with your name on them."

Then Joe chased her up the stairs and into the bedroom, where he proved that particular claim.

The doorbell rang. Willa dressed quickly and answered it. Phyllis, the police officer who'd taken her previous statement regarding Regina Gowl, stood outside the door. "Ma'am," Phyllis said politely, "so you know, I'll be leaving."

"Leaving?"

"Yes, they have the suspect in custody."

"The skank?"

Phyllis tucked her thumbs into her gun belt and rocked in place. "I wouldn't know anything about that."

"You'd be in the minority then. Where'd they find her?"

"The real estate agent was hiding out at a gentleman's house. Real slick fellow named—"

"*Phil Laslo*," Willa said, the words tasting like bile.

"Why, yes."

"*Skank.*"

Phyllis nodded. "If you say so. G'night."

Willa thanked her and closed the door. On the way to the staircase, an odd and unexpected lightness came over her. Brittany had done her a favor by wrecking her marriage to a liar and cheater. She was free of him, successful in her career, mostly happy in her private life. And as for her new leading man?

Joe stood at the top of the staircase, naked, aroused for more fun, and clearly smitten with her, only her.

So what if he's a vampire? she thought and skipped up the stairs and into his arms.

A tiny wedge of moon peered down through the clouds and seemed to study her through the part in the drapes. Willa's anxiety deepened. She sat up.

"What's wrong?" Joe asked. "Brittany's in police custody."

"It isn't just that." She pointed toward the window. "In a week, the moon'll be full again."

Joe moved up to his elbows. "You said this dude…"

"Race the Face."

"This *Face* just up and vanished?"

Willa nodded. "He's our only hope of finding a way to cure the curse."

"It doesn't sound like it. Doesn't sound like he was even aware he had the curse when he snacked on you."

She faced him in the darkness. "Did you try to undo your…dilemma?"

"I killed the monster who passed it on to me. It didn't matter."

"So you've given up trying?"

He caressed her bare shoulder. "Yeah. Until I met you."

She crushed her mouth over his, and then they made love again.

Early the following morning, they dressed, slipped out of the house, and drove to the downtown area in Joe's truck. The only place open at that dark hour was their destination: My Grains. The bakery was well lit and its particular industry underway. The air around the building smelled sweet and yeasty. Beyond the windows, Willa saw colorful trays filled with fresh pastries. Her stomach complained of its emptiness as, holding hands, she and Joe approached the front entrance.

"Now, I should warn you about the woman who owns the place," Willa said. "She's sort of prickly, like a cactus. I'm talking one of those big ones covered in long, sharp quills. Really long and sharp. Not like a cute, fuzzy houseplant cactus."

"I'm not worried," he said with confidence.

"Like I said, a cactus. Or a witch."

"Witch?" Joe repeated.

Willa opened the door. They'd only gotten a step into the bakery when Frau Krumpt appeared, blocking the way. Willa yelped. She couldn't be certain, but she thought Joe let out a little gasp, too.

"I don't serve *his* kind in my bakery," Frau Krumpt growled.

Willa composed herself. "His kind? You mean pilots?"

Frau Krumpt eyed Joe warily. "*Blutsauger.*"

Joe straightened and stared back.

"You don't scare me—and you have no power to bend me to your *vill*. I'm from the old country, you know!"

"We only wanted crullers and coffee," said Willa.

"There *vill* be no crullers and no coffee. *Geh veg!*" Frau Krumpt bellowed.

Suddenly, Joe was outside the open door.

"I ordered him to go away," Frau Krumpt said. And then she sniffed the air. "And you can join him, *Volf!*"

"Did you just call me a—"

Frau Krumpt lunged toward her. The ploy worked. Willa shrieked and ran from the bakery. Frau Krumpt folded her arms, a spare, triumphant grin spreading on her mouth. The door closed.

They drove back to Willa's house with less than an hour remaining until sunrise. "Do you believe that mean *potato*?" Willa griped.

"Hell of a date," Joe said. He picked up her hand and kissed her palm. "I was hungry for something else anyway," he said.

"About that…"

Joe pulled into his driveway and walked Willa to her front door. There, Quinn Montoya stood, looking exhausted in a rumpled suit which Willa noted were the same clothes he'd worn during his official visit the day before.

"Quinn, what are you doing here?" she asked.

Quinn cast a wary look at Joe. "Just some follow-up questions."

Willa got out her keys. "Come on in."

"Actually, Willa, it's your friend here I was hoping to speak to."

"What about?" asked Joe.

Quinn exhaled a humorless laugh. "Damndest thing. It's like the whole neighborhood's gone crazy. Kind of making me crazy with it."

Silence. Willa noted that even the crickets had clammed up.

"Brittany Barrows, your real estate agent," Quinn said.

"What about her?" said Joe.

"She claims you've got a coffin in your basement, and that you're a vampire. Silly, right?"

Joe flashed an amused smile. "You said it."

"I figure, if you don't mind, you could give me a little tour of the place. Just to put the claim to rest and prove what a loon she is. I mean…*a coffin*, right?"

"Totally nuts," Joe agreed.

"Or, even better, we could just stand out here for…what? Another fifteen minutes until the sun rises to prove you aren't a vampire."

Joe nodded. "We could. Or…"

Joe seized hold of Quinn and sank his fangs into his neck.

Willa froze.

Joe drank.

Ten minutes earlier, Mrs. Divia Winterton's Pekinese dog Chauncey had yipped her awake to be walked. Divia clipped the leash to Chauncey's jeweled collar and exited the house. Together, they wandered down the sidewalk, hastening past that dreadful Gowl woman's place—Mrs. Winterton was convinced Regina Gowl left traps to keep dogs off her lawn. And, of course, there was her recent arrest to consider.

While Chauncey watered the Slades' grass, Mrs. Winterton chanced to glance up at the writer's house. There, she spied a most peculiar sight—the writer standing frozen, a look of astonishment upon her face, while two rather attractive men canoodled. One had his mouth on the other's neck!

"*Kinky*," Mrs. Winterton mumbled and hastened Chauncey back to their home. "Honestly, more goes on here on Mistral Lane than in *The Paddington Murders*!"

"**W**hat did you do?" Willa demanded.

Joe sent Quinn away. In a daze, Quinn crossed the street and vanished into his and Wandalou's house. "Just a little basic hypnosis," Joe said. "He won't remember anything except what I tell him to."

"That's the problem, Joe—neighbors don't go around biting each other on the neck! Not good neighbors, at least."

"Willa—" He reached for her. She pulled away.

"You'd better get home," she said and tipped her chin up at the sky.

Joe followed her gaze. The black sky was graying—and quickly. He grumbled something that sounded like a swear and, between blinks, when Willa looked his way, Joe was gone.

At noon, the three friends gathered in Willa's front parlor. It was obvious that Wandalou had strong-armed Isis into attending—mostly because when Willa had answered the door, Wandalou had Isis's right arm pinned behind her back.

"*Ouch*," Isis complained.

Wandalou marched her prisoner into the front parlor. "Oh, stop being such a baby—or I'll really give you something to bitch about."

"Disemboweling, perhaps?" Isis spat.

"You gonna bring that up again?"

Wandalou released her. Isis assumed a defensive stance. Across from her, so did Willa. Wandalou stood between them.

"Enough. Far be it from me to be the voice of reason, but we've got a serious problem, and if it means me having to slap the piss out of the both of you—" Wandalou said. She raised her hand and took aim at Willa's face.

Willa shrank back. "Okay, all right!"

Wandalou turned to Isis. "Am I gonna have any more trouble or lip from you?"

"No," Isis surrendered, though she was still in a guarded pose.

"Are you sure about that?" Wandalou raised her hand again, now with Isis as the target.

Isis thawed. "Fine, I submit!"

"Good, because I just did my nails. Now make nice," Wandalou ordered.

Reluctantly at first, Isis moved a step closer to Willa. A threatening move by Wandalou, and Isis hastened forward and into Willa's hug.

"I'm so sorry," Isis sobbed.

"No, *I'm* sorry. You were right to be upset with me for not understanding your side of things."

Wandalou crossed her arms. "We done here, ladies? Anything else to say?"

"Yes," Willa said.

And then, using one of those moves that Sensei Schulman had taught her, she grabbed Wandalou's arm and pinned it behind her back.

"*Owww*," Wandalou griped.

"Make nice with Quinn and move out of their house," Willa said. "You're driving them all insane. And for the love of all that's holy, please invest in a pair of headphones!"

"**S**o," Wandalou said.

"So," said Isis.

"Yeah," Willa sighed.

They sat with tall cups of coffee, the tick of the mantel clock the only sound other than the October wind, which stirred through the changing leaves outside the house.

"About things…" said Isis.

"You mean those things we're no closer to fixing? *Those* things?" huffed Wandalou.

Willa leaned forward and clutched her coffee cup in both hands. "I'm starting to think poor Jessie-Marie is the lucky one. She's free from worrying about the full moon."

"Jessie-Marie," Wandalou whispered sadly. "She was trying to help us."

"Maybe she still can," said Isis.

In the Slades' living room they set up the Ouija board but after several tries to contact the dead gave up.

"It's no use. Even if she was here before, she's gone now," said Willa.

Isis contemplated that one obvious fact. "When you heard her, we were at the dog park!"

"Where they found her body," Willa said in a voice barely louder than a whisper.

Isis stood and packed up the game. "Come on." Then, to Wandalou, she said, "First, you have to change."

"What's wrong with what I'm wearing?"

"It's not very appropriate for the dog park."

Wandalou stood. "Okay, *Mom-jeans*," she fired over her shoulder. Then, turning, she added, "Influencer, remember? I'm just influencing!"

"I'll influence something," Isis grumbled from the corner of her mouth.

Fifteen minutes later, they exited the Slade house and where hopping into Isis's minivan when Quinn sauntered over. He nodded to Isis and Willa but motioned Wandalou aside.

"Can we talk?" he asked.

"What happened to your neck?" she asked.

Quinn covered the bandage strip with his hand. "Just cut myself shaving."

"Now isn't the best time, Quinn—we're sort of busy."

"When then?" Quinn pressed.

The sound of car doors closing shocked her out of her growing vulnerability. "I have to boogie—later, gator," she said, projecting calm even as her insides shattered.

They drove to the dog park. A few souls and their pooches leisurely strolled the grounds. A warm Indian Summer breeze clanked chains made of falling leaves and stirred the fragrance of autumn.

Isis strolled past the gazebo with the Ouija board game box tucked under one arm.

"Did you see the latest designs from Milan?" asked Wandalou in a casual voice meant for others to hear.

"Oh, yes, all that crepe and taffeta…simply *deeee-vine*," Willa said.

Wandalou's smile sharpened. "Yes, rother…" Then, in a lower voice, she added, *"Crepe and taffeta— seriously?"*

They continued down the path until they reached the end. The pile of dirt was almost unrecognizable beneath a thin layer of fallen leaves. Glancing around, Isis sat and opened the game box. "Come on," she said.

The others joined her and linked pinkies. Isis nodded to Willa. Willa cleared her throat. "Jessie-Marie, it's us. Are you listening, girl?"

The wind answered with a disembodied moan.

"Sister, we could really use your help. So if you're around…"

The planchette whipped around in a frenzy, spinning so fast beneath their fingertips that it blurred.

"That must mean something, right?" Wandalou said, her eyes wide.

The planchette stopped abruptly and pointed past them, into the woods.

"Not as much as *that*," Isis said.

"Jessie-Marie, what does it mean?" Willa asked.

The planchette jumped off the Ouija board onto the ground beside Willa, still aimed in the same direction.

"I think…" Isis said.

"Yeah," said Willa.

They stood. Then, together, they walked in the direction instructed. For some long while, they continued forward. They crossed old farmer's walls, the boulders covered in skeins of gray-green lichen, rounded past trees and plodded through meadows. At last, they emerged from the woods to find themselves staring up at that big, old haunted house found in every town, this one belonging to Hydrangea Heights.

"Um," said Willa.

"Um," echoed Isis.

And then a howl rose sharply from inside the ancient house wreathed in unmoved lawn.

"*Oh hell no!*" said Wandalou.

Chapter 15

The Lyin' the Witch & the Wardrobe

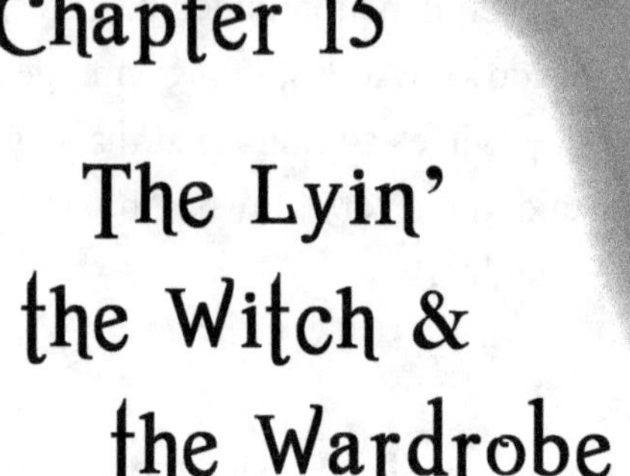

They spotted the car in the drive, a practical German model whose license plate read: *Kuchen.*

"I recognize that car," said Wandalou. "It's Frau Krumpt's!"

"That wasn't her voice we heard baying in there," said Willa. "It was a man's."

"Well, she is rather *mannish,*"

Wandalou caught the scowls of the other two as they hid in the overgrown grass. "I say we call in the cavalry. Let Hydrangea Heights's finest take it from here!"

"And tell them what, exactly? That a Ouija board pointed us in the direction of a potential murderer?" Isis asked.

Wandalou emoted, "Yeah."

Five long minutes later, they'd improvised the barest of plans to check things out and judge what would come next.

"Why me?" Wandalou complained.

"Because you are the only one to have a reason to be at that old witch's front door!" said Isis.

"Be silent!" Frau Krumpt hissed when a knock sounded at the front entrance. "If not, I'll return with the wooden spoon, and you know the *Schmerzen* that used to unleash upon your *Arsch!*" Whirling, she clomped up the wooden stairs and past the kitchen, taking the long hallway through the drab old house to its front door. She opened the door, loving its authentic creak. The October wind whistled into the house around a lone figure standing just outside.

"Hello, Frau Krumpt," said the miserable Trueheart woman. Blades of dead grass protruded from her visitor's long black locks. "Remember me?"

"Unfortunately, *ja.*"

Wandalou waved away the jab. "Oh, I bet you say that to all of your customers!"

"*Vhat* do you *vant?*"

"Me? Funny thing," Wandalou laughed. Not lost on her was the fact that Frau Krumpt's stony expression grew even tenser. "I'm here about a cake. You know, the *vedding* cake."

"*Vhat Vedding* cake?"

"Mine."

"I *vasn't avare* there *vas* a *vedding*."

"Oh, there is—a big, beautiful, last-minute *vedding*. And since you're the best pastry chef for *vedding* cakes—"

"Enough. Go *away*. This is my day off." Frau Krumpt attempted to close the door, but Wandalou's foot was in the way.

Wincing but maintaining her smile, Wandalou added, "I'll make it worth your while."

"How?"

"First," she said, "could you tell me again how you prepare the cake? We'll have guests who are gluten-intolerant and some with lactose issues." Then Wandalou began to laugh, and she knew straight away that Frau Krumpt had seen through her lies.

They slipped in through the kitchen door. Isis cast a quick look around and located a door with an ancient filigree knob. She pointed toward it. "According to my heightened powers of hearing, that cry came from the cellar," she whispered.

Willa nodded.

Halfway there, Isis honed in on the knife block and drew a blade for protection. From the other end of the house, Wandalou was in the middle of an intense fit of nervous laughter.

"Hurry!" Willa urged.

Isis snuck to the door and opened it. Wandalou's cackle masked the creaking of the old wood. The mildewed smell of basements wafted up from the darkness. Isis flipped the light switch and bulbs brightened, illuminating the cement floor at the base of the stairs.

"Come on," Willa said, leading the way.

Frau Krumpt's cellar wasn't filled with glass jars of preserved vegetables and jams; it more closely resembled a mad scientist's lair than anything else. Long tables beneath fluorescent light strips held test tubes, beakers, a microscope, culture dishes with agar agar, and one of those antennas between which electricity crackled. At the far end of the oblong space past windows that had been boarded over, another door was set into the rock wall. This was new, metal, and double-bolted from the outside.

Isis aimed the point of the carving knife at the door. Willa nodded. They approached.

Isis knocked. "Hello, is someone in there?"

A muffled man's voice answered. "Yes, oh, *thank God!* She's kept me prisoner in here for weeks. Let me out, please, let me out!"

Isis handed Willa the blade and dragged open the first deadbolt. She'd only gripped the bottom one when a clatter of heavy footfalls pounded down the cellar stairs at their back.

"Don't you dare open that door!" Frau Krumpt bellowed in a voice that rang in their ears.

Wandalou hastened down the stairs behind the witch. "Sorry, I tried to buy you more time, but she's got ears like a cat!"

"How dare you intrude upon my home?" Frau Krumpt roared.

"Nice place," Willa huffed. "And just exactly what does *that* thing do?"

She pointed the blade of the knife at the antenna and its endless waves of static electricity.

"That I'm not sure—I just liked the aesthetic," Frau Krumpt said.

"Who do you have locked up behind this door?" Isis demanded.

"No one," Frau Krumpt answered in an unexpectedly sheepish tone.

"Now who's lying, Frau Krumpt?"

A fist hammered the other side of the door. "Help! Help! Let me out!"

Frau Krumpt started forward. Isis retrieved the knife from Willa and raised the blade. The frau halted and cast a hateful look at the two women standing near the locked door and then another toward the one hovering behind her.

"You three…three *she-Verewolves!*"

Wandalou skirted around the wall away from Frau Krumpt and joined Isis and Willa near the door. "*Vhat? Vhy vould* you say that?" Then she corrected herself. "I mean, why?"

"Oh please, I can spot one from a distance!" Frau Krumpt said lightly.

"There are that many of us?" asked Willa.

"There *vas* at least one other in Hydrangea Heights."

"You killed Jessie-Marie, didn't you?" Willa spat. "The R! *Renate* Krumpt!"

Frau Krumpt's stony hauteur resurfaced. "You think me a murderer?"

"And a kidnapper," Isis said. She reached down and released the lower deadbolt. The door opened, revealing a stylish man's cave in the background complete with leather club chairs, flat-screen TV, and weight bench.

And, standing at the door, was Race the Face.

"Oh—" gasped Isis.

"—my—" said Willa.

"*Guguh*," Wandalou blathered.

His face was hairier, his silver eyes wilder, and a musky, male smell drifted off his musculature, presently clad in a gray tank top and black track pants. "*Ladies*," he growled, all cool, and stepped out.

"*Nein*," Frau Krumpt screamed. "No, *Hansel*."

"Hansel?" Willa repeated.

"It's 'Race' now," the prisoner spat. Race the Face grabbed the blade from Isis's hand, seized hold of her, and held the knife in front of her, pointing its blade at her chest. "I'm leaving this dungeon!"

"No, you're not," Frau Krumpt countered. "Soon, the moon *vill* be full. You cannot go."

Isis, hands raised in surrender, said, "By all means, please let him!"

"So he can continue his reign of destruction and bloodshed? I think not," said Frau Krumpt

"Mother, shut up!" Race spat.

"Mother?" Wandalou gasped.

Frau Krumpt shrugged. "Guilty."

"I knew she reminded me of someone. And speaking of guilty," said Isis pointing.

Race brandished the blade holding fast to his hostage. "I didn't mean to kill her, I swear. Your other friend…I wasn't myself…wasn't in my right mind. One of *her* potions did something to me!" Then his hand shook. "It was this very knife, too."

"I was only trying to cure you of the affliction before you did any more damage, *Sohn*," said Frau Krumpt. "Lower the knife and return to your room."

"You mean my *cage?* Never!" Race the Face spat. He motioned the others out of his way and forced Isis toward the stairs.

"Um," Isis said.

"You've broken my heart," Frau Krumpt said.

"You never had one!" Race fired back. "You're an evil old witch!"

"I've given my life to protect you," Frau Krumpt gasped. "But no more."

As Race moved past the nearest of the laboratory tables, Frau Krumpt reached for the base of the antenna. Isis ducked. Race raised the knife and came at her. Frau Krumpt zapped him. Race lit up, engulfed in the discharge. Sparks exploded around him. Jessie-Marie's killer shook and smoked. The stench of ozone and burnt hair filled the cellar. Frau Krumpt dropped the device. Race slumped to the floor.

He didn't stir.

Wandalou unstuck and reached for Isis, drawing her into a protective embrace. In the stunned silence that followed, Frau Krumpt only stared down at her son's body. "Oh, my Hansel," she said. And then she nudged the dropped and sputtering antenna with the toe of her sensible shoe. "So that's *vat* it does."

Willa joined Isis and Wandalou. "What happened on that night in September?"

"He broke free while I tried to treat his affliction, which he picked up on one of his late nights in Cincinnati. I attempted a mix of herbal remedies like Wolf's Bane and other plants…and some rather not-so-natural ingredients." She waved a pudgy finger at the chemistry lab. "He was in a rage. I pursued him to the dog park where, sadly, he met up with your friend."

"You mean his victim," Wandalou barked.

"I had to stun him and lug him back here. I'm getting too old for this—those fifty-pound bags of flour are difficult enough at *mein* bakery!"

"You buried the body?" asked Willa.

Frau Krumpt nodded. "I couldn't very well leave her there, could I?"

Isis reached for her phone. "You have to tell the police everything that you know!"

"Everything?" Frau Krumpt asked.

"Okay, leave out one particular detail," said Wandalou. "If you do, we will make sure to bring you treats in jail."

Frau Krumpt was led away in handcuffs. At the Hydrangea Heights Police Department stationhouse she confessed to helping her son, Hansel Krumpt, cover up his crime of murder committed under the influence of illegal substances. She left out the part about his madness fueled by recognizing another werewolf. In fact, she left out the entire werewolf part.

Isis, Wandalou, and Willa watched the police from the wood line before they quietly slipped back through the trees.

Quinn broke the news to Doctor Tim.

The next morning, long lines formed early outside My Grains, but nobody showed to unlock the door and the air about the center of town renounced its sweetness.

The three friends gathered at the grave of the fourth. Isis laid a bouquet of white roses beneath the new headstone. Wandalou scattered a scoop of decaf coffee—Jessie-Marie's favorite—across the grave. Willa unfolded the slip of paper and, clearing her throat, read:

"What is friendship but permission to love? Jessie-Marie Smyth, you gave your friendship—and love—to the three of us. And we hope you know how much you were loved as a result."

The wind gusted. "*I know*," it seemed to whisper.

Willa glanced around. "Did you hear that?"

"I did," said Wandalou.

"Me, too," said Isis.

They joined hands and reveled in the moment. Too soon, the sun set and the waxing Halloween moon drifted above the trees, nearly full and seeming to eye them with malevolence.

The date on the calendar arrived: *Ladies' Poker Night.*

Methodically and walking with invisible blinders on, Willa set up the folding table and chairs which showed their knocks from the last gathering, and placed the cards on the center. She pulled plastic cups from the cabinet and selected a bottle of merlot, aware of the ticking of the mantel clock which struck her as overly loud on this warm October day.

Across the street, Isis made a roast for the family and baked little fruit tarts, a practiced smile on her face.

"But I don't like roast beef," Marci moaned. " I want pizza rolls!"

"And I want sanity, so be a good girl and run along now, thank you."

Marci stomped her feet and waited, which Isis mostly ignored.

Darci tipped a look at Wandalou, who fiddled with her phone before snapping another selfie. "I like roast beef," the girl said.

Wandalou looked over. "Yeah, so I noticed. You kind of like everything, which could end up being a problem."

"*Wandalou*," Isis snapped.

"What? Influencer *influencing*," Wandalou said. She leaned over and pinched Darci's cheek. "Listen to your Aunty Wandalou…*celery sticks* if you want to wear designer threads, okay?"

Darci broke into a fit of laughter. "You're so funny, Aunty!"

Wandalou patted the girl's shoulder. "Good. Now *am-scray*."

Darci skipped over to Marci, who was still in the throes of her tantrum. "Come on, let's *am-scray*."

Marci stormed off. As the twin's departed, Bob's cherry red 'stang drew into the driveway. Isis pulled the roast out of the oven and covered it with foil. Half of the fruit tarts, cooling on a wire rack, went into a plastic container.

Bob entered, his tie unknotted, his shades still in place. "Superman's home," he declared, a wide smile on full display.

Isis greeted him with a kiss. "Dinner's on the counter. I've made dessert."

Bob's smile sagged. "Wait…you're not—?"

"Poker Night," Isis said. She picked up the plastic container and motioned for Wandalou to follow.

"But—?" Bob continued. "It's a school night."

"So help them with their schoolwork and make sure you drop them off at school on time in the morning."

"But—? The baseball playoffs are on tonight!"

"Enjoy the game," Isis sang. She tugged on Wandalou's arm with her free hand and maintained her smile until they reached the end of the driveway. There, her façade crumbled. Isis drank down a dry swallow of despair. Colored leaves crunched beneath their feet. Around them, the neighborhood had taken on the guise of the season. Cornstalks were tied to lampposts. Jack-o'-lanterns guarded front doors. Paper black cats and giant spiders in webs clung to windows. Mistral Lane was one gigantic haunted house.

"I can't do this," said Wandalou.

"You have to," Isis said calmly.

Wandalou dug in her soles and stopped on Willa's front lawn. "I can't be trapped inside that airless closet—that *wardrobe*—for another night let alone three. I can't go in there for an hour!"

"Wanda…"

Wandalou stood rooted to the spot. The sun sank lower. The sky had already surrendered most of the day's light at its edges, and Isis sensed her heart quickening its pulse.

Calmly, Isis backtracked, her smile partially restored but now sharp at the corners. "Dear, dear friend of mine. If you don't move your ass, I swear I'll drag you in there by your dyed locks."

Wandalou gasped. "*Dyed?* You wouldn't!"

"Try me," Isis said. "I have my family to consider."

Wandalou blinked first. "Fine, but it looked to me like you were ready to eat that one with the mouth yourself!"

They resumed their march to the plum-purple front door. Willa greeted them and welcomed them into the house. Then, together, the three friends marched without speaking up the stairs and behind the panic room's barricade.

"I made fruit tarts," Isis chirped. She scooped one each onto a paper plate and set it before the others.

"I wonder if they'll put Frau Krumpt in the prison kitchen," Willa said.

Wandalou snorted. "I suppose it's a good thing I won't be needing her services for a *vedding* cake."

The somber atmosphere grew heavier.

"Just fix things with Quinn," Isis said.

"I want to—but how can I with no hope of curing this curse and us being no closer to going back to something even remotely normal?" She cast a sour look at Willa. "And what about you?"

"What about me?"

"I thought you were so madly in love with your wingman over there." Wandalou waved her hand in the imagined direction of Joe's house.

"That's different," Willa said.

"How?"

"He's flapping bat wings."

"Even so, he's still a man—frustrating, aggravating, infuriating! Human or vampire, you slap a pair of peaches on them, and they're all ready to drive you to the asylum. *Oh*, that Quinn—he makes me so mad!"

"Don't get emotional, dear," Isis cautioned.

"I'm not getting…" Wandalou started. And then she burst into tears. Her sobs bounced off the tight confines of the panic room's walls.

Willa reached for her. "Don't cry!"

"I can't help it. I miss Quinn," said Wandalou between sips for breath.

They hugged. Willa joined in the waterworks.

"I miss Joe," she said.

Isis tsked and attempted to retain her composure. But a few seconds was all she managed. Her armor cracked, and tears fell. The three friends embraced.

"What are you getting all misty for?" Wandalou asked Isis.

"I miss my old soap opera!" Isis wailed.

The histrionics ramped up and then crested. Isis passed around paper napkins and they dabbed their eyes.

"After this is over, I'm marching right into that house and taking back my relationship with Quinn," Wandalou said. "That big dummy!"

"Oh, thank heavens," said Isis.

"What?"

"Nothing."

"I need him," Wandalou said while wiping at the inside corners of her eyes. "And he sure as hell needs me. You should see the chunk he took out of his neck shaving the other day!"

Willa coughed, suddenly and quite loudly.

"You okay?" Wandalou asked.

Willa forced a smile. "Yeah, just fine." She reached for her wine glass and downed its contents in a single gulp.

"So now?" Wandalou asked.

"Now, we wait," said Isis.

Not long after, Willa suffered the scratch of a tickle in her throat. "Oh God, it's starting. I can feel it."

"Me, too," said Wandalou.

"Make it three," Isis added. "Get ready, girls. And this time, try your best to not disembowel me. I know that it's almost Halloween, but Bob and I have that wine tasting night on the twenty-ninth, and next month is November, which means Thanksgiving, and I'd really like to—"

"I got it, okay," Wandalou said around a toothy smile. "And if I'm gonna rip through anything tonight, it's that damn door!"

She aimed a manicured pointer finger and its nail, painted like the others in a whimsical shade of rosy-posy pink, at the door. And as she did, a deep, single knock sounded from the other side.

The three prisoners of the new night yelped.

"Who the hell is that?" Wandalou asked in a voice barely there.

The unknown intruder knocked again.

Chapter 16

Season Finale

Willa froze. Someone was in the house uninvited, and that notion both terrified her and infuriated the beast working up from her guts and stretching its reawakened limbs.

"Who—?" she sputtered. Then in a deeper voice hot with anger, she barked, "*Who's there?*"

"Let me answer it," said Wandalou. She got up from her seat with such gusto that the folding chair toppled over backwards. Wandalou rushed at the door and tugged at the deadbolt.

"Wandalou, no," Isis called.

Both she and Willa stood up, but it was too late. The door opened, and Joe stepped in.

Willa growled. "What are you doing here?"

Joe's eyes glinted emerald-green in the glow cast from the overhead light. "I had to see you, Willa. You have to believe me when I say I love you—let me prove it!"

Willa cleared her throat. The wolf's howl powered up from her stomach. She let it out before responding. "Not really a good time," she calmly said.

"That's why I'm here. I think I can help."

"Help? How?"

Joe reached for Willa. His green eyes grew even brighter. "Do you hate the wolf inside you?"

"Well, *duh*," she said.

"Then put it back asleep. Look into my eyes, Willa. Believe that you can keep it quiet, *dormant*. Just like I made Quinn forget what happened that morning."

"What?" asked Wandalou.

Willa fell into the spell of Joe's gaze. Those magnificent twin emerald gemstones seduced her. "*Joe*," she sighed.

"That's right, Willa. I love you and want you to be as happy as you've made me."

Willa blinked. The itch in her throat flared on for another second before shorting out. She choked it down. "*Woof*," she said and then collapsed into Joe's arms. Joe caught her. Willa came out of it and straightened. "It's gone!" she exclaimed.

Joe smiled. "No, it isn't."

"What do you mean?"

"It's just repressed. In remission. There's no cure for what you three have except, you know…" He mimed croaking.

Willa stared at him, her face tense before breaking out with happiness. "I don't care—it's gone for now and that's all I could hope for!" She threw her arms around him. Joe scooped Willa up and kissed her.

Isis stormed over and separated them. "I'm sorry to break up this happy reunion, but…"

"Right," Willa said. "Joe, can you help out my two friends?"

"For you, babe, anything."

Isis stepped forward. "Hurry, if you don't mind. I'm starting to salivate. And crave human flesh."

"Hey, wait a minute," Wandalou interjected. "We're three tough, smart, and beautiful women, remember? We don't need a man swooping in to rescue us!"

Isis considered the gravitas in that statement. "She has a point."

Willa said, "Hate to throw your own words back in your face, Icy, but remember—my hot boyfriend isn't a man."

"Oh, yeah," said Isis. "Proceed!"

Joe took Isis by the shoulders and repeated the hypnosis. Isis faced Joe's unblinking gaze. Right as the first cracking of bones being reshaped shuddered through the room, Isis woke.

"It's gone," she said.

"No, it isn't," Joe said.

"It's gone for now," said Isis. "Thanks, Joe." Isis hugged him.

"And now, Wandalou," Willa said.

But when they looked behind them, the panic room door stood open and Wandalou Trueheart was gone!

Bones shattered and reformed. With her back arched, Wandalou spilled across Willa's front lawn. The she-wolf moaned, growled, and then recovered. Above the treetops festooned in colored leaves, the moon floated, obscene in its fullness. Ancient fire burned through Wandalou's insides and circulated in place of blood.

Thoughts confused, all save one.

"*Quinn,*" she mouthed around sharpened teeth.

Wandalou's vision blurred. She blinked away the dots and focused on the other side of the street—the house at Number 11. Their house. At the sound of footsteps behind her, Wandalou took off and sprinted away. Doorbell cam footage barely recorded the shadow as it streaked past.

Quinn popped the cap off a longneck and held the frosty bottle to his forehead. Lately, his neckties seemed to conspire to strangle him. Also lately, he'd pulled a lot of late nights at the station, because Hydrangea Heights was coming apart from an excess of crazy. First the Gowl woman, then Brittany Barrows, and now the German baker, whose wrists were almost too big for handcuffs. Worse than the arrests was his suspicion that there was more at work in all three of the cases than had been exhumed.

That nagging worry was keeping him up at night. And he missed Wandalou, who'd put up a mighty resistance to his demand for honesty. *Wandalou.* He could forgive her the one instance of cheating with a rookie cop under his supervision, but in denying him the truth? "Werewolves," he spat before knocking back a deep pull from his bottle.

He passed by the kitchen's row of windows and gazed up at the moon, which hung full above the backyard.

"Werewolves?" he repeated, this time in a whisper and tone not so dismissive.

Something rushed out of the shadows and into the moon's glare. It stood on two legs and, if he wasn't mistaken, a pair of Jeter Diletti strappy sandals exactly like his estranged fiancée owned. In fact, it looked like a werewolf, a legit Hollywood horror with its arms raised in a menacing gesture and saliva drooling from an open mouth filled with sharp teeth. The glowing, feral red eyes certainly added to the believability.

And it also looked like Wandalou.

"What the *fff—?*" Quinn got out right as the nightmare leaped at and through the nearest window.

Glass exploded like thunder. Shards sprayed the kitchen. Even before Quinn could finish his statement or scream in shock, the she-wolf had recovered and was in front of him. He smelled its hot, sour breath and fell into the terrible scrutiny of its mad eyes. A low, throaty growl followed the rush of breaking glass.

"*Quinn,*" the monster addressed in a guttural voice that sounded, underneath, like Wandalou's.

"*—uck!*" Quinn gasped. "Wanda…?"

The she-wolf tossed back her head and howled. The roar echoed through the kitchen and house and carried out through the shattered window and into the sky, all the way up to the moon. Wandalou stepped menacingly closer. The kitchen island prevented Quinn from farther retreat.

"Honey?" he asked around a nervous smile.

The she-wolf readied to lunge.

"*Wait,*" bellowed a man's voice, deep and powerful. Quinn recognized it as belonging to Joe Rhodes, Willa's pilot boyfriend, and also its authority—he'd used the same tone during interrogations.

Wandalou whirled toward the vacant window. Beyond the shattered pane, backlit by the moon and cloaked in shadow, stood a second dark figure. It stepped into the glow cast by the kitchen lights.

"*You*," Wandalou hissed.

Joe focused on Quinn. "Invite me in!"

"What?" Quinn asked.

"Hurry, before it's too late!"

"Dude, come on in for a brewski," Quinn said.

"Good enough," said Joe, and suddenly, he was past the blasted pane and standing directly beside Wandalou. "Look into my eyes, my eyes!"

"*No*," Wandalou yelped. "I don't want to!"

But she did as instructed. Joe blathered on about putting the wolf to bed or to sleep or something about rapture…it was difficult to be sure, because his voice played through Quinn's head with a soothing, haunting resonance. *A dream, that's all this is. I've put in so many hours on the job that I've snapped.*

Snapped.

Wandalou snapped her fingers and brought him out of the trance. "Hello? Anyone home in there?"

She stood in front of him, drool drying on her chin, her hair in a frizzy tornado, her clothes rumpled and torn. One Jeter D. strappy sandal hung askew off her ankle. She sported the makings of a decent five o'clock shadow.

"Hey, penis with feet," she said. "*Now do you believe me?*"

Quinn screamed.

They sat together in the house's front parlor.

"It was true, everything you said about Race the Face, Ladies' Poker Night…all of it?"

"Unfortunately," Isis answered.

Wandalou raised her hands. "At least it's over. The wolf is gone!"

"No, it isn't," Joe warned.

Willa took Joe's hand. "At least it is for now. You saved us, Joe."

Joe shrugged. "What can I say? I like this place. Mistral Lane's not nearly as boring as Brittany Barrows told me."

Quinn's eyebrows knitted together. "So that part's real, too? You're a…?"

"Vampire," Joe said.

Quinn touched his neck.

"The point is," Wandalou interrupted, "that you know all of it. Race went crazy after he escaped and killed Jessie-Marie, then his broomstick-flying mother helped him to cover it up, just like she said. Brittany Barrows—"

"*Skank!*" grumbled Willa.

"—tried to drive a stake through Willa's heart, and Regina Gowl wanted to blackmail us, so you've done your job with efficiency and, I might add, panache!"

Quinn shook his head, stood, and appeared to be on the edge of coming apart now that he was burdened with knowing the facts.

"Quinn!" Wandalou pleaded. She stood and moved toward him, but he turned his back to her.

"I had no idea," he said and shook his head. Then, turning back around, he added, "You went through all of that without me. *Alone.*"

Wandalou offered a weak smile. "I wasn't alone, Quinn." She briefly took Willa's hand, released it, and reached for Isis's. "I had the best friends a woman could hope to know helping me through it."

Quinn nodded. "And I want to be there, too, going forward."

Then he dropped to his knees before her and took Wandalou's hand. "Let's get married."

"Married? When?" Wandalou asked.

"As soon as possible. *Today*. Just as soon as you shave off that goatee."

She batted at his shoulder. "Okay, *yes,* Quinn, I'm ready!"

Willa said, "Any chance you can make it a night wedding?"

Wandalou tipped a look at Joe. "No worries, fly-boy."

Joe gave her a thumbs-up.

Wandalou held onto Quinn's hand. "Yes, yes, Quinn Montoya! I'm ready to be hitched!"

Quinn stood and held up Wandalou's hand to indicate her ragged fingers. "Good. Just make sure you get a manicure first. And, geeze, *please* do something about that beard!"

Frau Renate Krumpt sidled over to the table. The two inmates already seated there grabbed their lunch trays and scrambled away without complaint. Frau Krumpt sat and surveyed the lunch tray's contents. "*Schiesse*," she grumbled.

Another of Ladyville's newest residents boldly slinked up to the table. Frau Krumpt rolled her eyes. Brittany Barrows stood with her lunch tray in hand.

"Mind if I join you?" Brittany asked.

Frau Krumpt narrowed her gaze. "I remember you."

"You should. I sold you that spooky old haunted house out near the dog park."

"Ah, yes, charming place. It had all the comforts of home…until my idiot son caused all of this." She waved a pudgy hand around, indicating the room. "I had a life, a home, a business. And now, I am forced to subsist on…" she pushed the lunch tray away. "*Ass.*"

Brittany sat without being invited to, an action not lost on the Frau.

"Did I give you permission to join me?"

"Forget that. We have bigger matters to focus on."

"Like *vhat?*"

Brittany turned on the hard metal bench and waved at the next table. One of the numbers seated there hurried over and sat, also without the Frau's permission.

"Frau Krumpt, meet Regina Gowl," said Brittany.

"The one they call *the Pit Bull*," Frau Krumpt said. "Your reputation precedes you!"

"And I understand that they call you *the Rottweiler*," said Regina.

Frau Krumpt extended her hand in a horizontal fist. Regina knocked knuckles. "So *vhat* is this about, *Poodle?*" Frau Krumpt said to Brittany.

"It's about our mutual enemies back in our old stomping grounds," Brittany said.

"Please be more specific," said the Frau. "Do you mean the bureaucrats in Baden-Baden or the home cooks in Cincinnati?"

"No, Mistral Lane in Hydrangea Heights," said Regina. "Those three fornicating housewives!"

"You mean—?"

"Willa Forsyth," said Brittany.

"Wandalou Trueheart," said Regina.

"And the redhead, the one *mein* offspring tried to poof with my fish knife. Because of her, I *vas* forced to sacrifice my idiot son's life!"

"We all have scores to settle with them," said Brittany. "So I propose we work together."

"To *vhat* end?" asked the Frau.

"Revenge," said Regina. "Served cold. Served hot. Severed at room temperature. I don't care how it's served, just so long as it is!"

"Revenge," Frau Krumpt parroted. "Do you have a plan?"

Regina Gowl smirked. "Oh, do we ever!"

"Then let me in on it, *schnell!*"

"First, are we agreed, my new friends?" said Brittany.

"Friends?" Frau Krumpt said. "*Allies*, I suppose." She extended her hand, palm down, across the table. Regina added hers over the Frau's, and Brittany made it a pact of three.

On that warm Indian Summer night, my three dear friends gathered in the backyard of the Slades for the impromptu wedding of Quinn Montoya and Wandalou Trueheart. The back patio was decorated in pretty streamers and orange fairy lights, paper bells, and pumpkins. Candles and jack-o'-lanterns lit the venue, as did, of course, the moon on its second night of fullness.

A small number of guests gathered to help the bride and groom celebrate. Among those in attendance were Willa and her handsome boyfriend, Joe, in full pilot uniform, and my husband, Tim Smyth. The Slade Twins, each dressed in their Sunday finest, were given flower girl duties and scattered hydrangea petals before them. Bob Slade had stocked the large coolers, one with champagne bottles, the other with beer and plenty of ice. My dear friend Isis had spent all day baking a three-tiered *vedding*—I mean *wedding*—cake decorated in fresh strawberries over luscious vanilla buttercream. The best wedding topper they could come up with on such short notice was a pair of the twins' dolls—one female, the other male. The plastic dolls stood on the top tier, and the bride, who could be quite the diva at times, grudgingly approved.

The groom was decked out in classic black and white and looked quite dashing. The bride wore an elegant champagne-colored silk-satin gown and designer heels. She carried a bouquet of red roses and joined her groom. Isis, who was certified to perform the ceremony online, presided.

"We are gathered here today to witness the union of Quinn and Wandalou in joyous matrimony," Isis declared.

Vows were spoken, rings exchanged. When it came to the part about anyone seeing fit why the couple should not be joined in marriage, a nervous silence carried over the backyard, one broken only by the whisper of the wind.

"Get on, would you?" Wandalou urged none-too-subtly from the corner of her mouth.

Isis nodded. "Then, Quinn and Wandalou, it is my sincerest pleasure to welcome you as husband and wife!"

K-Pop blasted over Bob Slades's improvised backyard sound system. Couples danced. Neighbors complained and called in to the police station, but no cruisers were dispatched to the scene because they knew it was Detective Quinn Montoya's wedding.

While paint dried on the new accent wall, which Isis had hastily slapped on while the cake was baking and was, decided unanimously by those who stared in horror at it, the worst effort yet, she set out bowls of snack mix, platters of crudités and dip, shrimp and cocktail sauce with an aggressive bite of horseradish, scallops wrapped in bacon, and, for the flower girls, pizza rolls.

"But I don't want pizza rolls!" Marci whined. "I'm sick of them! That's all you ever give us—*pizza rolls!* I want sushi!"

"Then eat some shrimp, dear," said Isis.

"Shrimp? But that's fish! *Ewww,*" Marci complained. "I want sushi!"

Bob and Joe stood with Tim and Quinn near the grill. Bob had ribeyes sizzling on the flame.

"Love that sweet ride of yours," Joe said. "My dad used to own a 'stang—'67 convertible."

"*Dude,*" Bob said and offered a high-five. "She needs an oil change soon. Maybe you want to come over, help me out, get dirty."

"Make sure it's at night," Quinn said.

"What?" Bob asked.

After the music ended, the twins had gone to bed, and the steaks were eaten, Isis, Wandalou, and Willa sat around the backyard table. The fairy lights glowed. A gentle autumn breeze blew, and the neighborhood was quiet.

"That was a hell of a wedding," said Willa. "Thanks so much for inviting us."

"I like Joe," said Isis. "If he bites my husband or either of my girls on the neck, I'll drive a stake through his heart. But I like him."

"Noted," Willa said.

Wandalou reached into the bowl of snack mix on the center of the table and ate a handful of the crunchy offerings. "You know, my life is wonderful. I've got Quinn, you two…" She gazed around the table. "If only Jessie-Marie was here, it would be perfect."

"She is here," said Willa. "I feel her."

"Me, too," said Isis.

And I was, seated at the fourth, presumed empty, seat with the three best friends a woman could ever hope to know.

The joy of that moment proved to be brief. Wandalou's face contorted. "Oh, no," she gasped.

"What's wrong?" Isis asked.

"That tickle in my throat is back—do you feel it?" Wandalou asked.

They all looked up at the sky, where the full moon swam behind thickening clouds.

Then Wandalou coughed. "False alarm—wasabi pea!"

We all laughed, and how good it felt, how cleansing, even as a single light in Regina Gowl's dark house switched on across the hedge of roses and her new houseguest stared out at those gathered, flashed a sharp smile, and said, "Don't worry, my twins, your real mommy's home, and she plans to make them pay…"

But that's another story for a different season.

THE END

Maybe

The Coming
of
Going

Chapter 1

That Face in the Window

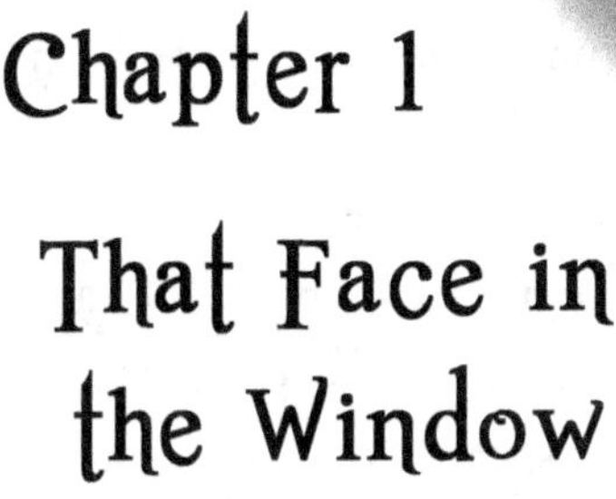

Three mornings before she gazed out Regina Gowl's bedroom window at the festivities taking place in the backyard next door, Lavinia Going who, in a former life, went by the name Joan Slade, sat staring up at the acoustic ceiling tiles of a rented office and forgot how to blink. The old desk chair complained with a sullen creak.

Screwed she was. More than that. Screwed was several off-ramps and nonexistent millions scattered to the Four Winds in the rearview.

"I'll do it," she shouted at the empty room. "I'll open that window and jump to my death! Think I won't?"

She stormed up from the desk. The hem of her shirt snagged on something grabby sticking out of the chair's lumbar area and snapped her back down. Lavinia grumbled in frustration and ripped herself free.

"I swear, I'll jump!" she shouted at the empty room. "And then you'll have to clean up one hell of a mess!"

She tensed near the window, steeled herself, and then threw herself into open air.

Less than twenty inches lower, she struck the soft cushion of the overgrown lawn and carpet of leaves dropped from the branches of nearby maples. "Stupid first-floor rental!" she said and spat out a yellow leaf that had found its way into her mouth. She sprawled across the ground and stared up at the sky, needing a sign—any sign—that promised an out to her predicament.

Something in her tight, white track pants pocket vibrated.

Lavinia yelped, "Snake!" Then she remembered her phone. Shifting, she drew it out.

"Ladyville Penitentiary?" she said after scanning the caller ID.

Fresh panic gripped her. Then she also remembered the rats hadn't convicted her of anything. Not yet.

With her free hand, she pinched her nostrils and answered. "Hello?"

The husky, board-up-the-butt woman's voice on the other end of the line asked her if she'd accept the call. Intrigued, Lavinia said yes. A brief silence followed.

"Joan?" her caller asked.

"*Lavinia*," she corrected in a voice that was all sealed nostrils.

"Sorry. I need the organization's help."

"Who is this?"

"An old friend. Neighbor, at least. It's Regina Gowl."

Lavinia released her nose and sucked down a cleansing sip of air. "Well, Regina, you know, we're so busy. So much charity work. So many souls to save from the wickedness of flesh. So much purity to—"

"Stow the purity shtick. And I don't care about saving souls. I'd rather crush them. Destroy them—including one in particular that you, yourself, would get your holy rollers off on flattening like a bug."

Lavinia sat up. "I'm listening…"

"Good. Come to Ladyville. Visiting hours start at one."

"I don't know," Lavinia said.

"There's a cool fortune in it if you do."

"See you at one."

In the upscale apartment whose rent had been paid by the organization until recently when all the cash dried up, some frozen by investigators, Lavinia showered, primped, and dressed in the most modest of white panties and bras, white trousers, and a white top that didn't reveal one molecule of cleavage. She gazed into the mirror, her makeup minimal, her hair restrained in a tortoiseshell chignon. The image gazing back was pure. Beyond pure—the purist of purity.

Ignoring the mess of eviction notices scattered across the length of granite counter, she calmly packed her luggage, stored it in the trunk of the luxury vehicle in danger of being repossessed if it lingered there much longer, donned her expensive shades—another of the organization's purchases—and drove away from her new life in the direction of her old.

She entered the industrial room, which smelled of decades of sweat and despair, and sat, feeling the oily residue cling to her pure, white raiments. Revulsion bloomed in her stomach and put that stink of toffee in her nose despite zero British blood. Clearing her throat, Lavinia glanced around. One of the miseries in prison garb smacked her lips suggestively in her direction. Lavinia's conceited expression tightened.

"As if," she said.

The security door buzzed open and another of Ladyville's unladylike residents strutted in. Regina Gowl moseyed over to the table where Lavinia waited and sat. They eyed one another across the distance of a yard.

"Regina," Lavinia addressed stiffly.

"Joan," Regina said unintentionally only to pivot. "Apologies—Lavinia, I'll remember next time. You always were such a chameleon."

"And you a yard bird."

"This?" Regina laughed. "Free Wi-Fi and three squares. And the entertainment—*As the Prison Turns*! I'm not complaining. Not about this part."

Lavinia pursed her lips.

"I understand that you, too, have suffered…how shall I put it? Setbacks."

Lavinia held her tongue.

"Laxative stocks, was it?" Regina offered. "A fortune in bad investments flushed right down the toilet, I heard. *Pppppllllloooopppppp!*"

The temperature in the room skyrocketed. The collar of Lavinia's shirt conspired with Regina's words to strangle her. Those cotton pants, too. Lavinia shifted in place. "Yes, there have been some setbacks."

"Setbacks? Sister, you're one tip to the feds from joining my prison shuffleboard team!" Regina clucked.

Lavinia glowered. "What do you really want, Regina?"

"Your help. You owe me, Joan."

"Oh? How's that?"

Regina fixed her with an unblinking scrutiny. "All those thousands I donated to the Purists of Purity because I believed in the message you were hocking. I ate the damned lima beans, rice…the disgusting pickled pigs feet! It didn't make me pure, only nauseous and quite gassy. But I believed and I wanted to be pure, like you instructed! Talk about a laxative!"

"Your point?" Lavinia pressed haughtily.

"My point, sister, is that you can finally repay me for all those trips to the Caribbean I helped finance. All those pilgrimages to spread the purity you took at five-star accommodations."

"I'm listening."

"Of course you are, because you need some fresh green lettuce—and Mamma's garden is in bloom!"

Lavinia shook her head. "What? You are talking actual money, right?"

"A fortune. Hidden in my house. But before I part with one cent of it, I want…no, I demand, your word! Your word that you'll strike back at my enemies. That you'll unleash fire and brimstone upon those three she-beasts who put me here!"

Lavinia beamed confidence. "Who, Regina?"

"Listen carefully. Willa Forsyth, the Writer."

Lavinia nodded.

"That hussy, Wandalou Trueheart."

The left corner of Lavinia's mouth sharpened with a grin.

"And finally, Isis Slade, your ex-husband's current wife and stepmother to those two brats you spawned eight years ago."

Lavinia's confident mask melted. "Peaches and Pickles?"

"No, Marci and Darci—Brat One and Brat Two."

"How dare you?" Lavinia spat.

"Oh, don't try to scam me, Joan—if you cared about those urchins, you'd be there now, not lamenting the laxative market plunge. This is your chance to stick it to that uppity redhead who's raising your kids!"

Lavinia willed the sharp smirk back onto her lips. "You make a tempting offer."

"And if you do care about those little moppets, you can take them with you when you flee the country to whatever new identity awaits."

"My daughters? That would be an interesting twist, now, wouldn't it?" Lavinia asked aloud. "Oh, and I must admit, I was never, ever okay with their baby-daddy remarrying…"

"So you'll do it?" Regina asked. "Do we have a deal?"

Lavinia sighed. "About that bonanza hidden in your house…"

Regina smacked her chops. "Upstairs, in the master bedroom's walk-in closet, is a fortune in merchandise…"

She located the spare key right where Regina said it would be—tucked in the folds of the sunbonnet left hanging on a peg outside the back door.

The music rising from the backyard of the house that once was hers masked her entrance into Regina's lair. Lavinia crept through the dark kitchen to the staircase, using the glow of the full moon through the windows to guide her and navigated up the stairs.

None of the revelers next door noticed the light come on in the upstairs bedroom of 19 Mistral Lane. Nor did they see the face that peered out to take in the celebration.

Lavinia scowled, offered a promise to her daughters, the twins, and then turned toward the walk-in closet and the fortune it secretly contained.

None of the wedding guests heard her scream when she flipped on the closet's light and saw what was entombed there.

"Dolls?" she posed aloud when she got herself back under control. "A fortune in dolls?"

Lavinia wanted to cry. Instead, she was soon laughing. A little research on the data made available by her burner phone revealed that Regina Gowl wasn't far off the mark in her claim. Okay, so she'd sell the dolls. And while she did that, she'd spread a little mayhem around the neighborhood.

Or a lot of it.

Chapter 2
Wedded Blisters

A ruckus of saw teeth and hammering jolted Wandalou awake on that late October morning. She opened her eyes to utter blackness and panicked before realizing she'd worn a Gunther Blue sleep mask to bed.

"Oh," she said and removed it.

The other side of the mattress was empty, the day bright beyond the bedroom windows. The unholy row that had shocked her out of her pageant-themed dream attained a jarring new level of exquisite sharpness as something metallic was yanked free of a wall, screaming every centimeter of the way loose.

She tore back the covers, slid her feet into the pair of Banolo Klonick mules with the glacier-blue ostrich feather details, and marched out of the bedroom.

"First victim of the day," she groused on her way down the stairs. With a model's grace, clad in dusty-blue satin sleepwear matching perfectly to her mules, Wandalou glided through the vast house's downstairs and stormed into the kitchen.

"What's the hell's that racket?" she demanded.

The buzz of a saw swallowed her voice.

"Huh?" asked Quinn Rodrigo Montoya, her new husband and intended target.

Quinn reclined against the kitchen island in a jaunty pose, clad in blue jeans and a basic white T, barefoot, coffee cup in hand. Two men wearing safety goggles stood at the gap blasting through the kitchen window and were in the process of replacing the damage.

"You're going to have to speak louder," Quinn shouted.

Wandalou's expression tightened. "Or maybe I'll just scratch something like one of you boys."

"Ewww," Quinn said. And then he scratched something.

The noise wound down. Both newlyweds glanced up to see the two carpenters' eyes trained on Wandalou and her skimpy attire. Quinn coughed to clear his throat, straightened, and shepherded Wandalou out of the kitchen. "Come on, babe."

"Don't you 'Come on, babe' me, Quinn!"

When they were out of eyesight, the sawing resumed.

Wandalou folded her arms. "Couldn't the destruction have started a little later?" she snapped.

"The destruction already happened—or do I need to remind you why the honeymoon fund is going to fixing the kitchen window? Along with a good part of the outside kitchen wall?"

Her scowl deepened. "Why couldn't you have just filed a claim with the insurance company and let them pay for it like any normal American husband?"

"Right, and tell them what? That my normal American wife turned into a werewolf and, in a fit of full moon lust, jumped through the window in order to rip out my throat?"

Wandalou's bluster deflated. "You have a point."

Still holding his coffee cup, Quinn patted the top of Wandalou's head with his free hand. "Why don't you run along to the girls for some you-time while the men-folk pick up the pieces."

"Do you know how condescending that sounds?"

Another screech of nails being yanked shrieked through the house.

"But you make another great point," she said.

Less than an hour later, Wandalou had showered, fixed her makeup and hair, dressed in her designer best— a pantsuit with a flattering low-cut top and Klonick flats—and was out the door for the Slades' house.

Coffee brewed. The tall cups were waiting beside the maker. The end-of-October breeze swept leaves past the windows of the cozy breakfast nook where the three friends gathered.

"Thank God that's over with," Wandalou said. "I swear my virginity grew back while I was imprisoned living here in your guest room—I could hear it squeak when I walk." She got up to pour coffee.

"What was that sound?" asked Willa, who sat at the table staring through an unflattering pair of reading glasses at her phone. "That squeaking noise?"

"It was my shoe—presently about to greet your ass," Wandalou said. "And what's with the ugly specs, Grandma?"

Willa looked up and squinted. "Huh?"

Clad in a tasteful ensemble of turtleneck and slacks, Isis wore her bright yellow apron with the chickens on it. She carried a tray of sandwiches over to the table. "Come, ladies, eat!"

Coffee flowed.

Conversations waned.

"Coffee and sandwiches," Willa sighed. "This is nice."

"Yeah, if it was the 1950s," Wandalou sniped, a sour look on her face. "What kind of bread is this?"

"Ciabatta, dear."

"Tastes more like *Chewbacca*."

Isis set down the brie and olive tapenade sandwich. "You're right, everything tastes so...bland. I wish My Grains was still open."

"It isn't just that," said Willa, who removed her glasses. "My eyesight and hearing aren't what they were when, you know..." And then she released a sharp little yip.

"You mean...?" asked Wandalou, who answered with a hearty wolf's howl.

"Shhh," Isis admonished.

Wandalou glanced around. "The twins are in school and Bob's at work. What gives?"

Isis sipped her coffee before answering. "It isn't Bob or the twins that concern me." She nudged her chin to the right, indicating that direction.

"You think the fridge is listening?" asked Willa.

"No. There's a car next door at Regina Gowl's place."

"Probably the fraud squad," Wandalou said.

"Involuntary manslaughter and blackmail," Isis sighed. "She still hasn't made bail and the trial is months away."

Wandalou tsked. "Can we not take the day any lower than it already is? About our flaccid senses—do you think it's because, you know..." And then she yipped.

"You mean...?" Isis asked and howled.

"Shhh," Willa and Wandalou cautioned.

"I think that putting the wolf to sleep means we're back to our boring old selves and lives," Isis said.

"Not her," said Wandalou, finger aimed across the table at Willa. "She's dating a vampire, flapping her wings and going all supernatural in bed."

Willa grinned. "Well, I don't want to brag…"

"Then don't," Wandalou threatened.

"Not even a little?"

Wandalou ripped another bite off her sandwich.

"Apart from that, I'm happy to say that life is nearly back to normal, and all the drama's over," said Isis. She raised her coffee cup. "To Jessie-Marie."

"Here, here," said Wandalou.

Willa made it three. They toasted the missing and missed fourth member of their loyal group, unaware at that moment how wrong they were about life on Mistral Lane returning to its former banality.

Wandalou entered the kitchen. The new window was in place. One of the workmen was in the process of sealing the corners with foam insulation. He looked up and smiled.

Smiling in response, Wandalou flashed the new rock on her ring finger. "Just married. To a fiery Latino with a temper who also happens to be a police detective in this blue blood berg."

The man, still clutching the insulator gun, spread his arms in surrender. "Ain't no thing."

"You mean, ain't no education," Wandalou said through a plastic grin.

"You're funny," he laughed.

"It's my defense mechanism."

"Speaking of defenses, it's like a nuke went off in that window."

"Werewolf incoming!" she declared and then mimed an explosion.

"Werewolf?" the man asked. "Your husband said it was a tennis ball."

He resumed working like talking about werewolves was as normal as walking the dog.

The new Mrs. Montoya found Quinn upstairs watching the sports news. "Hey," she said.

"Hey," he answered.

She hovered just inside the bedroom door.

Quinn glanced up. "Something wrong?"

"Not sure. So, great wedding, yeah. And the sex afterward has been…"

Quinn flashed a proud smile. "Some of my best work, right?"

"Oh, so good."

"You know it!"

"But…" she sighed.

His pride evaporated. "But?"

"I almost ripped your throat out. You saw me in full-on she-wolf mode, warts and all."

"Don't you mean pelt?"

"What?"

"Pelt and all, which explained all those mustache burns and the one where you yanked off the uni-brow. And—"

"Quinn, the sex has been *en fuego,* but don't you think we should talk about my odd condition?"

Quinn scowled. "No. And besides, it's gone."

"No, it isn't," Wandalou sighed. "It's only sleeping. And do I need to remind you, my inner werewolf's only sleeping because of our neighbor, the hot vampire?"

"You think Joe's hot?"

"Don't you?"

Quinn pondered the question and seemed to nod the slightest. "I suppose."

"My point is…we haven't talked about any of it."

"I don't want to," Quinn whined more like a boy than the man she'd married.

"So we just pretend it never happened?"

He was back again, all man. "Works for me."

An imperious look on full display, Wandalou agreed. "Fine."

Then she sashayed over to him and crushed her mouth over his. They fell upon the bed, untangled from their clothes, and made love while the workmen completed repairs, erasing the evidence of the crime from a few nights earlier.

Chapter 3
The Slade in the Shade

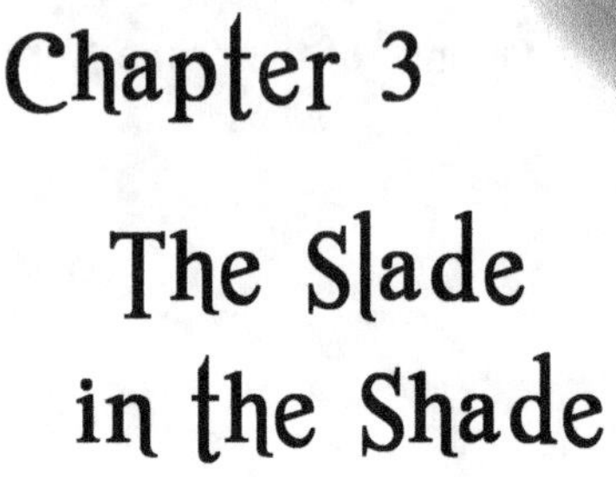

Humming to herself, Isis set the table. The chicken was roasted, the oven switched over to convection. The potatoes boiled. Fresh vegetables waited on the counter beside the chopping board to be diced and sliced into a salad, and croissant bread pudding cooled under aluminum foil.

What was more comforting—and wonderfully boring—than a chicken and mashed potatoes dinner? Her smile brightened. The long months following Wanda-lou's bachelorette party and the nightmare unleashed by Race the Face were over. If she never was forced to endure another full moon night imprisoned in Willa's panic room again, the loss of heightened senses and a gourmet palate were worth the cost.

Isis straightened, folded her arms, and glanced around. Outside, the short day had surrendered to autumn's early dark, and a sense of satisfaction filled her. The werewolf curse was gone.

"No, it's not," Bob said as he breezed into the kitchen, his tie unknotted, his shirtsleeves rolled up to his elbows.

Isis jolted. "What?"

"Daddy said we weren't having gazpacho for dinner," Marci whined. "I want gazpacho!"

"Do you even know what gazpacho is?" Isis asked.

"Yes, something yummy."

"We're having roasted chicken, mashed potatoes, salad, and croissant bread pudding for dessert."

Bob pecked a kiss to her cheek. "Sounds great, hon."

"Yuck," Marci complained.

Darci bounded in. "I can't wait!"

"I want gazpacho," Marci persisted.

Isis laughed. "Oh, I'm so glad to have things back to normal around here!"

Bob took his seat. "Me, too—now that our house-guest's in her own home again."

"I miss Aunty Wandalou," Darci giggled. "She was so funny! Especially when she brushed her teeth. She made a sound like a growling dog."

"That's your Aunty Wandalou," Isis said lightly. She set a pitcher of ice water and lemon wedges on the table. Bob poured.

"Girls, be seated," Isis sang. She whipped the potatoes and fixed the salad while Bob carved the chicken and arranged the parts and slices on a platter. Then the family took their positions around the table. Isis portioned out servings. Marci pouted.

"How was everyone's day?"

Bob shrugged. "Mine was unremarkable."

Isis rolled her eyes. "What a heavenly thought! Unremarkable days free from drama. I love you, Bob Slade."

He chuckled and stabbed his fork into the creamy potatoes on his plate. "Love you, too, hon." They eyed one another across the table.

"Girls?" Isis asked. "Care to share?"

"No, I don't like this dinner," Marci grumbled.

"Music to my ears. Darci?"

"My day was okay," the girl said.

"Mine wasn't," Marci carped. "If I don't get gazpacho, I'll scream!"

"Don't force me to tape your mouth shut, dear," Isis said calmly.

Briefly, three of the family members gathered around the table went about eating their dinner. Then Marci let forth with a bloodcurdling shriek that drew all eyes and attention to her.

"I will get out the tape—duct if I have to!"

But the girl's eyes were aimed past her step-mother and at the windows behind the table.

"Marci?" Bob asked.

Marci pointed at the windows. "Someone's out there! I saw a lady looking in at us. She was dressed all in white!"

Isis stood swiftly. "Bob!"

Together, she and Bob hastened to the French doors leading out to the patio. A waning moon hung over the backyard. The chilly October breeze gusted through bare trees and over their browning lawn. No woman in white prowled the night.

Neither concerned parent saw Lavinia crouching low on the other side of Regina Gowl's rose hedges.

She paced the floor of the dark living room, anger rising hotly up her throat to infect her cheeks. "Bob," she spat, the name tasting like lava. "Oh, that Bob!"

I only wanted a glimpse at the twins, Lavinia told herself. Curiosity, nothing more. But when she'd crept up to the window and peered in, saw them all seated around the table, all so happy, something in her had snapped.

Lavinia sold herself on the lie that what she'd felt when looking at the twins was a mother's purest love, but what she really suffered was base jealousy. She didn't want the little brats so much as she didn't want Bob and what's-her-name to have them.

What's-her-name...Athena? Juno? Pocahontas?

"Isis," Lavinia growled, and, screaming into the cover of her right arm to muffle the sound, cemented her plan for revenge.

Calmly, quite calmly, she glided up the staircase under cover of shadows, switched on the bedside lamp, ignoring the mess of dolls and vacant stares from her cataloging progress, sat on the very edge of the bed that reeked of Regina Gowl's embalming fluid perfume, and opened her phone screen to the internet.

Chapter 4
Bat-shit
Crazy in Love

Captain Joe Rhodes leaned against the doorframe in a jaunty pose, a confident smirk on his handsome mug, naked apart from the pilot's cap upon his head of dark hair.

"Woof," Willa said.

Joe uncrossed his arms, removed his cap, and, his smirk widening, hastened over to the bed where Willa waited in a state of equal undress.

"I'm so glad you're back," she said between kisses.

"The captain's glad to be back," Joe growled.

She took his face in her hands gazing up at his handsomeness. Joe's eyes glinted like twin emerald gemstones in the brewing early November darkness.

"Thought the great writer, Lena LaFleur, would approve," he said, so cool.

"Oh, right to my heart!" Willa said.

Joe pulled her into his arms. They settled beneath the covers, flesh close, souls closer.

"How have things been in my absence?" he asked.

"Quiet," Willa said while twirling the fingers of one hand through Joe's chest hair. "There's been absolutely no sign of…you know…"

Joe tossed back his head and howled.

"Yeah, that."

He gazed down into her eyes. "That's what you wanted, right?"

"Yes, of course. And without, you know…" Now, Willa howled. "Life is back to its boring normality here on Mistral Lane."

Joe gently brushed Willa's cheek with his thumb. "Is your life boring, Willa Forsyth?"

"Not in the least," she said.

They made love. In the bed. On the ceiling. At one point, he took her outside, floating over the dormered peak of the roof until the cold night air forced her to complain. They returned to the bed, Joe's masculine body protecting hers.

In the darkness, Willa rolled over, the little spoon to Joe's big. "G'night," she tittered.

"Night, Willa," Joe said.

"Oh, I'm gonna sleep like the dead after that."

"Ouch," he said.

"Sorry."

Joe kissed her shoulder. Willa closed her eyes. An instant later, her cell raised its alert. Willa's eyes snapped open.

"What is it?" Joe asked.

"I'm not sure."

Willa sat up and reached for the little offender. The alert was warning her of the first review posted for her latest Lena LaFleur romance novel. Willa scowled. One star? The reviewer, **goingmad@19**, wrote:

> *Written so poorly that the author makes me pine for a world of anti-romance and the purist of purity—convent life, here I come!*

"What?" Willa huffed.

Joe shifted up to a seated position beside her. "What's wrong?"

She showed him the phone's screen. "Look!"

"Yikes," he said. "Do you want me to hunt this goingmad down and go medieval on them?"

"Yes," she said. Then she sobbed, "No. They have a right to their opinion."

"Wrong though it is," Joe comforted. "And it's only one review."

Willa nodded. "You're right. I've gotten bad reviews before. One doesn't much matter."

She set her phone back on the nightstand and attempted to ignore the sting.

"You are a talented novelist," Joe soothed. "And the hottest babe on the planet!" His big right hand caressed down to her outer thigh. Willa trembled. "Better?" he whispered.

"Much. I'm over it already."

Joe lowered to kiss her. As their lips connected, Willa's phone bleated the same alert. Over the course of that long night, it warned her eight more times that Lena LaFleur had collected as many scathing, one-star reviews of her romance novels.

"Oh dear," Isis cooed. "Rough night?"

Willa sat at the breakfast table, her head hung in shame. Isis hurried over with a tall mug of coffee. Willa guzzled that first cup down without cream or sugar, her usual choice. "You could say that."

Wandalou breezed in from the direction of the downstairs powder room dressed impeccably in the latest LeeLee Lime ensemble. Two steps into the Slade kitchen, she skidded to a stop on her Walther Wibble heels and made no effort to hide her horror.

"Be kind," Isis threatened.

"It's just that…" Wandalou gasped. "She looks like a cat that never bothered to groom itself!"

"I said be kind!" Isis admonished through clenched teeth.

"I was being kind," Wandalou said. Then, breaking focus with Willa, she narrowed her eyes on Isis. "Fashion influencer, remember? I'm influencing."

Slowly, as though approaching a frightened stray that was ready to bolt, Wandalou stepped closer to Willa, a counterfeit smile projected. "Hello, friend," Wandalou said. "My, that's a lovely purple sweater you've got on."

"Oh, shut up," Willa huffed.

Wandalou dropped all pretences and took her seat. Isis refreshed everyone's coffee and joined them.

"What's up with this?" Wandalou tsked.

"Last night, Joe and I—"

"So it was his fault?" Isis interjected.

"No, it wasn't Joe's doing. My new novel got shredded in an online review. And then the shredder left the same kind of scathing feedback on all of my novels."

The others gasped.

"Not *Diva in Denim*," Wandalou said.

"Yes, even *Diva in Denim!*"

"Bastard!"

"And you only like that one because I based the character of Diva Sinclair on you!"

Wandalou acknowledged the charge with a roll of her eyes and a tilt of her head.

"The person who did this…it was like they had a personal grudge against me. A score to settle!"

Isis set a hand on Willa's arm and offered comfort. "Can you have the reviews removed?"

"They've already affected me badly. My sales are down. The damage is done!"

"I'd like to get my hands on their neck," Wandalou said. "Or, if you found out who left those reviews, have your boyfriend attend to their neck."

"Joe already volunteered to do that."

"Oh, good," Isis said. "I'm sure this is all fixable."

Willa sniffed. "I suppose. And after all, look at how many reasons I have to be happy with my life. I've got both of you, my career, Joe, and we're no longer, you know…"

Wandalou howled. "Way to go, girl," Wandalou said after clearing her throat. "Glass half full outlook. Only for the love of all that's holy, would you please run a brush through that rat's nest of yours?"

Both Isis and Willa glared at Wandalou.

"What?" Wandalou asked.

Unknown to them at the time, one house over, Lavinia was now ready for the next step of her revenge scheme.

Some of the ugly little freaks were special editions, others rare. Those select monstrosities born in porcelain were highly valued among the doll collector community.

Lavinia snapped photographs, listed the best for sale, and sat back to watch the bloodshed as one loser in Walla Walla and another in Caribou, Maine, waged a bidding war over the hideous relics in Regina's walk-in closet. She'd already scored a small fortune on the spoils of that combat—enough to get her where she'd go next once this work was completed.

There was much more to do before she made her grand escape into a new identity.

While the coast-to-coast battle over Bobby the Bridegroom continued to be waged online, Lavinia turned her attention to the next phase of the local campaign.

"Wandalou Trueheart, I'm coming for you," she sighed, a sharp little smile twisting on the corners of her mouth.

Chapter 5
Influencing

"**A**s brisk as an autumn breeze blowing," Wandalou stated. "And remember to keep it fashionable and fabulous—or you'll get the look." And then she flashed it for the camera, that silent, icy, and cutting stare that could make instant cubes during the height of August. Another video done, Wandalou switched the camera off and checked herself in the mirror. The Castillo top, trousers, and Lizzy Lester shoes fit her physique as though her clothes worshipped her.

"Influencing," she announced aloud to the room, "and conquering bad fashion one caftan and pair of mom jeans at a time!"

She poured the contents of the water bottle into a goblet and pulled a grape from the bunch on the tray. Even if a proper honeymoon was pushed to the horizon over finances, a decent dinner wasn't out of the question. For the first time since the night of the wedding, she felt rather peckish. Quinn would indulge her in such an unexpected treat. He never denied her, not even after learning of her and the girls' dark secret. Yes, a nice dinner at an upscale restaurant. After all, she looked too stunning for only the purview of her video channel.

Sarki's maybe, or the Hydrangea Heights Country Club. She'd endure the boujee to be seen looking so hot on the arm of her detective husband, who'd solved the notorious murder of Jessie-Marie Smyth, local resident and wife of a doctor. At that thought, Wandalou's façade cracked.

"Oh, Jessie-Marie, we miss you," she said to the room, afraid the sudden tears would ruin her makeup.

Jessie-Marie was gone—apart from her Ouija board visitations. But Willa was still here and hurting thanks to some overzealous reviewer. Steeling herself, the influencer reached for her phone. Her intention was to call Willa and brainstorm ways to minimize any further damage and unleash unholy hell on the reviewer. But before she could dial, the doorbell gonged.

"Get that, would you, Isis?" she shouted to the otherwise empty house. Then Wandalou recalled that her recent roommate days were over. "Oh…"

She glided down the staircase. November sunlight glinted on the other side of the windows. She opened the door. Standing outside was an unfamiliar woman dressed in a severe white pantsuit and the hair-don't to match.

"Dear gawd," Wandalou cringed.

The woman maintained a spare smile. "Hello, I'm here about the orphans," she said.

The words were past her lips before she could trap them. "I see that. Didn't anyone tell you we passed Labor Day weeks ago? I mean…is all that vanilla on purpose?"

Her visitor's expression tightened. "My clothes, you mean?"

Wandalou made a gagging noise and nodded.

"You don't say. Please, tell me more…"

"First, what's up with the hair? It looks like rats ran through it and scared away all the color. Next, I want to pluck those wiry guitar strings you call eyebrows. I mean …seriously? What are you, saving them up for some concert violinist in Eastern Europe? If I weren't so overbooked for time, I'd help you out. My tweezer finger's itching to start yanking as we stand here!"

"No fooling?"

Wandalou crossed her heart and then made a jerky grab at the other woman's face. She pulled the one hand back with the other. "Next, that face! Are lemons a regular part of your diet?"

"Lemons?"

"Because you look like you're sucking on one at this very second. Trust me—lemons are great in ice water, but unless you've got scurvy, you don't want to overdo it. And while we're on the subject, be careful of them in meringue pies." She tipped a look down at the woman's hips. "Trust me, we've all noticed. The lemon meringue pies, I mean. Forever on the hips. And the ass, too."

The woman grumbled and folded her arms. "Is that all you've got to say?"

"Oh, I could go on. I'm thinking of engaging in an emergency seam rip just so you can breathe. And are those breasts of yours bound?"

"That's my under-wire!"

"More like barbed wire, sweety. And I have to tell you, you look like an albino sausage that's about to explode. That is not a flattering fit on you."

The woman's jaw dropped.

"You know how they teach you to rub two sticks together to make a fire if you're lost in the wild?" Wandalou continued in spite of her visitor's agog expression. "You'd better stick to the sidewalk until you get out of that asbestos suit, because those bird legs look chafed enough to me to unleash one of those cataclysmic wildfires they get out west every summer. We're talking scorched earth in your case. Please be careful not to light up this neighborhood with those killer matchsticks. And as for the shoes…"

"What about my shoes?"

Wandalou folded her arms and narrowed her eyes. "No, seriously, I could be here all day. And a good part of the night. I get paid for this expertise. You figure it out."

Silence briefly fell between them.

"What was it you said about orphans?" Wandalou asked.

The woman flashed a sharp, slippery grin. "Oh, nothing."

"We're done here then?"

"Oh, quite," the woman said. "You've been most helpful."

"That's what I do," Wandalou laughed. "Fashion influencer…influencing. Good talk."

As the woman turned and strode down to the sidewalk, Wandalou thought she heard her say, "That certainly was easy!"

"Ta," Wandalou called after her, waving. "And remember what I said about those human flamethrowers of yours. I can see stray sparks shooting off those sandpaper legs as you clomp around. Remember, moisturize!"

Wandalou closed the door, a proud smile on display.

Lavinia continued up the sidewalk to Number 19 Mistral Lane. She wrestled her own smile under control until she was back inside Regina's fortress.

"Please let that have worked," she whispered in prayer to whatever dark deity was taking on new clients on her way to her laptop.

The tiny camera secreted into the top button of her shirt had more than done its job. Now, all she needed was a little creative editing, and her target would fall.

Quinn chose the country club for its steaks. She ordered the grilled prawns. A vase with autumn flowers decorated the white tablecloth. Light muzak drifted over the snooty ambiance. "You look beautiful," Quinn said around a mouthful of sirloin.

"And you look like you need a feedbag," Wandalou said through a fake smile.

Quinn set down his fork and oversized knife and wiped his mouth on his linen napkin. "Seems to me, I recall a few recent nights when you could have appreciated a bloody cut of meat."

Wandalou toyed with the bitter endive in her salad. "I thought we weren't talking about that."

Quinn swallowed and reached for his beer glass. "Not unless you want to go for my jugular."

"Oh, please—you know this is just the way I'm wired. Besides, Willa's hot pilot boyfriend already got there first."

"What?" he asked.

"Huh?" This brought them eye-to-eye. Wandalou waved a hand in dismissal. "Forget it. Can't we just enjoy a lovely night out together as husband and wife?"

Quinn extended his hand across the table. Wandalou accepted it and squeezed.

"After all, not only is your new wife a knockout," she continued, "but she even gave vital, free advice to an orphan about the dangers of dry skin and flash fires!"

As though timed to that precise instant, Wandalou's cell bleated for attention from inside her House of Menkez designer clutch with the trademark black onyx zigzag.

"Ignore that," he said.

"I plan to," she answered.

But then it complained again and twice more after that. On the sixth repetition, Wandalou reached in and removed the offender.

"What is it?" Quinn asked.

Wandalou scanned the message. "It says I've been locked out of my channel…for violating the provider's standards and ethics? *You will not be permitted access while we review and investigate the incident on November…* But that's today!"

"What incident?" Quinn asked.

Wandalou clicked on a link. A video played, one that showed her clearly at her front door offering sage advice. Only the delivery wasn't as she remembered, the script different, out of sequence.

"I'm collecting for the orphans," her visitor in white could be heard saying off-camera. *Camera*—the whole time she'd been recording!

"…I want to pluck out those wiry guitar strings you call eyebrows…"

Quinn listened, stunned. So, too, did the nearest of their fellow diners. As the video continued, the shocked reactions around them deepened to disgust.

"You said this to an orphan?" Quinn asked.

"No, to a fashion emergency. If you saw her—"

"I just saw the whole thing."

Wandalou switched off her phone. "What am I gonna do? Without access to my video channel, how am I expected to tell my followers this is a set up and move past it to keep influencing?"

Quinn set down his cutlery. "I think you've had enough influence."

She glanced across the table "We're talking my entire livelihood, Quinn!"

"I'm talking the stares we're getting," he said. "Not only from the upper crust but the wait staff. And I'd really prefer they didn't lick the ice cubes in our water glasses when we're not looking."

Wandalou chanced another glance at her phone. By then, the video had gone viral and the Internet had labeled her *The Fashion Influenza*.

Chapter 6
Round
One

Wandalou entered Isis's kitchen clad in a black cape that fully hid her face from the others. Isis screamed. Willa tossed both hands ahead of her on instinct—another sweet move earned at Sensei Schulman's dojo.

"Relax, Cobra Kai, it's me," Wandalou snapped.

Willa lowered her fists.

"I thought you were Death," Isis said while heaving to catch her breath.

Wandalou emerged from the cloak. "I intend to throttle that **goingmad@19** if I ever get my hot little hands within striking distance."

"What did you say—**goingmad@19?**"

"I plan to wake up the wolf within and see what happens!" Wandalou raged before answering the question. "Yeah, that's the name of the puritan who showed up at my door two days ago. The whole thing was a setup! Then this ratchet in white posts the video even after my account is frozen. **goingmad@19** is a dead woman walking.”

“That’s the name of the reviewer who trashed my books!” Willa said.

Isis folded her arms. “This is no coincidence. Ladies, I think we have a common enemy.” She poured fresh coffee, set out maple biscotti, and then the three friends gathered around the table.

Wandalou crunched down and made a face. “These cookies are stale!”

“I know, dear,” Isis said. “They’re supposed to be.”

Willa made a show of dunking her biscotti into her coffee.

“Oh,” Wandalou said and did the same.

“So who is this **goinmad@19**, and what possible grudge would they harbor against us?” Isis posed.

All three eyed one another, and then, in unison, they tossed back their heads and howled.

“But who knows about that besides Joe and Quinn?” Willa said.

“Frau Krumpt,” said Wandalou.

Isis’s face screwed with a scowl. “All because of her son, Race the Face.”

“But she’s behind bars,” Willa said. “This going-schmuck isn’t.”

“And there is one more piece that neither of you has mentioned,” Wandalou said. “That schmuck’s already gone after the Purple Pen over there and me. But if you're correct about this being a three-fer…"

Isis choked down a swallow drier than her biscotti. "That means I'm next. But whatever could **goingmad@19** possibly want from me?"

Later that day, Isis shopped at the organic co-op. She purchased vegetables, the very best, and distracted herself from thoughts and worries that a new shadow-player was in town and working misery behind the scenes. She selected squash, apples, blueberries, and all else required for Thanksgiving pies. She ordered a fresh turkey at the butcher shop—twenty-seven pounds, which she hoped would be enough for eight guests. She doubted Joe would snack upon the bird—so long as he didn't snack on anyone other than Willa, she was fine with it. Then, on schedule, she arrived at school to collect the twins.

Beaming a sunny smile, she waited for the girls to buckle their belts and then pulled away from the traffic line. "And how was your day?" Isis chirped.

"Fine," Darci said. "We got to read in the library."

"Oh, what fun. And you, Marci?"

Marci pouted. "I hate the library! It smells like books in there!"

And so it continued for the two-point-seven-mile drive down Pleasant Street until they reached Mistral Lane.

"What's for dinner tonight?" Darci asked.

"I have a wonderful homemade mac and cheese planned—with four different cheeses! And we'll have salad and my famous chocolate-chocolate chip cookies for dessert."

Marci stretched against her seatbelt's constraint. "I don't want macaroni and cheese! I want pâté."

"Do you even know what pâté is, dear?"

"Yes, and I want that instead! We never get to eat anything I want. You're mean!"

"That's right, Marci—I am. And if you complain with one more word, I'll show you just how mean and serve paté for dinner."

They pulled into the driveway. Isis put the van in park and switched off the engine. "Now, if you'd both be so kind as to help me carry in the bags."

She located her house key, shouldered the strap of her tote, and popped the hatch. Then, with two canvas shopping bags in each hand, she walked up the pavers to the front door. A brisk breeze blew across the neighborhood. In the time it took to drive from the school to home, the sky had turned overcast.

"Hurry up, young ladies—there's a storm brewing."

She unlocked the front door and keyed in the security code to disable the alarm system. Isis set the bags down and returned for more. The first drops of rain pelted Hydrangea Heights.

Just in time, she thought, but the positive notion got snuffed out when she rounded the minivan where the twins lingered and a woman dressed all in white knelt at the girls' level. Something jolted through Isis, a mix of shock and hot adrenaline. She recognized the latter emotion instantly—her mother tiger instinct kicking in at full fury.

Flashing a snarl, Isis assessed the stranger, an intruder, who'd gotten so close, too close, to the twins. "Hello," she said loudly.

The woman straightened and parried with a sharp smile. "Isis Slade?"

"Yes. But you have me at a disadvantage. I don't know you."

Their gazes locked, and Isis saw in her opponent from this staring contest a level of clear menace.

"She's our first mommy," Darci said.

"Our *real* mommy," Marci added, and oh how that sentence pierced Isis almost as much as the unexpected revelation.

The smug sharpness in the woman's smile deepened.

"Joan?" Isis gasped.

"I prefer Lavinia—my middle name."

"What are you doing here?"

"Isn't that clear?" Lavinia said, her body language that of a victor. "I'm here to see my kids."

But they aren't your kids anymore, Isis thought. *You walked away years ago!*

Darci attempted to hug Lavinia's leg. Like the rest of her body language, not lost on Isis was how her opponent flinched and stepped away, not wanting the girl's touch.

"Girls, come inside," Isis ordered.

Darci disentangled from Lavinia and bounded over. Marci held her ground.

Isis cleared her throat. "Marci, dear, do as I say."

"You don't have to, Peaches," Lavinia challenged.

"Peaches?" Isis parroted.

"Yes, it's her real name," Lavinia said. And then she faced Darci. "And you don't have to either, Pickles."

"Peaches and Pickles," Marci cracked up. "That's so funny, isn't it, Pickles?"

Darci laughed too. Lavinia smiled. Isis's insides froze.

"Your sister's name is Darci, Marci," Isis said. Now the mother tiger had dug in its claws. She faced Lavinia. "I want you off my property immediately!"

"Not without *my* property first," Lavinia lobbed back.

Isis hiccupped something that tasted of wet wool and raw meat. Only after she'd gotten the girls into the house, Marci complaining en route, did she understand that it was the dormant she-wolf within, opening her eyes in response to a threat she'd never imagined possible.

Less than an hour later, Bob entered the house smelling of the brisk November rain. He pecked a kiss to Isis's cheek. She stood stiff and glacial. The smells of dinner he'd expected were absent to welcome him home.

"Hey, Icy," he said. "What's wrong?"

Isis pointed into the living room. Seated in one of the Queen Anne chairs set before the hideous yellow accent wall was a woman dressed all in white. Bob did a double take. He unknotted his tie and narrowed his gaze.

"Who—?" he posed aloud. Then, stepping closer, he said, "Joan?"

Lavinia stood and flashed a smile filled with lemons and vengeance. "Hello, Bob. And I go by my middle name now."

Bob thought it through. "Lavatory, was it?"

"Lavinia."

"What are you doing here?" he asked.

As if on cue, a wild stampede sounded over their heads. Isis glanced up and tracked the clomping of feet from one end of the upstairs hallway to the other and back again. That glance had a decidedly sad undertone.

"The twins?" Bob gasped.

"Why else?" Lavinia said. "Certainly not for that old car of yours—I see you're still driving that heap around."

"It's a classic," Bob defended.

"I want…no, I *demand* to be part of Peaches's and Pickles's lives."

"Peaches and…?" Bob sighed.

Isis's fury returned. "Their names are Marci and Darci."

"Says you."

"No, says their legal mother, Joan," Isis said.

"Lavinia. And you're only high and mighty because I was strong-armed out of my daughters' lives!"

Bob made a face. "You said you were going out for ice cream and never came back."

"Well, I'm here now—and I will have what I want!"

Isis surged at the woman in white and, lightning-quick, had her backed against the ugly accent wall, forearm pressed to her throat. "You don't want to piss me off," Isis growled. "I can get rather hairy, shall we say, when it comes to anyone threatening my family and friends."

Lavinia's eyes showed shock and all smugness vanished from her expression. When the surprise passed enough for her to rationalize her next move, she extracted herself from beneath Isis's show of dominance and hastened toward the door.

"You're nut-so, lady," Lavinia said. "And no court on Earth will deny me shared custody…maybe sole. You'll be hearing from my lawyers!" Lavinia escaped through the front door without bothering to close it behind her. The brisk, damp November breeze gusted into the house, its voice the only one, at first, daring to speak.

Fuming, Isis stared at the accent wall. "You know, that is really a hideous shade of sallow." She turned to face Bob, who'd held his breath and forgotten how to blink.

He unstuck and did both. "I've never loved you more," he said.

Isis took him into her arms.

"Joan Lavinia Going Slade," Bob sighed.

Isis tensed and broke the hug. "What did you say?"

"Her name."

"That woman's maiden name is Going?"

"Yeah, why?"

Isis didn't answer. Her gaze traveled to the open door and the dark autumn night that brooded outside.

Lavinia sat and waited. The security door buzzed open.

In walked Regina Gowl, her mouth in a constipated pucker of a smile, her stride confident.

"Well?" Regina asked.

"Round One completed successfully," Lavinia said. "All three enemy agents have been targeted and acted against."

Regina chuckled beneath her breath. "And now to begin Round Two."

Lavinia scowled. "Do I really have to sue for custody of those girls? They're such aggravating little brats!"

"Focus," Regina snapped. "My two associates have some disturbing intelligence you need to hear."

"Disturbing? How?"

"First, the Writer's boyfriend, that pilot…one of my sources claims he isn't only a pair of stones with a mustache."

"What is he?" Lavinia asked.

Regina leaned across the table and whispered her response.

"I'm sorry…it sounded like you said *vampire*."

"I did."

Lavinia gaped.

"Oh, sweetheart, that's nothing," Regina continued. "Wait until you hear what my other associate has to say about those three she-devils. Or, should I say, those three *she-wolves*…"

Chapter 7
Round Two

Getting the words past her lips hadn't been easy. Once Isis had, both Willa and Wandalou's ears seemed to have difficulty processing them.

"She wants to sue for custody," she added. "And her presence has already confused the twins and made them act up more than usual. You should have seen the spectacle this morning while getting them to school—I almost needed a whip, a chair, and a lion tamer's hat!"

"Does this Joan beyatch stand a chance?" Wandalou asked. Before Isis could answer, she added, "And what kind of name is that anyway? Joan—it sounds like a fart in a bathtub. Joan. *Joooooone.*"

"She doesn't go by Joan anymore. She's using her middle name, Lavinia."

Willa cringed. "She sounds like a woman vampire who swoops down out of the trees to bite the necks of unsuspecting innocents."

Wandalou cleared her throat. "Uh, girl, forget who you're dating?"

"Right," Willa whispered.

"There's more. Lavinia's maiden name is Going. Get it? **goingmad@19!**"

The other two women's shock melted in fresh rage.

"The reviewer?" Willa said.

"That fashion crisis who ruined my enterprise?" Wandalou hissed.

"One and the same, I'd say. Which backs up our earlier fear that someone is targeting all three of us." Isis folded her arms and moved before the accent wall, where the new coat of paint had nearly dried. "Hmmm, I think I got it right this time."

"You know, I think you're right," Willa said.

Instead of baby diaper mustard or a putrid acid yellow, the color appeared sunny and inviting; finally bright without being neon.

"Don't jinx it—it hasn't dried fully yet," laughed Wandalou. Then her voice tightened. "So this Lavinia shrew wants a fight, let's give her one. She can't attack our livelihoods and threaten to take your kids, not without some good old-fashioned Mistral Lane justice. I'm talking hellfire, ladies! Where is she? I say we go over there and smack her around!"

"In those shoes?" Willa challenged.

Wandalou glanced down at the spectacular Pedro Pretty heels with the jeweled vamps. "Maybe not these.

But I have Pedro's combat boots, too, for some serious ass-kicking!"

"She doesn't want the twins and never did. They're just a way to get to me. Chess pieces, that's all they are to her. "

"In lieu of violence, what do you plan to do?" Willa asked.

"Bob's talking to our attorney today. All we can do is wait."

Silence filled the Slade house.

At one point, Isis grew aware of the gallop of her heart broadcasting beats in her ear. "There is that other matter."

"You mean…?" Wandalou asked and followed the truncated question with a weak wolf's howl.

"The full moon is in two nights," Willa said. "I haven't felt anything. My vision and hearing suck."

"So does that ensemble," Wandalou said.

"What?"

"Never mind."

"And I haven't had any cravings for raw meat."

"Even so, we will need help. When is Joe back from the friendly skies?" Isis asked.

"Tomorrow night. He knows to be on standby just in case you-know-what awakes." Willa added her howl to the stillness inside the house.

"Good. I think we'll be all right," Isis said. "I haven't experienced any of the tells."

"Too bad," said Wandalou.

"Excuse me?" Isis questioned.

Wandalou's expression sharpened. "I doubt she'd be so eager to cross you if she knew, you know…"

Isis howled and then coughed to clear her throat.

In the shuttered fortress of Number 19 Mistral Lane, Lavinia plotted and planned her next moves. Sailor Billy stared at her through unblinking eyes. Lavinia ceased her pacing and glanced at the hideous little doll dressed in sailor whites with a porcelain dimple and tiny red mouth.

"If you weren't worth a fortune, I'd smash your ugly face into the hardwood floor," she said. "And I'd enjoy it!"

The sale of Regina Gowl's doll collection was resulting in quite the payoff—enough for her to travel far from this miserable place. She'd never liked Hydrangea Heights with its rules and snooty appearances. She was a free spirit—if she didn't want to mow the lawn or chose to paint the house electric lime, who were the overlords who thought they owned the block to tell her she had to or couldn't?

Some place safe. Maybe she'd be able to sell the two brats there. Live girl children surely would sell quickly.

They were tainted anyway—spoiled little princesses who'd grown up pampered by Bob's new wife. *Bob's new wolf,* her inner voice corrected.

"Werewolves?" Lavinia wondered aloud.

It seemed that in addition to embracing a life of crime, old Regina Gowl had gone a bit loony in recent months.

"Vampires?"

He sleeps in the basement, according to Brittany Barrows, Regina carped in her thoughts.

As part of the deal, she would pony up Regina's bail. Then steal the brats and sell th…er…*lose* them. It wasn't about maternal rights so much as sticking it to her idiot ex-husband and his toity second wife. Make off with a bonanza in filthy doll loot. Lounge on a beach somewhere, safe from persecution and responsibility.

"Wolves and bats," she laughed. But in the brooding silence, a shiver teased the nape of her neck. She fought it, failed, and the chill tumbled down her backbone.

The next morning, winter white blanketed Hydrangea Heights. The first snow of the season sent neighborhood children racing around to catch flakes on tongues before school and frustrated commuters out early to scrape windshields. For Lavinia, it was the perfect camouflage.

Head aimed low, she snuck down the sidewalk, blending in with the white. She passed the Slade house, crossed the road, and scooted beyond Willa's with its purple mailbox to the old Dunkel place where the pilot now lived.

Lived? Not according to Regina, she thought.

A black pickup sat parked in the driveway. No lights shone from inside. Even as she vanished from the sidewalk and cut into the backyard, she questioned the sanity of her actions. Stick it to the Writer. Another shot fired at the former model and beauty queen. And then the final offensive that would win the campaign—the twins.

"Oh, well," Lavinia harrumphed.

She snuck up to the back door. Picking the lock with her toolkit proved little hindrance—she'd opened better protected doors. Lavinia entered into a cold, empty room that lacked refrigerator, stove, or any signs the house was occupied.

"Hello?" she called out, ready to deliver her charity and orphan spiel if anyone answered.

The echo confirmed her suspicion and fear. An attempt to open the door to the basement further supported Regina's claim—locked from the inside. The light snow upped its tempo outside. The undercurrent of wrongness in the house thickened.

Get out of here fast, her inner voice urged. But, technically, it was daylight, and the vampire sleeping in the basement was vulnerable. If she left now, the Writer's dead pilot boyfriend might wake up at dusk and scent her presence in his lair, track her to Regina's house, and exact revenge.

Lavinia gripped the lock picking tools she'd pulled from beside the weapons secreted in the large inner pocket of her jacket. Twenty minutes after she started, the lock gave, the hardest one she had ever come up against. Its release struck her ear like thunder. Lavinia gasped. Straightening, she tried the door. It creaked open. Darkness brooded beyond. She located the light switch and flicked it on. A bald yellow glow illuminated stairs leading to the concrete floor.

"Hello?" she called again.

Nothing.

Lavinia started down. She reached the cement floor. It was your typical, lackluster basement with slab walls. The only element that marked it as different was the oblong black coffin propped on wooden pallets at its center.

She gasped again. A long minute later, Lavinia melted from her shock and stormed over to the casket. "What kind of neighborhood is this?" she spat and threw open the lid.

Stretched out inside with one hand tucked under the waistband of his pants was an athlete's body clad in an expensive jogging suit and kicks. Fighting terror and going on automatic, Lavinia checked for the rise and fall of the man's chest. Seeing none, she removed the rest of the day's vital tools from inside her coat—the stake she'd fashioned from one of Regina's wooden kitchen spoons and a rubber mallet. Sucking in a series of deep breaths, she set the sharp end of the improvised stake where living men had hearts and raised the hammer.

"You can do this, Lavinia," she whispered to herself.

Right before she brought the hammer crashing down, the man opened his eyes. They glowed green and pinned on her. Lavinia screamed, swung. The hammer struck the stake. She felt the point go past the fabric of the man's track shirt and into the flesh of his chest.

Joe bellowed.

Blood gouted.

Lavinia brought the mallet up for a second strike, but Joe grabbed at her, the spray of blood struck her face, and she lost her nerve.

Joe roared again; a wounded animal's sound. Lavinia dropped the hammer, turned, and staggered back up the stairs. She pushed out through the kitchen door and into the swirling whiteness. *"Ohmygod, ohmygod ... Ohmygodohmygod!"* she blathered, wiping the gore from her face.

But she'd nailed him! Lavinia Going had gotten that undead sumbitch!

On the sidewalk, she passed an old woman dressed to the nines walking a Pekingese dog. Lavinia hastened by.

"I say, Chauncey," Mrs. Divia Winterton sighed as the bloodied woman in white passed her. "It really is like *The Paddington Murders* in Hydrangea Heights!"

She paced the house. Her cell phone rang. Lavinia jumped up and screamed. Calming, she answered it with a sharp, "What?"

"Don't snap at me," Regina Gowl said.

Lavinia downed a cleansing breath. "Sorry."

"Just wanted to thank you for coming through on my part."

"You can thank Nancy Jean the Nurse Doll for paying your bail."

"I'll be coming home tonight after the red tape's over. Can't wait to get in on all the fun you've been up to."

"Fun?" Lavinia asked. She killed the call.

A glance out the kitchen door showed the snow had let up. She needed to get out and fast. Out and as far away from Hydrangea Heights as possible. Screw Sailor Billy—she'd take him with her, sell him while on the road from Here to There. Anything to be as far away from vampires in the basements of high end constructions as possible.

Lavinia's gaze drifted to the Slades' backyard. There, the two brats were attempting—and failing—to build a snowman from the November flakes.

"Try harder, Pickles," the mouthy one said.

"I am—and you try harder, Peaches."

This cracked both girls up.

Lavinia opened the door, willed a plastic smile onto her mouth, and stepped out.

"Girls," she whispered. "Oh, girls…"

It was time to make her escape.

Chapter 8
Going,
Going...

$\mathbf{A}$ November full moon drifted up from behind the trees and thinning snow clouds. Its cold, silver light swept over the backyards and sidewalks and crept past drawn curtains.

Willa raised her reading glasses, squinted at the screen of her laptop, and then lowered them back into place. The words blurred. She'd read the same paragraph three times before she set down the laptop and stood, restless in a way that was different from how she remembered other recent full moons. No tickle teased her throat. Certainly none of her senses were honed to sharpness.

And still, her flesh prickled and breaths came with difficulty. Boldly, she nudged aside the plum-purple curtains and peered up at the moon, displayed in its fullness. No fur sprouted across her palms or face.

"Willa," a pained man's voice rasped from somewhere that sounded a thousand miles away.

Willa whirled. "Joe?"

No reply came. The malaise settled thicker atop her skin. Her pulse raced. The next few seconds ticked past with the weight of minutes. A slow scrape and shuffle across the floor sounded at her back.

Willa spun around and there, dragging himself toward her, was the emaciated, bloodied corpse of Joe. His eyes glowed green. His mouth hung open. She saw the improvised stake jutting out of his chest and screamed.

The wrongness around her exerted its pull. Willa gathered herself together right as Joe collapsed and caught him. On the floor, he opened one hand. In it was a torn-off chunk of white fabric.

"Who did this, Joe?" Willa sobbed, though she suspected the answer.

"**G**irls," Isis called up the stairs. "Peaches and Pick—"
She caught herself short and clenched her teeth before continuing."Marci, Darci, dinner in ten minutes."

Neither twin answered.

"You know the silent treatment won't work on me. I simply adore peace and quiet. Ten minutes. One second after that and I'm coming up there ready to rain Old Testament fire on you."

She cast an eye at the sunny yellow accent wall and smiled. Then, humming to herself, Isis returned to the kitchen, stirred the gravy, and glanced out the window at the full moon. Her smile endured. So did the tune on her lips—until a rapid hammering on the French doors drew her out of the illusion that all was well.

Wandalou waited outside, her eyes frantic. Isis opened the French doors. Wandalou stormed in growling. "That *beyatch!*"

"Language—the girls might hear!" Isis admonished. "What's wrong?"

"Quinn just called. Someone lodged an ethics complaint against him with the mayor's office! Take one guess who filed it."

"*Beyatch!*" Isis exclaimed and them clamped both hands over her mouth.

"Another shot fired by that Lavinia Going!" Wandalou said. "And that isn't all. I've been doing some detective work of my own—**goingmad@19?** Nineteen? I think she's holed up next door at Regina Gowl's place, which likely means that vinegary old trout's behind her being here!"

"No," Isis gasped.

"Yes. How about we go over there and confront her? Preferably armed with a pair of our husbands' baseball bats!"

Isis folded her arms and assumed a defensive stance. "Are you suggesting violence, dear?"

"I'm not suggesting it—I'm ready to rip out that woman's hair!"

"It's a bad idea, Wandalou. These matters need to be resolved through proper channels. By lawyers and the letter of the law. I have a family to think of."

"That psycho dressed in white's trying to steal your kids!"

Isis huffed out a sigh and turned to the staircase. "Girls, hustle your butts down here at once! Call me crazy, but I prefer to eat dinner while it's still warm!"

When she turned back, Wandalou was gone.

"**W**hat about our toys?" Marci asked.

"You'll get new ones," Lavinia said. "Anything you want. And new clothes, too—ones more suitable for young ladies than what they've dressed you in."

"And can we eat what we want for dinner, not what we're forced to?"

"You can have ice cream and cotton candy seven nights a week for all I care. But we have to go now!"

Marci hesitated. "Without saying goodbye?"

"Goodbye? To that woman?"

"She's our mommy," Darci said.

"I'm your mommy," Lavinia sniped. "I'm the one who carried you in my tummy for nine months, not her!" Lavinia's gaze narrowed in the living room's shadows. She saw that Pickles held something in a tight embrace. "What is that?"

"A doll. He's so cute, and I love him!"

"Sailor Billy?" Lavinia asked. "Give him to me!" She reached down and seized hold of the doll. "Do you know how valuable he is?"

Darci held onto the doll. Lavinia pulled harder. Sailor Billy flew out of the girl's grip and struck the floor. The crunch of Sailor Billy's face unleashed a minor burst of thunder through the tense air.

Lavinia fumed. Magma ignited in her gut. She made a paddle with her hand and raised it, intending to strike the girl's face. "You rotten little brat! Do you know what you've done?"

Both twins screamed. Lavinia readied to bring her hand down, hard, across the urchin's cheek. But when she moved to swing, a force clamped around her wrist. She whirled. The Trueheart woman stood there, holding her back with a vice-like grip.

"You harm one hair on my nieces' heads, lady, and I'll bitch-slap you all the way to Saturn!"

"How dare you," Lavinia spat as she pulled free.

"Girls, get behind me," Wandalou commanded.

"Yes, Aunty!" both twins said.

"No—Peaches and Pickles, we're leaving!"

"Don't call us that—those aren't our names!" Marci shrieked. "And you're mean!"

Lavinia shot a hate-filled look at Wandalou.

"Girls, go home—your mom's got dinner on the table."

"I'm their mom."

"You're a mother, that's for sure," Wandalou said. Then to the girls, she added, "Go home to your *real* mom. Now, scoot—before I remind you both how much I hate kids."

The twins raced to the kitchen and out through the back door, into the night. Both opponents sized one another up in the dark living room lit only by the full moon's silver light.

"You've got quite the big, brass pair on you, Lavinia," Wandalou said. "You come here, attack the three of us. You're lucky it isn't last month—we'd have kicked your ass!"

"Is that supposed to frighten me? The full moon's out, and you don't look particularly *wolfish*."

The creak of a footstep sounded behind them. Wandalou turned to see Willa standing in the moonlight, pale and traumatized, her eyes wide.

"You," Willa hissed.

Lavinia raised her chin with arrogance. "What's the matter—boyfriend troubles?"

Willa froze.

"You mean Joe?" Wandalou asked. Then she again faced Lavinia. "What did you do to Joe?"

"Put him out of his misery while the sun was still out," Lavinia proudly declared.

Wandalou gasped.

"She tried to stake him through his heart. Luckily, she didn't get all the way there. I pulled out that sharp wooden spoon and let him feed. He's recovering at my house. But as for you…"

"Let me guess, you're here for revenge. What are you planning to do? Make me a villain in your next crappy book? Hah—it takes more than that to frighten Lavinia Going!"

Another footstep sounded behind Willa. All tracked it to the third arrival to Number 19 Mistral Lane. Isis walked in and pinned Lavinia in her wide-open gaze, which glinted red around the edges.

"You tried to steal my children?" Isis asked in a low voice not much louder than a whisper.

"You should thank me for ridding you of those monsters!"

Isis answered with a humorless laugh. "They're not the monsters, Lavinia." Then coughing to clear the tickle in her throat, Isis dropped to all fours on the floor. A cracking of bones shuddered through the room.

Willa followed suit. As Lavinia watched, horrified, the Writer contorted, grunted, and grew less human in appearance with the passing seconds.

"Oh shit," Wandalou said. "It's waking up!" She, too, sprang to the floor and transformed.

Lavinia roused from her paralysis and hastened toward the front door. "Screw this—I'm out of here!"

The Isis-thing sprang in front of her. "I don't' think so, Lavatory!" And then it tossed back its head and howled.

Lavinia screamed. Willa chuckled in a juicy wolf's voice. Wandalou's fangs chattered and her mouth salivated. The three she-wolves circled Lavinia Going and, snapping, were upon her.

The taxi pulled up to Number 19 Mistral Lane and dropped off its lone passenger. Regina Gowl stepped out and straightened triumphantly. She cast a look around the neighborhood and savored a rush of satisfaction. Oh, the residents of Mistral Lane would pay and pay dearly for their sins against her. Her revenge had only begun.

Nose aimed high, she produced her house key and marched up to the front door.

"Lavinia," she called into the dark house.

Regina flipped on the hall light switch. She took another step into the living room and froze. Three hairy horrors were in the process of gorging themselves on the bloodied remains of a skeleton picked mostly clean. The monsters looked like werewolf versions of Isis Slade, Willa Forsyth, and the Trueheart woman.

"What the—?" Regina sputtered, suddenly not so confident.

She got off one shriek before they ate her, too.

Before sunrise, Joe again put the wolves to sleep. He recovered and drove Lavinia's car to the airport, where he left it in the extended parking lot. With the same precision in which she kept her own house—and plenty of bleach—Isis scrubbed up the mess in Regina's as Joe went to sleep and healed.

The general belief was that both Lavinia and Regina had made their escape before authorities could catch up with the leader of the Purists of Purity and her accomplice, who'd skipped out on her trial and charge of involuntary manslaughter in the death of Jessie-Marie Smyth.

Reviews were taken down, locked accounts unlocked, and baseless complaints deleted.

Isis baked.

She baked a pumpkin pie, a pecan pie, a blueberry pie, and an apple pie. She fixed homemade cranberry chutney, slow-roasted the gigantic bird in the oven, and prepared all of the expected sides—fluffy whipped potatoes, butternut squash, green bean casserole, creamed baby onions, sage stuffing, and glazed carrots. She set the dining room table for eight with their fine holiday china, linen napkins, the antique silverware that had been her grandmother's along with elegant goblets.

"Why do we have to eat so late?" Bob complained.

Isis flashed her patient smile. "So Willa and Joe can join us. You know he's a night owl."

Bob's expression scrunched. "What is he, a vampire?"

To this, Isis cackled and told him to go watch the game. She set out baby rolls and butter and added another bottle of wine to the table.

"But I don't want turkey!" Marci moaned. "I want goose!"

"And I want to send you to an all-girls school in the Swiss Alps, dear," Isis calmly responded.

"I like turkey," Darci said.

"You would, Pickles," Marci groused.

Isis maintained her smile and passed the gravy.

They sat around the exquisite table—the Slades, Willa and Joe, Wandalou and Quinn. Candles flickered. Wine got poured. All was well.

"I'm so glad she's gone," Wandalou said while digging at the portions heaped onto her plate.

"Me, too," Willa tsked.

Joe smiled and unconsciously patted his heart.

"Not eating, Joe?" Bob asked.

"No, allergic to turkey," Joe said.

"I'm not," Wandalou said. "Thanksgiving is my favorite. Icy, you've outdone yourself."

"Thanks, dear."

Quinn eyed her from his seat. "And you outdid yourself three bites ago. What gives?"

"I'm hungry," Wandalou snapped.

"You're a cannibal," Quinn said lightly while reaching for his wine glass.

Wandalou set down her knife and fork and shot Quinn a look. "You eat *one* human being and suddenly the whole world thinks you're a cannibal!"

Willa held up a pair of fingers. "Two," she whispered beneath her breath.

"Huh?" asked Quinn.

Wandalou flashed a counterfeit smile and cackled. "Just using a figure of speech. Eat up, babe."

Slowly, conversation returned around the Thanksgiving table, most of it about ordinary subjects like sports and the weather.

Later, when alone in the kitchen, the three friends raised their glasses and made a vow that though life on Mistral Lane was back to normal, they would still have their Ladies' Poker Nights once every full moon.

The End

About the Author

Raised on a healthy diet of creature double features and classic SF TV, Gregory L. Norris writes regularly for numerous short story anthologies, national magazines, novels, and the occasional episode for TV or film. Gregory novelized the NBC Made-for-TV classic by Gerry Anderson, *The Day After Tomorrow: Into Infinity* (as well as a sequel and a forthcoming third entry into the franchise for Anderson Entertainment in the U.K.), a movie he watched as an eleven-year-old sitting cross-legged on the living room floor of the enchanted cottage where he grew up. Gregory won HM in the 2016 Roswell Awards in Short SF Writing and was a 2022 Finalist. He once worked as a screenwriter on two episodes of Paramount's *Star Trek: Voyager*. Kate Mulgrew, *Voyager*'s "Captain

Janeway," blurbed his book of short stories and novellas, *The Fierce and Unforgiving Muse*, stating, "In my seven years on *Voyager*, I don't think I've met a writer more capable of writing such a book—and writing it so beautifully."

In late 2019, Gregory sold an option on his modern Noir feature film screenplay, *Amandine*, to the new Hollywood production company Snarkhunter LLC, owned by actor Dan Lench, a devotee of Gregory's writing. In late 2020, Snarkhunter optioned Gregory's tetralogy Horror film based upon four of his short stories, *Ride Along*. Twice Norris has been nominated for the Pushcart Prize. He is the author of the novel *Ex Marks the Spot* (Woodhall Press) and the forthcoming release of SF tales of wonder and adventure stretching from Sol to Pluto, *The Solar System* (September 2022), and a delightfully dark dystopian novel, *The Lost City of Books*.

Gregory lives and writes at Xanadu, a century-old house perched on a hill in New Hampshire's North Country with spectacular mountain views, with his rescue cat and emerald-eyed muse.

Follow his literary adventures at:
www.gregorylnorris.blogspot.com

Love Books?

SUPPORT AUTHORS – buy directly from independent publishers. This puts more royalty dollars into the pockets of your favorite author – and gives them time to write their next book.

Visit us for links to our other books as well as many other vibrant publishing companies to find the book for you.

Send a note to join our **Book Launch List.**

Director@vanvelzerpress.com

These ARE The Books You've Been Looking For.

Vanvelzerpress.com

www.ingramcontent.com/pod-product-compliance
Lightning Source LLC
Chambersburg PA
CBHW071205210726
48293CB00002B/295